Texas Rose *forever*

ALSO BY KATIE GRAYKOWSKI

The Marilyns

Place Your Betts

Getting Lucky

The Lone Stars

Perfect Summer

Saving Grace

Changing Lanes

The Debra Dilemma

PTO Murder Club Mystery

Rest in Pieces

A TEXAS ROSE RANCH NOVEL

Texas Rose *forever*

Katie Graykowski

Montlake Romance

This is a work of fiction. Names, characters, organizations, places, events, and incidents are either products of the author's imagination or are used fictitiously.

Text copyright © 2016 Katie Graykowski
All rights reserved.

No part of this book may be reproduced, or stored in a retrieval system, or transmitted in any form or by any means, electronic, mechanical, photocopying, recording, or otherwise, without express written permission of the publisher.

Published by Montlake Romance, Seattle

www.apub.com

Amazon, the Amazon logo, and Montlake Romance are trademarks of Amazon.com, Inc., or its affiliates.

ISBN-13: 9781503950740
ISBN-10: 1503950743

Cover design by Mumtaz Mustafa

Printed in the United States of America

For Uncle Virgil—southern gentleman, cattleman, lover of children . . . I miss you.

CHAPTER 1

CanDee McCain leaned over to get a better look at the framed marriage license hanging on the wall. Carlton Rose had married Prudence Althea Lehman in 1867.

That was a freaking long time ago.

Maybe if she stopped living and writing in the past, she could murder some modern-day people. Her mailman, for starters, and then there was the lady at the DMV. She definitely had it coming.

Or Phillip. If anyone deserved to be murdered in some horrible fashion, it was her ex. Not only had he stolen the first draft of her mystery novel, he'd published it under his own name and now it was a *New York Times* best seller. He deserved beheading by spork . . . a dull one. Or possibly hanging or submersion in acid. She nodded to herself. Acid it was.

She pulled a yellow legal pad out of her battered leather tote, intending to make a note of the marriage date. She dug around for a pencil. Where was it? She shuffled through sticky notes, breath mints, tampons, more sticky notes, receipts, one pearl earring, lip gloss, a travel-sized deodorant, a letter opener. A letter opener? What the hell?

Damn, she could never find her pencil or her car keys. There had to be some mystical vortex that sucked up her pencils and keys. That was the only explanation. She gave up. She'd just come back later and take notes. Hell, she was scheduled to be here for the next six weeks, and it wasn't like this picture was going anywhere.

The Rose family was paying her a nice chunk of change to research and write their family history. Six weeks away from her latest mystery manuscript wasn't a lifetime . . . and she'd have money to pay her bills. Really, six weeks was nothing. Only, her heart wasn't in genealogy—it was in psychological thrillers with lots of twists and turns.

What were the chances that the Rose family's history would have twists and turns? She rolled her eyes. This was her fifth nonfiction book and second large-family-ranch genealogy. Genealogy wasn't mystery, but a girl had to eat. She wanted to murder people in gruesome ways, but alas, she was stuck on a ranch out in the middle of nowhere, writing a family history that no one outside the family would ever care to read.

She flipped her pad back to the front page. According to her notes, the Texas Rose Ranch was a multibillion-dollar operation. At eight hundred thousand acres, it was the second largest ranch in Texas—a mere twenty-five thousand acres smaller than the King Ranch, but a hundred times more profitable. Her definitive work on the King Ranch was currently ranked at 1,800,092 on Amazon Best Sellers. It held the spot right under *1040-ME: Memoirs of an IRS Part-time/Seasonal Employee* and right above *Colorectal Bleeding: It Anus Your Fault.*

It was good to know that she'd edged out colorectal bleeding . . . that was something. She moved on to the photo to the left of the marriage certificate. It was a tintype of two men. She glanced down at the typed plaque underneath.

Col. Lacy Kendall Lehman and his wife Brunhilda Arndorfer Lehman (née Hitzler)

"Which one of them is Brunhilda?" She leaned in closer and flipped her cream-colored rhinestone cat-eye glasses to the top of her head. Surely the one with the bushy mustache wasn't female.

"She's on the right."

CanDee just about jumped a foot in the air as her heart hammered against her rib cage. She'd been sure that she was alone in this sixteen-by-five building the family called the "museum," which housed a freakin' lot of photos. "You scared me."

She turned around and came face to chest with the tallest man she'd ever met. In her stockinged feet, she was six feet. In the heels she was wearing now, she was six feet five. She tilted her head up. He had to be close to seven feet tall. He made her feel small . . . that was a first.

"Sorry to scare you, ma'am. I bet you're here to see me." His voice held just enough Texas to be charming, and his aqua-blue eyes crinkled at the corners in merriment. His skin was tanned from years baking out in the sun, and his chambray shirt and faded Wranglers were dusty. His thick black hair was dented all the way around from the battered white Stetson he was now holding. He was a ranch hand. She'd met more than her fair share on the King Ranch.

"No worries." She turned back to the picture. "Are you sure Brunhilda's the one without the mustache?"

"Yes, ma'am. I've been told she was even more dour in person." He pointed one callused finger at the picture. "Supposedly she made the best peach preserves around."

She settled her glasses back on her nose. "I'm still not convinced."

She glanced over her shoulder.

He grinned and dimples popped out on both cheeks. "Now that I really look at her, I'm inclined to agree. She is definitely the more masculine of the two, but Lacy Kendall Lehman is sitting on the left."

"Lacy? That must have been a tough name for a man. I bet he got beat up a lot." And Kendall wasn't much better. It was funny, now the Kindle was a device that had taken the place of paper books. The spelling was different, but the pronunciation was the same as the name. "Thanks for your help. I'm CanDee McCain."

She held out her hand.

A slow smile crept across his face.

"Cinco." He transferred the Stetson to the crook of his left arm. He couldn't have been more than thirty-five. He held more than shook her hand and his gaze stayed on hers. He was handsome in a rugged cowboy way, and she'd been known to mix a little business with pleasure, but she wasn't looking to make this assignment any more complicated. Too bad—he looked like he'd be good at pleasure. She fought the urge to run her gaze down his lanky body.

"Nice to meet you, Cinco." She'd met all sorts of oddly named ranch hands. At the King Ranch alone there'd been a Snake, Dumbo, Puddin', Two Fingers, and Bunchy . . . even a Snatch. She'd learned not to ask how they'd gotten their nicknames.

"Likewise, ma'am." He finally dropped her hand, but his gaze stayed on her. He wasn't massaging her with his gaze so much as drinking her in. "Want to get started?"

She looked down at her notes. She was supposed to meet with Dr. Lucy Rose—the matriarch of the family. According to her research, Dr. Rose was a busy surgeon at the local hospital. Maybe something had come up and she'd sent Cinco instead? He seemed to know a lot about the family.

"Okay, sure. Let me find my pencil." She dug around in her leather bag some more. "I know it's here somewhere."

"Allow me." There was a slight tug on her hair, which then fell in one long wave down her back. Duh, she'd shoved her pencil in her French twist to hold it up.

"You have beautiful hair. It's the color of a shiny penny." He handed her the pencil and his gaze moved to the V of her cardigan sweater.

This morning, she hadn't been able to find the shell that went under it, so she'd buttoned it all the way up. Well, except for the top three buttons that were missing. It showed a respectable amount of cleavage—she glanced down and cringed—if she were working the pole on amateur night. Her sweater gaped open. If she pulled it together, that would draw even more attention to her chest. She was damned if she did and damned if she didn't, so she just stood there with her boobs practically falling out.

She took the pencil and moved the notepad so that it blocked his view. Problem solved.

"I like this whole naughty-librarian thing you've got going." His gaze finally made it up to hers. "Are the glasses real? They look real."

"I beg your pardon?" This was the strangest family interview she'd ever been on.

"I expected the shoes, but the boring black shirt and pink sweater aren't what I'd pictured." He walked over to the door, plucked up a wooden straight-backed chair, set it down in front of her, and sat. His grin was downright sexy.

She'd expected him to offer the chair to her. Apparently his manners only went so far. She checked her watch. It was three in the afternoon. Maybe he'd been on his feet all day and was tired.

So he didn't like her outfit. Who cared?

"Okay, um . . ." She unlooped her bag from her shoulder and set it on the floor next to the wall. She leaned against the wall and flipped to a clean page on her notepad. "How long have you worked for the Roses?"

He scratched his jaw and then pointed to her pad. "You're really into this. I like that."

She wasn't sure what that meant. Clearly he'd been out in the sun for way too long. "I take my job very seriously."

He laced his fingers behind his head and stretched his legs out in front of him, crossing his left ankle over his right. "I'm counting on it."

She tried again. "How long have you worked for the Roses?"

"All my life, sweetheart." He nodded absently. "Wouldn't you like to get started? These questions really add to the whole mood, but I'd rather cut to the chase."

The hair on the back of her neck stood up. "I'm sorry?"

"No need to be sorry, sweetheart, but I'd like to get this show on the road. I've been in the saddle since six this morning, I need a shower, and then my brothers are throwing me a surprise birthday party after the official party my parents are hosting. I half expected you to be at the after-party. That's usually how it works."

"What?" She took a step back. "A party? I don't know—"

"Don't you have some music? If not, that's okay. I'm flexible." He pointed to the front of her sweater. "Why don't you start with your sweater? Undo the buttons slowly and take it off."

She glanced down at her sweater. "What the hell?"

"I don't mean to tell you your craft, but all this talking is starting to get on my nerves. I know they ordered a sexy librarian, but it's time to get down to business. Maybe this will help." He pulled a roll of money out of his back pocket and swiped off five bills. They sailed to her feet.

She couldn't help but notice they were hundreds.

She sucked on her bottom lip. That would pay off her American Express card. She was halfway tempted to pick them up. "I think there's been some sort of mistake. I'm here to—"

"Sweetheart, I know you're my birthday present. Last year my brothers got me a midget—excuse me, little-person—stripper. She also did acrobatics." He shook his head. "This year I can see they went more . . . you know . . . average."

"Wait a minute—"

"There's nothing wrong with that. You're easy on the eyes . . . that's all that counts." He sat up. "I bet you're a gymnast or a fire-breather. There's bound to be more to you than just those sexy glasses."

She took another step back and banged into the wall. A framed photo came crashing down and bounced off the floor, and the glass shattered.

"Don't worry about that . . . keep going." He nodded his head to the rhythm of some imaginary music. "Don't worry about the music, I've got some going in my head."

"I'm not a stripper. I was hired to—"

"Sorry, I didn't mean to offend you. Exotic dancer." His gaze fastened on her chest as his head continued to nod to some song that only he could hear.

With a name like CanDee McCain, this wasn't the first time she'd been mistaken for a stripper—at least on paper. Once they saw her, there was no doubt that stripping wasn't her profession. She wasn't particularly well endowed, and apart from her long legs, no man had ever really commented on the rest of her body.

"I can see that the music is an issue for you." He pulled an iPhone out of his back pocket. He swiped his finger across the screen and Katy Perry's "Roar" roared out.

"I would have never taken you for a Katy Perry fan." Somehow this seemed more ridiculous than his taking her for a stripper.

"I'm a very complex man," he said over the music as he stood. "I can see that you're new at this. I'll start."

He gyrated his hips—it was part hula-hoop and part seizure. Whatever rhythm he was dancing to wasn't coming out of his iPhone. He added some arm movements that looked like he was flapping his wings to take flight. He moved into a hop-shuffle thing that reminded her of Tripod, the blind, arthritic, three-legged dog she'd had as a child. She couldn't help but stare. It was like driving by a car wreck. She tried to look away but ended up rubbernecking.

"What in the hell is going on?" A female voice called from the front door. A petite woman marched more than walked up to them. She grabbed the phone out of Cinco's hand and turned off the music. She had penetrating aqua eyes and a razor-sharp blond bob.

"Trust me, you're not going to want to stay for this." Cinco pointed to CanDee. "CanDee McCain here is my birthday present. You're not going to like it."

The woman's eyes turned as big as teacups and she turned to CanDee. "I'm Lucy Rose." She stuck out her hand.

CanDee shook it once and then dropped it.

"Miss McCain, I am so sorry. I can't apologize enough for my eldest son. Usually, he's more respectful of women." She went up on her tippy-toes and tried to smack him on the back of the head, but only made it to the middle of his back.

CanDee picked up her leather bag, debated a split second about the hundreds on the floor, chose to ignore them, and shoved her notepad into the bag. "I think it's time for me to leave."

"Please stay. I don't know what this imbecile has done, but I can assure you it won't happen again." The woman shot Cinco a mom death-glare.

"Hold on . . . she's not a stripper?" He looked from CanDee to his mother and back again. "Your name really is CanDee McCain?"

"I'm too short to smack him on the back of the head." Dr. Rose let out a long, labored breath. "Can you please do it for me?"

CanDee shrugged. He did have it coming. She walked over to him, took out her notepad, used it to smack him hard on the back of the head, and stepped beside Dr. Rose.

"Ouch." Cinco rubbed the back of his head. "That hurt."

"You deserve so much worse. What were you thinking, Lacy Kendall Lehman Rose V? You better get on your knees and beg her to stay." Dr. Rose's eyes turned mean.

Cinco looked like a caged animal. The blood-red flush that had started at his collar was now working its way up his face. She had never seen a grown man blush. It was both charming and grotesque.

Dr. Rose stabbed her index finger in his direction. "You will apologize right now. You've humiliated her and me."

"It's okay, Dr. Rose." CanDee bit her bottom lip to keep from laughing, but laughter slipped out anyway. She couldn't help it. His look of drop-jawed bewilderment combined with the glow of the blush on his face made him look like one of those Christmas nutcrackers minus the coat and tails. She turned back to the hundreds on the floor, bent down and scooped them up, folded them in half, and tucked them in the waistband of his Wranglers. "Thanks for the dance. What you lacked in rhythm, you certainly made up for in creativity."

Silence crackled through the small building.

"I like you." Dr. Rose laughed. "Call me Lucy."

"Okay, call me CanDee."

"Whew." A bleach blonde with obviously surgically enhanced cantaloupe-sized breasts ran in on ten-inch-tall hooker heels. "Sorry I'm late. I got so lost."

It was amazing that she kept herself upright, considering the size of her chest and the thinness of those heels. She defied the laws of physics. It was interesting to watch.

"Just give me a minute to set up." She hitched a pink duffle bag off her shoulder and dumped it on the chair. Several things inside the bag clanked against each other. She unzipped the bag and pulled out swords of different lengths.

Lucy crossed her arms. "In my mind, I'm running through different scenarios where swords would be involved, but I can't come up with one that makes sense . . . Well, I can, but it's disgusting and painful."

"I'm a sword-swallowing contortionist. That adds a little extra something when I strip." She flashed her electric-white teeth. "I didn't know this was a mixed party. It's okay. I like girls too."

She winked at Lucy.

CanDee turned to Cinco. "See, your brothers didn't let you down this year. They got you a bisexual sword-swallowing contortionist. That beats the little-person acrobat from last year." She patted him on the shoulder. "Have fun."

Lucy linked her arm in CanDee's and they walked out the door. CanDee had never met a stranger family. Maybe the next six weeks weren't going to be nearly as boring as she'd thought.

CHAPTER 2

How exactly did a man apologize for confusing a total stranger with a stripper? Cinco Rose picked another bluebonnet to add to the bunch he'd gathered on his way to the cottage. Flowers were a good start, and there would probably be some groveling.

Normally, he didn't grovel, but CanDee McCain was owed some. It had been an honest mistake, but he felt bad . . . really bad. In fact, he was missing his birthday party just to come apologize. That had to count for something.

He picked some firewheels and a couple of blackfoot daisies and added them to the ever-growing bouquet. CanDee was a looker. A fiery redhead with huge golden-brown eyes and a full bottom lip that was ripe for sucking. It was a wonder his eyes had made it off her face long enough to take in her body. She had a nice one, legs up to her armpits, but it was her face that kept popping into his head.

And her laugh. She had a nice laugh—full and genuine.

CanDee had spirit. He'd give her that. She should have decked him, but she'd only laughed. He liked a good sense of humor.

Now that his bouquet was so large that he had to hold it with both hands, he felt stupid for having picked them. Wildflowers were hokey. She was a city girl. He looked down at them. This was a bad idea.

"Are those for me?" CanDee sat on the porch swing right outside of the cabin where she was staying. He'd been so focused on the flowers that he hadn't seen her. "Or is a love of wildflowers just another indicator of your complex personality?"

She wore a silky dress the color of ripe peaches, which came mid-thigh because she was seated, showcasing her mile-long legs. Her coppery hair curled around her shoulders.

"For you." He stood in front of her and extended his hands. "By way of an apology."

She tilted her head to the left. "Did your mother put you up to this?"

"No, ma'am. The flowers are all me." He felt like a fool standing there holding a giant bouquet of wildflowers.

Slowly, she stood and took the flowers. "Tell me, is the charm part of the whole aw-shucks-ma'am cowboy thing you've got going on or is it real?"

Was he being charming? No one had ever accused him of being charming—surly, yes, but never charming.

She brought the flowers to her nose and inhaled. "They smell wonderful. Bluebonnets are my favorites."

It was crazy to be this happy at having made her smile, but here he was, probably wearing a stupid grin. He needed to get out more and start dating. It was past time. His divorce had been final for more than five years. Several women in town had showed interest, but none of them seemed as much fun as standing here and staring at CanDee McCain.

"Can you get the door?" She nodded to the closed front door. "My hands are full."

Manners, crap. He'd forgotten his.

He opened the door and stepped aside to let her in first. "I'm sure that my mother told you, this was the first house built on the ranch. Lacy Lehman built it for Brunhilda after she got tired of living in the dugout. When Prudence Lehman married Carlton Rose they lived here for a while until he built her the big house."

He'd always loved the cabin. It was one giant room with a huge, round wood-burning stove in the center. Over the years, the stove had been converted to a fireplace, a bathroom was added off to the side, and everything had been updated with electricity and modern appliances, but it still held the spirit of the old place.

"Dugout?" CanDee glanced over her shoulder at him. "Like dugout-of-the-ground dugout?"

"Yes, ma'am. It was three rooms and quite cozy, from what I've heard. I seem to remember there's a box of letters and old newspaper clippings around here somewhere that talks about it. I think there's even a picture taken right before it caved in." He followed her into the kitchen alcove.

She pulled out a plastic pitcher from under the sink, tucked the flowers inside, and filled it with water.

"How charming. A photograph right before it caved in." She shook her head. "No wonder Brunhilda looks so angry in that tintype with her husband. He'd probably just told her about his grand plan to build her a dugout. She must have loved Lacy a lot. People do strange things for love. Personally, I draw the line at dugouts. It must be impossible to keep the floor clean with it being made of dirt and all."

It was on the tip of his tongue to ask her what crazy thing she'd done for love, but he didn't know her that well. That he wanted to know her that well struck him as odd. She was easy to talk to, which he didn't find most of the time in women—or men, for that matter. It wasn't that he was shy, it was just he didn't have much to say.

"Then again, maybe it wasn't love. Don't take this the wrong way, but your however-many-times-great-grandmother was not a handsome woman. In fact, I'm going to go out on a limb here and say that she's the single ugliest person that I've ever seen. I'm guessing that men weren't lining up to marry her." She leaned against the counter next to the sink. "Come to think of it, was Lacy a sighted man? Apart from a mustache that was the size of a small dog, he wasn't half bad looking. Maybe Brunhilda was from a really wealthy family or like you said, she made spectacular peach preserves."

Laughter made his chest shake. "Are you always like this?"

"What?" Her eyebrows arched.

"Saying what you're thinking . . . always looking for the motivation behind things." With the exception of his mother, women rarely said what was truly on their minds. At least Naomi, his ex-wife, hadn't. She'd professed all her love while screwing his best friend . . . and that hadn't come close to the worst thing that she'd done.

She shrugged. "I guess. I've never really thought about it. I'm a writer. Motivation is everything."

"Really? What's my motivation for missing my party to come here?" He liked her. True, she said the most bizarre things, but at least they were never stupid, only clever.

Her eyes narrowed in contemplation. "Let me see." She tapped her right index finger against her closed lips. "Off the top of my head, I can think of three reasons. The first and most obvious is that your mom probably threatened you with bodily harm unless you came over and made things right."

She shook her head. "But I don't think that's your primary motivation. I don't know you that well, but based on the whole noble-cowboy thing you've got going on, you couldn't stand the idea of offending a lady."

She'd nailed it. He'd known CanDee three whole hours and she already knew him better than his ex-wife ever did. "What's the third thing?"

She smiled mischievously. Whatever lipstick she'd used made her lips look like shiny ripe peaches. "You want to find out if I secretly videotaped you dancing and if so, if I've posted it on YouTube. I'm betting you're prepared to kill me and hide my body in that caved-in dugout if I don't turn over the video."

"Are you kidding?" He matched her grin. "I'd have to dig out the dugout. That's too much work. I thought about strapping some concrete blocks to your ankles and throwing you in the quarry lake."

"That's pretty good, but you forgot one small detail." She walked over to the kitchen table, which was littered with papers. She riffled around in the papers until she came up with something that looked like a brochure. "Scuba divers come from all around to dive your clear-watered quarry lake. They'd find me in a heartbeat."

Were they really standing here discussing the ways he'd get rid of her body? Strangest conversation ever. "Okay, what if I throw your body into the stump grinder and then feed you to the hogs?"

Yep, strangest conversation ever. "Oh." Her face lit up. "That's good. Can pigs really eat bones?"

He nodded once. "I've seen them chew through a deer's leg bone like it was nothing more than a handful of pecans."

She picked up a legal pad from the table and shuffled some more papers until she found a pen. "I'm writing a mystery. Okay if I use that?"

She mashed her lips together like she hadn't meant to say that. She had nothing to fear—his mother wouldn't care if she wrote another book on her own time. Based on the amount of papers scattered on the table, she'd already started on the genealogy.

"Help yourself." He shoved his hands in the front pockets of his jeans. Was it inappropriate to ask out a woman whose gruesome murder he'd just planned? "I don't suppose you'd like to go to a birthday party?"

"Your mom already invited me. I was headed that way when I saw you walking across the yard." She walked to the door and leaned down to pick up a pair of brown super-high-heeled shoes. She held them instead of putting them on. "I decided to stick around to see what kind of apology you'd come up with. At first when I saw you picking wildflowers, I thought you were dancing again. I'm not going to lie, it was scary."

"What are you talking about? I'm a terrific dancer." He ruined his indignation with a laugh.

"Do a lot of dancing at the Texas School for the Blind, do you?" She grinned up at him. He had a strong urge to kiss her . . . just a taste, but she pulled the door open and the moment was gone.

"Are you coming?" She stepped through the open doorway. "I'm sure everyone is wondering where the birthday boy is."

He glanced down at her bare feet. Tiny little Texas flags were painted on her toenails. "Aren't you going to put on your shoes?"

"Not until we get there." She waited for him to shut the door.

"Why?" He pointed to the shoes. "You've got shoes."

She hunched her shoulders. "They hurt my feet."

"So wear different ones." In his experience, women liked to complicate simple situations.

"These are the only shoes that match my dress and they make my legs look fantastic." The *duh* in her voice was implied.

"You have some pretty nice legs, you don't need shoes to make them look good." If his gaze lingered on her legs, it wasn't his fault. She'd brought them up.

He offered her his elbow as they walked across the yard to the main house.

"Yes, but these shoes take them to the next level." She took his elbow.

She smelled faintly of cinnamon and vanilla. A strand of her hair curled around his shoulder.

"Here I go, thinking that you're the coolest girl I've ever met, and then you go and wear shoes that hurt your feet. That just knocked you back down to average. I hate to do it." He shook his head. "Unfortunately the shoes thing is average and a cool girl would have worn ugly but comfortable shoes."

She put her hand over her heart. "Average . . . me?" She hip-bumped him. "You're going to eat those words when you see me in these shoes. FYI, you're probably going to have to carry me home because I'll be crippled, but it'll be worth it."

"I doubt it." He glanced down at the shoes. "They're pretty average."

"Since your opinion of me has fallen so low, I have a confession to make." She was all seriousness. "I'm just working as a writer until my stripper career takes off."

"You could have fooled me." Screw the party, he just wanted to hang out with her. He couldn't imagine that the party would be any more fun than he was having with her.

"I was a little intimidated by the bisexual sword swallower." She sighed long and hard. "It appears that you Rose men only hire the best. I'm going to have to step up my game."

"I look forward to it." He couldn't wait to hear what would come out of her mouth next.

"I'm thinking something with flaming batons, or maybe a mime." She nodded like mime was the way to go.

"I hate to burst your bubble, but they got me a mime year before last." He shook his head. "It wasn't nearly as exciting as you'd think."

"What about magic tricks?" She waved her hand in the air. "I yell *abracadabra* and then my clothes disappear."

"If would be neat if they appeared on someone in the audience," he added to be helpful.

"That's a good idea." She nodded. "I'm thinking of starting small. Thought I'd work a couple of the VFW halls to cut my teeth and then move on to bigger venues like the Elks Lodges or maybe the Freemasons."

"Sounds like a great business plan. Who knows? In a couple of years, you might even work up to bachelor parties."

"I don't know. That's brass-ring territory, but I plan on keeping my eye on the prize." She transferred her shoes to her other hand. Her left breast grazed his upper arm.

His gaze went to her face; she didn't seem to notice the contact.

"I like ambition in a woman." His arm tingled from the accidental boob-graze.

"You gotta have goals."

They reached the front porch of the main house. Using his shoulder for stability, she slipped on her shoes. She walked up the steps and turned around and modeled for him.

"What do you think?" She walked seductively back and forth.

"Stretch, you've got legs all the way up to your earlobes." He sucked on his top lip. "I take back everything I said about those shoes."

"So you're a leg man." She turned around and threw him a saucy smile.

"I am now." He'd never met anyone who put him more at ease than CanDee. She didn't take things too seriously and she made him laugh more than he had in the last five years. All of a sudden, he had a powerful need to tell her everything he knew about the Texas Rose Ranch. Hell, he might even make up some stuff just so he could spend more time with her.

CHAPTER 3

CanDee had never seen a house quite like the main house. She glanced up at the turrets. The house was at least four stories, made of cut limestone, and appeared to have been modeled after both an English castle and the Alamo.

Cinco twisted the enormous wrought-iron doorknob and pushed the left side of the double front doors open. "Welcome to Rose Manor, my family home."

The house actually had a name. She looked around for a butler. A house that had its own name needed a butler.

He waited for her to walk in, then followed and closed the door. "I don't live here. I have my own house down by the river."

"So you don't live with your parents. That's good to know." She took it all in. A good bit of the limestone outside had made it inside as well. Besides that, the house was surprisingly homey . . . very Pottery Barn. Overstuffed brown-leather chairs and dark green velvet curtains were mixed with lots of potted plants and off-white area rugs. This was much better than the outside.

"My mother hired a decorator who said he could work wonders with the inside, but the outside was beyond even his abilities." Cinco put his hand on the small of her back and led her into a huge living room.

She'd missed having a man lead her into a room. Phillip had done that. He'd done lots of things that she'd liked and even more than she'd hated. Slurping his soup, for one, and then there'd been all of those women. He'd claimed to want only her, but every time he cheated on her, he all but told her that she wasn't enough.

On second thought, she'd didn't miss a man doing anything for her.

"I have a friend who could make the outside just as beautiful as the inside. Her name's Justus and she's landscape designer." Justus could use the work. Not that CanDee was pimping her friend out, but Justus was really talented.

"Really?" He leaned close to her ear. "My mom's birthday is in a couple of months. My brothers and I were talking about doing something like that for her as a gift. Can I get your friend's number?"

"Sure, or I can give her a call first thing tomorrow. I know she's finishing up a job so she should have some time in the next month or so." She noticed his gaze venturing south. "Are you looking down my dress?"

The blush started at his neck. "You caught me. I couldn't help it."

She arched an eyebrow. "Couldn't help it?" Actually, he was the first guy tall enough to look down her dress while she was standing. It wasn't often that she came across men who could beat her six-five in heels.

"Okay, I didn't want to help it." He shrugged. "You have a nice body. It's not everyone who gets mistaken for a stripper."

"Wow, you just insist on digging that hole a little deeper." She shouldn't enjoy his discomfort, but she did.

"I'm so sorry. That sounded so much better in my head." His face was glow-in-the-dark red.

"I'm just messing with you." She whispered close to his ear, "You have a nice ass." She smacked him lightly on it. "Now we're even. I'm going to the buffet."

His look of total shock was priceless. He followed her. "Wait a minute."

"Boiled shrimp, my favorite." She picked up a plate and filled it with boiled shrimp and cocktail sauce. She appreciated good food but it wasn't important enough for her to actually cook it. She could cook, she just chose not to. When she was working, yogurt would suffice, but ice cream was better.

"You can't smack me on the butt and walk away." At that moment there was a lull in the conversation around them, so Cinco's voice carried and a few heads turned their way.

"Why not?" She twirled a fat shrimp in the cocktail sauce and then popped it into her mouth.

"Because . . . well . . . because . . ." He was at a loss for words, but clearly he wasn't a quitter so he kept on going. "It's just . . . well . . . women . . ."

"Double standard much? You can look down my dress and confuse me for a stripper, but the minute I slap you on the butt, you're offended. Really?" She popped another shrimp into her mouth.

"I apologized about the stripper thing, I thought we were over that." He looked a little lost, like he couldn't quite figure out how the conversation had taken such a turn.

She cocked her head to the left and shot him a look. "Please, I'm female. That means in my mind, I'm recording and cataloging every mistake you make so I can use it against you later." She tried to keep the "you idiot" out of her voice, but come on, he should have learned this long ago.

"What?" Bless him, he looked so helpless.

"It's the way of the world. Fifty years from now, we'll run into each other at the grocery store and I'll bring up the stripper thing just to make you feel bad—not because I'm still mad about it, but because I'm mad that you took the last package of Double Stuf Oreos off the shelf. While you're busy apologizing again, I'll steal the Oreos and put them in my basket. It's your classic female bait and switch. Frankly, I'm surprised you've made it this far in life and haven't figured it out." She licked cocktail sauce off her thumb.

He picked up a plate and piled boiled shrimp on it. "I don't like Double Stuf Oreos. Too much stuff."

She drew in a dramatic breath and put her hand over her heart. "You don't like Double Stuf Oreos?" She shook her head sadly. "I don't think we can be friends anymore."

"That's kind of harsh, don't you think?" One corner of his mouth curled up in a half smile.

"Maybe . . . Where do you land on Reese's Peanut Butter Cups?" It was an olive branch—that was the best she could do.

"I like them frozen. I have some in my freezer if you need proof." Instead of pooling his cocktail sauce, he just dumped a lot of it all over his shrimp.

Impressive. It seemed a messier but more efficient sauce-delivery method. Maybe she'd try that next time.

He moved on to the fajitas.

She thought about his response for a second. "I can live with that."

"Thank God, I was starting to feel bad."

"You know, the King Ranch has King Ranch Chicken. Y'all really should have something—maybe a Texas Rose Ranch Dip?" She examined the crudités. They really could have used some Texas Rose Ranch Dip.

"We make wine. Have you tried our Rancho Red Reserve? It just took the gold in the San Francisco International Wine Competition." There was quite a bit of pride in his voice. "My brother Rowdy is very proud of our wines."

"I'm sure it's very good, but I'm more of a beer girl myself." Until a year ago, she'd been forced to drink wine because Phillip loved wine. But now that he was out of her life, she didn't have to pretend to like it. "Have you ever tried cheesecake brownies and beer? It works—I don't know how, but it does."

"I see that you two are getting along better than the last time I saw you." Lucy smiled from across the table.

CanDee glanced up to find that several people were watching them.

She looked around. The whole room seemed to have stopped talking and was now staring at both her and Cinco.

She tried her hand at ventriloquism and whispered around the bright smile on her face. "Why is everyone staring at us?"

"It's because Cinco is usually a man of few words. In fact, I believe that he's spoken more to you at this party than I've heard him say in the last two months." Lucy grinned.

"You should dance for them and then you won't have to talk. Let your body do the talking, that's what I always say." She winked at him.

He threw back his head and laughed.

Lucy looked from her son to CanDee and back at her son. Another smile, slower than the last one, dawned. "That's the first time I've heard him laugh in a very long time."

"Really?" CanDee shook her head knowingly. "It's probably because of the Double Stuf Oreos . . . he doesn't like them. That can lead to depression, schizophrenia, and in extreme cases, gout. You're a doctor and on the frontlines, surely you've seen the devastation." She nodded toward Cinco and whispered loudly, "I think we're talking an intervention situation here."

"If I agree to try them again, will you get off of my back?" he asked through the tears of laughter streaming down his face.

CanDee rolled her eyes. "That sounds like an empty promise." She shook her head. "I can practically see the wheels turning in your head. You're planning on scraping half the stuff out before eating the Oreo. You're impossible."

"Just think of all that extra stuff waiting for you to claim it." He nodded. "See where I'm going with this?"

"Oh." She returned his nod. "Good point." She turned to Lucy. "The intervention's off."

"If you think that's best." Lucy looped her arm through CanDee's. "I'd like to introduce you to my other sons."

"Here." CanDee shoved her plate of food at Cinco. "Hold this. Don't eat my shrimp."

"Okay." He grinned at her. "You are so odd."

"This from a man who freezes his Reese's Peanut Butter Cups. Everyone knows they're supposed to be refrigerated." She shot him a sympathetic look. "Like my grandmother used to say, that's the pot calling the kettle a dumb ass."

"What does that even mean?" He shook his head.

She shrugged. "I don't know. My grandmother is crazy, but she makes fantastic banana bread." If only more people judged their peers based on banana bread, Grammie would have a lot more friends.

"So much makes sense about you now." He grinned. "Clearly derangement is a family thing."

"Look at you using your big words." She blew him a kiss. "It's so cute."

Lucy's blue eyes looked like aqua-colored drink coasters. "I think the next six weeks are going to be very interesting," she said with a grin before leading CanDee to a huge man with dark hair and kind, light-blue eyes.

"This is my husband, Bear." Lucy said.

CanDee noticed that she didn't introduce him as Lacy, which was completely understandable because his barrel chest and full beard made him look like a bear.

Bear held out his huge paw for her to shake. "It's so nice to meet you."

His eyes crinkled in the corners. He was like a hairy younger Santa Claus.

"It's nice to meet you too. You have a lovely home and what I've seen of the ranch is amazing." She shook his hand and found the handshake firm but not bone crushing. Grammie had always said that she could tell a lot about a person by their handshake. Based on Bear's firm but gentle shake, CanDee was willing to bet that he was a firm but gentle person.

"Thank you." He leaned in close to her ear. "I've never seen my oldest son flirt. It's pretty funny."

"Really?" She turned to look at Cinco, who was watching her. "He's very good at it. Maybe he practices when you're not looking."

"Nope, I think he hasn't found a woman who can bring him out of his shell." Bear nodded to himself. "Until now."

So Cinco didn't bring women home to meet his family often. Not that he'd brought her home to meet his father. CanDee was on the verge of making a joke about shelling Cinco like a pecan, but thought better of it. She was pretty sure the sexual innuendo was something his parents wouldn't appreciate.

Bear wrapped his arm around his wife and called across the room, "Rowdy, come meet CanDee."

A tall man in a navy three-piece suit grabbed two glasses of what looked like champagne off of a tray held by a caterer and walked over to them. Rowdy had his mother's coloring and eyes, but he must have gotten his six-foot-five height from his father. He was polished, not a single blond hair was out of place, and looked more businessman than rancher. He looked too tame to be named Rowdy.

"I'm Houston Rose, but my friends call me Rowdy. It's so nice to meet you." He handed her a glass. "This is our new Hill Country Sparkling Wine. Tell me what you think."

All eyes turned to her. She took a sip and found it to be fruity and not too dry. For a beer girl, she liked this wine very much. "I love it. I'm not much of a wine drinker, but this is fantastic."

He put a hand on her arm. "How about we get out of here and I take you on a personal wine tour?"

"Rowdy, stop hitting on her just to make your brother crazy." Lucy stood on her tiptoes and smacked him on the back of the head. She barely reached, but she managed to ruffle his hair. Clearly Lucy had been disciplining her sons with a smack to the head since her boys were children. CanDee wondered if she'd have chosen something else if she'd realized they were going to outgrow her.

"But driving him crazy is so much fun." A mischievous smile curled on Rowdy's lips. "Plus, you always said that you'd let us fight until we were two bloody spots on the carpet. I'm still waiting for that day."

"I've been pulling you two off of each other since the day you were born." Lucy rolled her eyes. "Clearly adulthood has done little to change things."

Rowdy winked at his brother. "He started it."

Cinco walked over. "Did not."

Lucy folded her arms and rolled her eyes skyward like she was asking for some help from upstairs. "When the two of you start throwing punches, I'm zapping you both with my stun gun."

Rowdy turned to his father. "Damn it, Dad. Why did you buy that thing for her in the first place?"

"Leave me out of this. I'm just an innocent bystander." Bear hugged his wife closer.

Clearly Lucy had been and still was the disciplinarian in the family. She might be tiny, but she was definitely mighty.

"Cool, a fight," a male voice said from behind CanDee.

She turned around to find two gorgeous men who looked just alike . . . identical twins. They were closer to Rowdy's height, had dark hair and baby blue eyes, and were in their late twenties. They smiled and matching dimples popped out on their cheeks.

"I'm Dallas," said the twin on the right, who then he pointed to his brother. "This is Worth—well, really it's Fort Worth, but we call him Worth."

"You don't have nicknames?" CanDee shook both of their hands in turn.

"No, ma'am, with names like Dallas and Fort Worth, they already sound like nicknames." Worth said. "Sorry about the whole stripper thing."

"Thanks for bringing that up." Cinco sighed like the weight of the world was on his shoulders. "Next she'll start grilling you on Double Stuf Oreos."

"Did someone say Double Stuf Oreos?" a baby-faced bear of a man with sandy-blond hair and brown eyes asked as he walked into the dining room. "I love Double Stuf Oreos."

"Finally, someone with taste." CanDee held out her hand. "I'm CanDee McCain."

"Nice to meet you, ma'am. I'm San Antonio Rose, but everyone calls me T-Bone." He was soft-spoken almost to the point of being shy.

Rowdy put him in a headlock and ruffled his hair. "This is the runt of the Rose litter."

T-Bone had to be at least six feet tall.

CanDee turned to Lucy. "You don't make small humans, do you?"

"Clearly their father's DNA is dominant." She smiled at her boys and her face held nothing but pride.

Had her mother's face held pride when she'd looked at CanDee? Her parents' faces were nothing but a blur. They had died when she was four, so she'd been raised by her grandmother. Grammie lived her life by her own set of rules—unfortunately those rules made sense to no one but her. Like Hallowthankmus, a combination of Halloween, Thanksgiving, and Christmas. Every single year, CanDee had to explain to Grammie that Christmas caroling in a Freddy Krueger mask made others uncomfortable. And, dressing up the Thanksgiving turkey as a Christmas elf wasn't the same as turkey and dressing. After Grammie had joined that coven, Halloween got to be its own holiday again. Thank God or Gaia or whoever. Even though the loss of her parents caused a hole that she felt she'd never been able to fill, she was grateful to Grammie for making her childhood so fun . . . and weird.

"Rowdy, let your brother go." Lucy went to slap him on the back of the head, but he was too fast for her and let his brother go. "I swear, if you'd been born first, we wouldn't have had any other children." She glanced at CanDee. "He was a difficult child, and it's been downhill from there." She laughed when she said it.

"I couldn't help but notice that you didn't name any of your children Austin." CanDee smiled.

"We all went to Texas A&M. Austin is a place that we tolerate, but rarely mention." Rowdy stepped beside her. "You're not from Austin, are you?"

"As a matter of fact, I am. Born and raised." She mashed her lips together to keep from smiling. "Want me to leave now on my own power, or would throwing me out satisfy your sense of collegiate loyalty?"

Rowdy turned on the charm. "Now, Miss CanDee, we wouldn't throw you out. We'd only suggest strongly that you vacate the premises immediately and never return."

"Can I kill him now?" Cinco pleaded to his mother as his hand found the small of CanDee's back again. It felt more than a little possessive, but she kind of liked it. "When I was ten, you said that one day you'd let me kill him, and today's as good as any."

"No murder in the living room." His mother took everything in stride. "Take it outside."

"She's right. Blood is so hard to get out from between the cracks in the wood floor. Grass, on the other hand—all it takes is a hose and some water to make that mess disappear." Either Dallas or Worth was speaking—she couldn't tell them apart.

"I went to Texas State instead of the University of Texas. Does that help your opinion of me?" CanDee liked the big, loud Rose family. Every touch and jibe showed how much they loved each other.

"Well, that's something." This time it was the other twin. "I guess she can stay."

"Let me introduce you around." Cinco put a small amount of pressure at the small of her back, urging her forward.

CanDee looked around. Besides her and Lucy, there didn't seem to be any other women. "Does this party seem a little male heavy?"

Not that she was intimidated, it was just a little strange. She'd been to a couple of parties at the King Ranch and even they hadn't been this XY-chromosome laden.

"Female ranch hands are hard to come by." He shrugged. "The guys would love it if I hired more women, but cowgirls don't grow on trees."

A Christmas tree with cowgirls as ornaments popped into her mind. "That's an interesting image . . . the cowgirl tree. I bet harvesting them would be difficult."

Cinco just grinned and shook his head.

"Good to know that you're an equal-opportunity employer." CanDee smiled at the group of men they were approaching. "There's something I don't understand. There's supposed to be an after-party, right?"

"In the bunkhouse."

"So why didn't your brothers hire the stripper for the after-party? Wouldn't that have been a better choice than having her drop by this afternoon?" Not that stripper scheduling was CanDee's forte, but a little common sense went a long way.

"Scheduling conflict. She said something about doing a CIA gig this evening." He bit his top lip. "Just so you know, I sent her home after you walked out."

"I bet your brothers weren't too happy that you didn't enjoy their present." It was really none of her business, but she was a little relieved that he'd sent the stripper home instead of enjoying the show. It was interesting that she felt relief—or anything about someone she'd just met.

"I think it's time my brothers and I created a new tradition that doesn't involve strippers for my birthday." He was dead serious.

"My birthday's in a few weeks. Can you ask them to get me a stripper?" She grinned. "I want a dude, though, maybe dressed as a cop."

She glanced up at him. The horror on his face was hilarious.

"And he needs to be able to dance. I don't mean a little either. He needs to have more than two moves that he does over and over. I expect some pelvic thrusts in my direction before he yanks off the pull-away pants. It is my special day." She had a hard time keeping the giggle out of her voice. Cinco was such an easy mark.

"I'll see what I can do." He sighed like his burden was great.

"You're a good man." She patted his cheek.

It was too early to tell, but she wanted to believe that he really was a good man.

CHAPTER 4

CanDee put a hand on Cinco's shoulder and leaned against him as she slipped off her shoes. "I told you I was going to be crippled by the time your party was over."

What were the chances that he'd carry her? She glanced down at her dress. It was kind of short. If he Rhett Butlered her, the bottom of her dress would hang open. If he fireman-carried her, the back of her dress would ride up. The only answer was a piggyback ride and since she wasn't eight years old, it seemed like a bad thing to ask of a man who'd she'd only met a few hours ago.

"I'm willing to admit that the shoes were worth it." One corner of his mouth turned up. "I could stand to see you in those shoes again."

"Are you asking me out on a date?" She tried her hand at coy as she elbowed him playfully.

His cheeks turned a nice shade of red.

"Yes . . . no . . . maybe." His voice was high and squeaky. He cleared his throat. "The man likes to do the asking."

"You don't get out much, do you?" She patted his upper arm. His was nothing but hard, lean muscle.

He offered her his elbow and she took it.

"I'm willing to admit I don't date much, but I still believe that men should do the asking, open doors for women, and pick up the check." He shrugged. "Call me old fashioned."

"I'm not going to lie, I mostly agree with those things too, but since you haven't asked me out yet, I'm about to change my mind." She waited. "I'm not getting any younger here."

"I'll ask you out when I'm ready." He grinned. It seemed that he was messing with her.

"So I guess now's a bad time to bring up our sex life." She could give as good as she got. She had a PhD in messing with people.

"What?" His voice was an octave higher than normal. He cleared his throat. "What?"

"I should tell you that I don't like to mix business with pleasure, so when we sleep together you're going to have to sneak out before sunup." She bit her bottom lip to keep from laughing as he led her down the front porch steps and into the cool grass covering the yard.

She noticed that he'd avoided taking her down the granite walkway and went onto the grass instead because she was barefoot.

"Wait . . . no . . . wait, what?" he sputtered. In the fading light from the porch, she could just make out the blush staining his cheeks.

"We are not sleeping together," he whispered.

"Why are you whispering?" she whispered back.

"Because . . ." He looked around. "I don't know."

"So back to our sex life: you have to sneak out because I'm not walk-of-shaming it in the morning from your place. Call me old fashioned, but I think it's the man's responsibility to hit it and quit it before the sun comes up." This was a relatively new rule for her since all the men she'd woken up beside in the past had betrayed her in some way. She was determined to kick the next guy out of her bed before she could wake up to find that he'd stolen her money, her car, or worse, her heart.

"What about breakfast?" He guided her around a tree.

"I'm happy to send you on your way with a tub of yogurt, but the spoon is your responsibility." She was firm on the spoon. God knew she'd lost more than her fair share over the years.

"What if I want to stay?" His voice was quiet, thoughtful.

"Sorry. I like my space." After her last relationship, she'd vowed to date like a man. Besides, she wasn't going to be here that long. Her heart had been broken and she wasn't eager to repeat that experience anytime soon. "Don't you have another party to go to?"

"Yes." He seemed relieved that she'd changed the subject.

She was happy to give him a reprieve . . . for now.

"I bet your next party involves lots of booze, some poker, and maybe a hooker or two. It's a shame your stripper had a previous engagement." She patted his arm. "I hope you have fun anyway."

He glanced down at her. She winked at him.

"You got the liquor and cards right. No prostitutes or strippers." He was whispering again.

So he was a prude when it came to sex . . . interesting.

"Have you ever been with a hooker?" She, however, was not a prude when it came to sex or just about anything else.

"No." He sounded scandalized. "Have you?"

"No, but I'd love to know if they're better at sex than a nonprofessional. I wish I knew one to ask." She shook her head. She'd always been a live-and-let-live kind of person and she sure as heck didn't begrudge anyone making a living. "I'd love to interview one. Do you know any?"

Abruptly, he stopped and stared down at her. "No, why would I know a prostitute?"

"You're right. Just because you're a man who spends a lot of time around other men doesn't mean that you know any hookers." She nodded. He'd caught her in a stereotype. "Sorry, it's the writer side of me. We like to know what makes people tick." She sucked on her bottom lip. "Mind if I ask around the bunkhouse if anyone knows a hooker?"

They resumed walking.

"Yes, I mind. I think you hanging around the bunkhouse is a bad idea and I sure as hell don't want you talking about"—he whispered the last word—"hookers."

She shook her head. They were back to whispering.

A minute or so of silence passed between them.

"So, are you going to kiss me goodnight on the porch?" She hip-bumped him.

"You're relentless." This time he laughed.

"I prefer *focused*." She hunched her shoulders. "Tomayto . . . tomahto."

"I don't kiss on the first date." He tried his hand at serious, but the grin on his face told another story.

"You think this was a date?" She sighed long and hard. "Maybe if we were in high school. For the love of God, you just took me to your parents' house for dinner." She hunched her shoulders. "You did bring me flowers, but since they were an apology, they don't count."

"Looks like we're back to square one." He looked up at the night sky. "Nice stars tonight."

She glanced up. Out here in the middle of nowhere, light pollution wasn't a problem. The night sky was a black velvet cape studded with millions of rhinestones. "Beautiful."

"Wanna see something really spectacular?" He slowed their pace.

"I don't know." She sucked in a breath. "This isn't where you pull out your smartphone and show me creepy pictures of your penis, is it? Because . . . been there, done that. I met a guy online. On our first date, he took me to Cheddar's and before our waters arrived, he pulled out his phone and showed me pictures of his new hobby—penis puppetry. It was disturbing."

"Sounds painful." He shivered.

"You have no idea. He had little costumes. To be fair, the Cher one really did look like her." She'd never been able to figure out how he'd gotten the black, spiked wig to stay on the head of his penis—glue? Tape? Both sounded really horrible.

"Penis puppetry aside, no, I was talking about the lookout tower." He pointed to the sky. "It's the best place to see the stars."

"A lookout tower—like the kind in a castle turret where they watch for an enemy invasion?" She glanced back at the main house. Maybe there was another castle somewhere on the property? Personally, she thought one castle was more than enough.

"Not a castle tower, but a lookout tower—the kind used to spot fire before we installed cameras everywhere. My great-great-aunt had one built in the early 1900s after a fire took out the main house and several hundred acres." He pointed off to the right. "It's a couple of miles that way. We can take the golf cart to my house and then take my truck."

"I'm so glad you have a truck. I'd hate to think of you tootling around in a Chevy Malibu or a Volkswagen Beetle. Don't get me wrong, I like for people to surprise me, but that would be too big of a shock to overcome." She leaned into him. "So, are you planning on kissing me at the top of the lookout tower?"

"This is like the Double Stuf Oreo thing, right? You're not going to drop it." He tried to pull off an accusatory tone, but his broad grin was a dead giveaway.

"Now that you reminded me, I need to drop by the cottage on the way." She needed to pick up dessert.

"You've finally come to your senses." He nodded to the shoes she held. "I'm going to miss those."

"Huh?" She glanced down. "Oh yeah, I should probably pick up some different shoes while I'm there."

He stopped at the cottage front porch steps. She clomped up and inside the cottage. She grabbed a pair of socks, some purple Converse high-tops, and a bag of Double Stuf Oreos.

She headed back outside. Cinco opened the door for her before she could get it.

"You're really serious about your Double Stuf Oreos." He closed the door behind her.

"It's time to put up or shut up, Cowboy." She sat on the front steps and set the cookies and shoes down next to her. She unrolled the sock ball and was about to slip one on when he took the sock from her.

"Allow me." He slipped the white sock over her left foot and then took the other and slipped it over her right. He grabbed a shoe.

"You a foot-fetish man?" She tried to keep the revulsion out of her voice.

"I take it you're not into feet." He slipped on the left shoe and tied it for her.

He reminded her of the shoe salesman at the mall, only he was missing that stool-shoe-rampy-thing and that flat silver metal plate thing they used to measure feet. Both made her cringe. "I'm pretty open minded when it comes to sex, but I don't do feet. Once, I dated this guy who was really into feet. After we'd spent the day tromping around downtown Austin for South By Southwest, he took off my sandals and started sucking my toes. All I could think was how dirty my feet were and that he really shouldn't be driving and sucking my toes at the same time."

She couldn't help but gag. It was nasty.

"I'm trying to picture the driving and sucking the toes, but I can't get he mechanics down." He slipped the shoe onto her right foot and then tied it for her. He offered her his hand to help her up.

She grabbed the Oreos and took his hand. "He had a convertible and I'm very flexible."

Actually she'd just had her back against the door and her feet in his lap. It had started with a foot rub and things had gone downhill from there.

He guided her to a big gunmetal-gray barn. "This is where we keep the golf carts and ATVs. If you need one, just sign it out. The clipboard's over there." He pointed to a clipboard hanging on a nail beside a closed door with *OFFICE* spelled out in stick-on letters. "Try to return it when you're finished so that Lefty, our mechanic, can make sure to keep it gassed up."

"Do I want to know why his name is Lefty?" She followed him to the barn.

"I have no idea." He lifted the small metal bar serving as a lock and pulled the sliding barn door open.

He flicked a switch and a legion of fluorescent lights flickered on. The barn had to be at least two stories and was cleaner than an operating room. Six golf carts, seven ATVs, and several other small vehicles, including an old white Ford truck, each had their own parking space. Tools hung on the back wall in perfectly outlined spaces. The gray concrete floor looked to have been freshly swept.

"Wow, Lefty is a neat freak." Not that she knew a lot of mechanics, but she'd spent more than her fair share of time having her old Toyota Corolla repaired and she'd never seen any garage—or, for that matter, many houses—as clean as this.

"You have no idea." Cinco stepped inside and slid behind the wheel of the closest golf cart. "Once, I didn't park exactly in the lines and he revoked my golf cart privileges for a week. I had to walk everywhere. It sucked."

"He works for you. How come he has so much power?" Clearly ranch politics were very complicated.

"He was my grandfather's best friend. Lefty's been around longer than I have. He's family." He turned the key and the gas-powered motor came to life. He drove it out the door and stopped a couple of feet from the barn.

CanDee pulled the barn door shut before he could jump out of the seat and help her. She liked for men to close doors for her, but she wanted to show him that she could do it too.

"I could have gotten that." He stepped out from behind the wheel.

"I know, but it was easier for me to do it." She walked over to the cart and took the passenger's seat.

Cinco sat back down. He put the cart in gear and gently mashed the gas pedal.

"My house is a mile or so down that path." He pointed back over his left shoulder and then turned the cart toward the path.

"Do you all have houses?" Clearly the family was close. They all still lived on the ranch. It was like the Kennedy Compound, only bigger and less snotty.

"Yes . . . and no." He turned onto the path. "Over the years, many houses have been built for ranch hands and foremen and family. My house was built in 1900 for my great-great-aunt. She was quite the cattlewoman."

He hadn't mentioned her husband. So he'd had an old maiden great-great-aunt.

"With all of these men around, I wonder why she never married." It was kind of sad. CanDee chewed on her bottom lip. Maybe some horrible tragedy had taken her beloved. "Was there some sort of accident that killed her fiancé?"

"I didn't say that she didn't marry . . . she was a lesbian. Her partner's name was Edith Grover. They did get married . . . sort of." He sounded matter-of-fact.

"I bet that was hard for the family to handle back in the day." Even now, she wasn't sure that it was easy for a family to handle.

"Not really. Back then homosexuality was called 'mutual solace.' I'm told that Great-Great-Aunt Mel—short for Mellifluous—was a much better businessman and a way better shot than her three brothers. She ran the ranch while Edith took care of the house. Mel threatened to shoot her brothers if they interfered in the cattle business. I never met her, but I think I would have liked her." She could tell he was proud of his family and would be a great resource for the genealogy. Picking his brain was going to be so much fun.

"I wish I'd remembered to bring my legal pad. I need to jot down these facts so I can research them." It wasn't that she was absent minded, it was only that she forgot things.

"I believe that you'll find their marriage certificate in the family museum. It used to hang on the wall, but I think the frame broke, so I'm not sure where it is."

"How were Mel and Edith able to get married?" Gay marriage had just become legal.

"I believe that I mentioned Mel was good with a gun." He laughed. "Apparently, Edith refused to live in sin, so they were married. Edith took the Rose last name. It was all very official."

"Wow. Your family history is way more interesting than I'd thought it would be." She was itching to dig into the research. When it came to research, she was a demon. That's why *Murder, Mayhem, and Madness* had been such a runaway hit. She'd left no Internet stone unturned and had taken several trips to remote Texas towns to get the feel just right. It might have been fiction, but it was factually accurate fiction. Too bad her ex, Phillip, was the one raking in the cash from her labor of love.

"Just on my father's side. My mother's side is pretty boring. They're all doctors . . . every single one of them." He turned the corner and a huge three-story Victorian house came into view. An outdoor light illuminated the huge wraparound porch and lots of white frilly carpentry, but the most intriguing part of the house was the bubble-gum-pink exterior.

She turned to Cinco. "You are a man of mystery and great confidence. I can't imagine living in a pink house is easy out here amongst all of these cowboys."

"Edith liked a lot of froth. In her will, she stipulated that the outside of the house and barn should remain pink or she'd haunt whoever lived here." He pulled around the front of the house to the huge matching pink barn. "It's common knowledge that Mel hated the pink and threatened to change it as soon as Edith died."

"Did she?" She took in the white trim. The house reminded her of scoops of strawberry ice cream.

"No, she died a couple of months after Edith."

CanDee put her hand over her heart. "That's so sad. She died of a broken heart."

"Nope. Lung cancer. She smoked something like fifty hand-rolled, unfiltered cigarettes a day. It was amazing she lived as long as she did." He set the brake, turned off the ignition, and came around to offer his hand to CanDee.

She took it. "I keep trying to make her out to be a romantic and she keeps shutting me down."

"I'm pretty sure romantic was the exact opposite of Mel, but I could be wrong. Maybe you'll unearth some notebook of her love poetry, but I wouldn't hold my breath if I were you." He led her to the side of the barn where a lean-to housed a brand-new fancy pick-'em-up truck, a four wheeler, a motorcycle up on blocks, and an old metal Coke machine that appeared to be in the middle of a restoration. So he was a fixer-upper. As Cinco revealed new facets of his personality, she was able to place another piece of the puzzle. She loved figuring out puzzles, and he was an especially intriguing one.

Her grandmother was also a fixer-upper; unfortunately, she also wasn't much of a finisher, so half-finished projects cluttered her house, garage, and backyard. Hopefully, Cinco was not only a fixer-upper, but was strong out of the gate and gave it his all until the job was done.

"Do I get to see the inside of your pink house?" She was ready to jump into his life with both feet and see what made him tick, which had the potential to be another in a bad series of decisions when it came to men. Hadn't she talked herself into taking things slowly?

"Another time, Stretch. The cleaning lady comes tomorrow and I'm afraid you'd run away screaming if I took you in there now." He opened the passenger-side door of his truck for her.

She noticed the logo as she climbed up. "This is the Texas Rose Edition. I didn't know y'all had moved into leather interior too." The King Ranch had been providing quality leather products for Ford trucks for years. Now it seemed that the Texas Rose was doing the same for Chevy.

"It's another revenue stream. Chevy came to us wanting something to compete with the King Ranch Edition. I was more than happy to sell them some leather." He closed her door and walked around the hood of the truck, opened his door, climbed up, and closed it. He started the truck and backed out.

It just occurred to her. "Why do I get the feeling that you spend more time on the business side of things than you do with the cows?"

"It's true, unfortunately. Long days in the saddle are getting fewer and fewer." He sounded sad.

"Wait a minute." She turned to him. "Shouldn't you be at your birthday party?"

"I'm sure it'll still be going strong when I get there." He pressed his index finger and thumb to the bridge of his nose.

She got the distinct impression that he was tired and wanted nothing more than to go to bed.

"We don't have to do this tonight. Sounds like you've had a long day. Why don't you take me back to the cabin?" It was his birthday, he should be able to do whatever he wanted. "You sound tired."

"I am. Did I say that long days in the saddle were few and far between . . . well, except for today. I've been up since four this morning." He sighed long and hard.

"That's just crazy talk." She pulled an Oreo out of the bag and munched on it. "I'm pretty sure that serial killers and drunk frat boys are the only people up at four."

"I love the random bizarre things that come out of your mouth." He pulled onto a wide dirt road.

She had to admit that made her heart go pitter-patter. Phillip had hated her chattiness and oddball sense of humor. He'd done a lot of eye rolling every time she'd opened her mouth, so she'd learned to bite her tongue. It said a lot about their relationship that she couldn't be herself around him. If only she'd noticed it before he'd run off with her debut novel.

"You look tired. It's okay to do this another time. Looks like you need to go to bed." It was a shame. She liked his company and wasn't eager for the night to end.

"Always trying to get me into bed." He grinned. "You have a one-track mind."

"A girl shows a little concern and your mind goes to the gutter." She watched his face turn red. He was so much fun.

"Um . . . I didn't mean . . . to . . . you know."

"You're such an easy target," she teased as she unbuckled her seat belt and turned to face him. She had her back to the door.

"Put your seat belt back on. Buckle up, it's the law."

Was he kidding? Was he worried about her or was he a staunch rule follower? He didn't strike her as a total conformist, so she couldn't help the smile. Aside from her grandmother, no one had shown concern for her in a long time.

"I'm pretty sure there aren't any cops on the ranch. Besides, you're going maybe four miles an hour down a road you could probably navigate blindfolded. I'll take my chances."

She pulled one of her legs up, straightened it so that it was almost in his face, and pointed her toes. "You wanted to know how the toe-sucking happened."

With her shoe, she tapped him on the shoulder.

"You are limber." A slow smiled worked its way across his face. "Nice."

"Yoga. You should try it." She reached over and patted his thigh. "Work out those tight muscles."

Then again, Phillip had tried yoga and the yoga instructor.

"Yoga's too girlie. Nope, horseback riding is all the exercise I need."

"This from a man who lives in a pink house and probably listens to Taylor Swift?" Her shoulders shook with laughter. "If you have enough man points to cover that, yoga is nothing."

"I don't know why haters gotta hate." He shook his head. "Maybe you should 'Shake It Off.'"

"I never thought I'd hear a grown man quoting Taylor Swift." She hunched one shoulder. "It's not as frightening as I'd thought it would be."

She leaned over and hit the power button on the radio. Katy Perry's

"Teenage Dream" roared out. She switched it off and laughed so hard her eyes watered.

"What?"

"I'm just picturing you at a Katy Perry concert in the front row, dancing to the songs." She patted his thigh again. "It's just so darn cute."

He picked up an Oreo and shoved it in her mouth. "Chew on this for a while."

So he was sensitive about his music. She chewed on the Oreo and then swallowed.

"Now, it's your turn." She fed him one.

He chewed and chewed and chewed. Finally, he swallowed. "It's just too much stuff."

He picked up another one and popped it into his mouth. He chewed and chewed and chewed. "Yep, too much stuff."

"Are you kidding? There's never enough stuff. That's like saying, 'Gosh, I have too much money.'" She popped one into her own mouth. The stuff-to-cookie ratio was perfect. Come to think of it, he probably did have too much money. Given her history, that would be a switch, and she wasn't sure how she felt about it. According to Phillip, money was all she'd had to offer, but since he was a narcissistic asshole, his opinion was right up there with tonsils or pantyhose in the usefulness department. A person didn't need them, so what was the point?

Apart from Cinco's hatred of Double Stuf Oreos and his possible overabundance of money, he seemed like an okay person.

Up until now, life had dealt her some crummy cards, but as she glanced at this strong, sensitive, and sweet man who didn't want anything from her except her company, it occurred to her that maybe . . . just maybe . . . her luck was starting to change.

CHAPTER 5

Cinco was exhausted, but he just couldn't bring himself to end the evening with CanDee. There was something about her that made him smile . . . like an idiot . . . all of the time. There weren't any awkward conversational pauses because there was always something to talk about. And he'd just about laughed himself hoarse for the first time in a long time. He had a feeling that she was going to be important to him.

He glanced at the clock on the dash. It was after nine. The closest restaurant was Dairy Queen and it was over an hour away. "Hungry?"

"Not really. You?" CanDee picked up the bag of Oreos and waggled it at him. Moonlight streamed in from behind her and made her skin glow.

"Not so much." He pulled up to the fence surrounding the lookout tower. So much for the receipt. He'd find something to keep with him so the night never ended.

He jumped down from this truck and picked up the combination lock, rolling the tumblers until they clicked in place and the lock sprang open. After pulling the chain free, he swung the large metal gate open, secured the chain and lock around the handle, and returned to the truck.

The driver-side window rolled down. "I'll pull through and you can lock the gate."

As the man he felt like it was his job to take care of the details like driving through, but it was nice that she wanted to help out. He moved aside and let her pull into the pasture before locking the gate.

CanDee put the truck in park, turned off the engine, and opened the door. "I didn't even have to move your seat."

She handed him the keys. The headlights stayed on, lighting up the zigzag of stairs leading all the way up to the top of the lookout tower. He went to the passenger side, opened the extended-cab door, and pulled out a blanket and a large metal flashlight.

"Isn't the blanket a little presumptuous?" He could tell that she loved messing with him.

"Nope. The entire building is made of metal and this time of year it gets cold. If we're going to lie down and watch the stars, we should be comfortable."

He flicked on the flashlight and pointed it at the metal stairs. "Ladies first."

She ran up the first flight of stairs and turned back to look down on him. "I bet you had me go first so you could look up my skirt."

He ran up the flight behind her. "No, but do you always wear tiny lace underwear?"

It wasn't that he'd been looking, but the wind had blown her skirt up and he'd gotten a pretty good look at that tiny excuse for underwear. He'd only gotten a view of the backside. Was the front as itty-bitty? He wouldn't mind having the opportunity to peel them off of her.

This time it was her turn to blush. By the light of the flashlight, he could make out two dots of rose-petal pink—one on each cheek.

"Pervert. I've agreed to watch the stars with a total pervert." She held out her hand. "Give me the flashlight and you go first."

"Why?" He grinned. "I'm enjoying the view."

"A little too much." She pointed to the flashlight. "Hand it over."

"But if you stumble, I won't be able to catch you if I'm in front." That really was the reason he'd had her go first; the lacy panties had just been a bonus.

"It's a risk I'm willing to take to keep your eyes off my thong." She folded her arms.

"OK." Gently, he turned her around. "I'll follow closer and I promise not to look up."

She rolled her eyes. "Fine."

She started on the next flight and true to his word, he was right behind her.

"Do you always wear a thong?"

She bumped the flashlight as she turned around and looked down her nose at him.

"What? I'm not looking at them. I just wanted to know for future reference." He'd tried to get Naomi to wear a thong, but she hated them. So there were women who actually wore them because they liked them? He grinned to himself.

"Why are you so interested in my underwear?" She stomped up the stairs.

"Just making conversation. My ex-wife wasn't into frilly underwear." His ex-wife hadn't been into much except spending his money on everything except lacy underwear.

"You were married?" She looked back over her shoulder.

"Five wonderful . . . peaceful years." He hadn't meant to sound so cynical.

"Don't believe in marriage?" She turned back around and continued up the steps. She wasn't even breathing hard.

"I didn't say that." He'd never really thought about it before. "I do believe in marriage. I just don't believe in marriage to Naomi."

He dreaded the next question . . . the one where she asked what happened. Should he lie and tell her that they'd grown apart or should he tell her the truth and risk looking like an idiot because he hadn't known his wife was cheating?

She nodded. "Makes sense. I've learned a thing or two from my exes. Although, I was lucky enough not to have married any of them."

He waited for the "what happened" question but it never came.

"You neglected to mention the four hundred flights of stairs when you brought up stargazing." She still wasn't out of breath, but she'd slowed down. "My thighs are burning."

"Must be all of that yoga that keeps you so in shape." He couldn't help it. Sparring with her was so much fun.

"Put up or shut up, Cowboy. Yoga at the cottage at noon tomorrow. Show up or I'll know you're afraid."

"You're on." He'd do it just to watch her do yoga. Hell, he'd show up just to watch her stand there and read from Dictionary.com.

"Good God, how many more steps are there?" She looked up and grimaced.

"Only four more flights to go."

"You don't have to sound so cheerful." She stomped up the steps.

"I'm a complex man with lots of layers. I find humor in the strangest things." He was struggling to keep up with her. His thighs were on fire too.

"I thought your mom said you weren't much of a talker. Now I can't get you to shut up." She stomped up another flight of stairs.

"You bring out my inner teenaged girl. Want me to text you? Later, we can braid each other's hair and post the pictures on Instagram." He grinned.

"Lucky me." She climbed the last flight of stairs and threw her arms up like Rocky taking a victory lap. "I haven't climbed that many stairs since my ex decided to be a personal trainer and thought I needed to get into shape. Thank God he'd only wanted to be one long enough to get the certification."

It was on the tip of his tongue to ask what had happened with the personal trainer, but she hadn't asked what went wrong with Naomi, so she deserved the same courtesy.

He climbed the last stairs and used the flashlight to point her in the direction of the observation deck.

She followed the beam of light to the rail and looked up. "Okay, this is worth it."

He spread the blanket out and sat.

She turned around and leaned against the rail. "So, you bring all of your women up here?"

She made it sound like he'd had dozens.

"No." He thought about it as he patted the real estate next to him. "You're the only one."

"Uh huh." She sat beside him.

"No, really." He looked up at the stars. He pointed up. "That's the Big Dipper and there's Ursa Major. See, there's the head. It's supposed to look like a big bear, but I think it looks more like a turtle."

"I guess you learned all about the stars on all those cattle drives. Spending the night under the stars and all of that." CanDee lay down on her back and stared up at the sky.

"No, there's an app on my iPad. You hold it up to the sky and it maps the stars."

Her hair spilled all around him and the scents of peaches and coconut drifted up. Her full bottom lip was ripe for sucking. With the moonlight dancing off of her creamy skin, she was impossibly beautiful. He wanted her in his bed with her hair scenting his pillow and he wanted to wake up next to her with his arms tangled around her.

When he was seventeen, Cinco had been pretty sure that he loved Jenny Drake, but before he fell all over himself telling her, he'd asked how his father had known that he loved his mother. His father told him about their first date. His mother had been an exhausted resident working a rotation in the ER when his father had brought in a ranch hand who'd broken his arm. His father asked her to have dinner with him and she'd turned her back on him and left the room. He had shown up at the ER every single night until she had agreed to get coffee with him in the cafeteria. When he got to this point in the story, Cinco's father pulled out something from his wallet to show Cinco. It was the crumpled hospital cafeteria receipt from his first date with his mother, which he still kept in his wallet to this day. His dad had told him that night was special and as long as he had the receipt with him, the magic of the night would never end.

More than ever, he wished he had a receipt like his father had to remember this night. Cinco understood now how important it was to have something tangible to mark this night because he knew it was the start of something special. His feelings weren't logical or even practical, but he knew this was a beginning and he never wanted the magic to end. Nothing he'd ever done with Naomi felt this special. He took out his phone, scooted up next to CanDee, pulled up the camera icon, and held it out at arm's length. "Smile."

The flash went off and then he turned the camera around to see the picture. His thumb made a tiny appearance off in the left corner, but mostly—well, minus half of his left ear—the picture was of two smiling people who looked happy. He hadn't thought of himself as happy, or for that matter seen himself happy in a very long time. Just the thought of CanDee made him grin and want to do things like bring her flowers and drop by the cottage just to see what she was doing and to call her just to hear the sound of her voice. Oh God, he was turning into a girl.

"Now that I'm blind"—she rubbed her eyes and turned her face toward him—"how bad is the picture?"

He turned his face toward her.

"Really good, actually." And much better than a receipt.

His mouth was inches from hers. He could feel her warm breath on his cheek. It occurred to him that he wouldn't mind spending the next million nights doing this . . . just sitting here with her. She made him laugh. In his mind, that made her the perfect female. The itty-bitty panties didn't hurt either.

"In case you're getting lost in your head, I'd like to point out that this is the perfect kissing moment." She grinned up at him. "Just FYI."

He inched closer to her opened mouth and gently ran his lips from one corner of her mouth all the way to the other.

Under his hand, the muscles of her shoulder tensed up and her breathing turned heavy. Fear, not pleasure radiated off of her. Not the reaction he'd expected.

"Please tell me that's your finger that just slithered up my thigh." Her voice was a frantic whisper. He held up both of his hands for her to see and then grabbed the flashlight and pointed the beam at her lap.

"Don't be alarmed." He jumped up, grabbed the snake, and tossed it over the railing. "There was a snake on your leg."

"Oh my God." She jumped up and did her best to climb up the front of his body. "A snake?"

He patted her back. "It's fine. I threw it over the side. It's gone."

"There's probably more. Oh my God. We're in the middle of a snake pit or den or nest or something." She wriggled her way back behind him. "It's just like that scene in *Indiana Jones* when they were dropped in the snake pit. Is the floor moving?"

She wrapped her legs around his waist piggyback style.

Gently, he pried her hands from around his neck and held one in each of his. "Hush, it was one snake. It's gone. They climb up here sometimes from the trees next to the lookout. Usually, they're all out hunting during the night. I guarantee you that snake is more afraid of you than you are of it."

"I seriously doubt it. I hate snakes, especially ones that slither up my leg." Her voice was frantic and he could feel her heartbeat pounding away in her chest.

"So I guess you're piggybacking it down the stairs." He bent at the knee with her still on his back, let go of one of her hands, and grabbed the blanket. He rolled it up in a ball and tossed it over the side. He couldn't carry her and it down all of those stairs.

"That's my plan." She locked her feet together. "I hope you don't have a bad back because while I'll feel terrible about making it worse, I'm not prepared to set foot on the lookout."

"It's going to be fine. You're going to be fine." He used the tone he reserved for skittish horses and scared females. "Grab hold of my shirt. I need both of my hands to reposition you."

"Okay." She took two fistfuls of his shirt and pulled on it so hard that it came untucked, rode up, and was choking him.

With both of his hands, he reached around behind him and grabbed two handfuls of smooth, round ass. Apparently her dress had flapped open and his hands had traveled under it. His fingertips brushed the tiniest scrap of soft lace.

He repositioned her more firmly on his back. "You weren't kidding about the thong."

"I should be embarrassed, but since fear kicks embarrassed's ass every time, I'm going to pretend that your hands aren't caressing my bare butt." Her fingers loosened and she flattened out the wrinkles she'd put in his shirt. She ran her hands up and down his shoulders. "You have nice shoulders."

"Stop fondling me and loop your arms loosely around my neck." Was he really going to have to carry her down ten flights of steps? She was kind of heavy—not that he was going to mention that. He had a highly developed sense of self-preservation and knew what not to say to a woman.

"I'll stop picturing you shirtless when you get your hands off of my butt," she said close to his ear. "You know, you're the first guy who's managed to get your hands under my skirt before we've actually kissed."

"I kissed you." Slowly, he moved his hands down her thighs and around to the tops of her shoes.

"No, you didn't." She looped her arms loosely around his neck. "Wait . . . maybe you did. But the whole snake episode ruined it. Besides, I didn't get any tongue. It's not a real kiss unless there's tongue."

"Has anyone ever told you that you're pushy?" He bent down and picked up the flashlight.

"Now that you mention it, I do believe Thomas Murray-Carter accused me of that in the seventh grade. It was something about being too intimidated by me to ask me out." She leaned forward and rested her chin on his left shoulder. "Come to think of it, I didn't get any tongue from him either."

"What ever happened to Thomas?" He used his hands on the stair rail to steady himself as he started down the stairs.

"He and his wife are big swingers . . . not the dance kind. He's bald and pudgy now. He and his wife hit on me profusely when I ran into them at Amy's Ice Creams about a year or so ago."

"I'll never understand Austin. I would never share my wife with anyone." The irony was that he hadn't had to because she'd shared herself with everyone but him.

"Yeah, I can tell you that it's a conversation I never hope to have again. While I'm pretty much a live-and-let-live kind of person, I really didn't want to know that much about their personal life. Now I can't walk into that Amy's Ice Creams without throwing up a little in my mouth. It sucks because that's the closest Amy's. Now I have to drive to one farther from my house." Her voice tickled his ear.

"You could just get your ice cream from the grocery store like the rest of the world." There was nothing wrong with store-bought ice cream. He had a half gallon of cookies and cream in his freezer at the moment.

"You're skating on very thin ice cream here. I haven't forgotten about the Double Stuf Oreos. Right now, all that's keeping you in my good graces are some frozen Reese's Peanut Butter Cups and the ability to carry me down ten flights of stairs." She laughed and the sound made him smile.

"All roads lead back to the Double Stuf Oreos."

"They are the center of the universe." He heard the shoulder shrug in her voice. "My life revolves around them. I don't make the rules."

He hoofed it down another flight of stairs and then the next.

"So, you're really planning on carrying me down all ten flights of stairs?" Her voice was as dark and rich as the Rancho Red wine that his brother was so proud of.

"You're a lady in distress, I'm saving you." It was as simple as that.

"I figured I was good for two, maybe three flights, but you're in it for the long haul. I admire that level of commitment." She sniffed his collar. "You smell good. What is that?"

He thought she smelled pretty damn good too. "Tide laundry detergent and Dial soap. Real men don't wear perfume."

"That should be a T-shirt—Real Men Don't Wear Perfume." She rested her head on his shoulder.

"Real men don't wear T-shirts that say 'Real Men Don't Wear Perfume.'" He was almost halfway.

"So many rules. Here I thought women had all of the rules . . . no white after Labor Day, no horizontal stripes, chunky heels are out, and no pleated pants because they make our butts look fat. But really, it's you men who have it hard." She patted his shoulder. "You can put me down anytime."

"No, ma'am. Hauling you around is good exercise. I call it the piggyback workout. I need to keep in shape. Occasionally, I have to pick up a calf and move it. You weigh less than that." He pulled her legs tighter around him.

"Good God, I hope I weigh less than a cow. How flattering." She tightened her arms around his neck.

"You're choking me."

"That's the point." She loosened her grip.

"What I was trying to say, was that you . . ." He'd already stuck his foot in it and he was smart enough to know when to walk away. "I'm going to quit while I'm ahead."

"Who said you were ahead?" she said close to his ear.

"Good point."

"You can put me down now, anytime." She jiggled a little like she was going to climb down.

"I'm good." He hadn't given a piggyback ride in twenty years. And he'd never enjoyed it more than he did right now. She was warm and he could stand to have her legs wrapped around him for a whole lot longer.

"Okay, suit yourself. I'm just along for the ride." She stuck her nose next to his collar and inhaled deeply. "You really do smell good."

He glanced up just in time to see a meteor skitter across the sky. "Did you see that?"

She leaned forward shifting his balance and he grabbed the rail before he toppled forward. "What?"

"The falling star."

"Really?" She shifted again, but this time he was ready.

As he clomped down another flight of stairs, he kept his eyes on the sky. He stopped halfway down the next flight. "There's another one."

CanDee gently shook off his hands from around her ankles and climbed down. He missed her weight. There was something to be said for that knight-in-shining-armor stuff. Playing the role of her hero had felt fantastic.

She stood next to him and watched the night sky.

"There's another one." Her finger followed the path of the meteor hitting the earth's atmosphere.

He liked *shooting star* better than the scientific explanation. Her shoulder was only a few inches shorter than his. It was nice not to have to bend down to talk to her.

"Now would be an excellent time to put your arm around me." She cut her gaze over to him and smiled. "You know, in case that's what you were mulling over."

"I was thinking that it's nice not to have to bend over to talk to you." Or kiss her.

"I like that you're tall too. It means that I still get to wear heels." She turned to him, leaned up on the balls of her feet, and lightly touched her lips to his.

"It's a man's job to initiate the kiss," he said against her mouth, but her only reply was to suck on his bottom lip.

His hands went to her waist and he pulled her into him. Her hands slid into his hair as her tongue slid into his mouth. She molded her body to his. This time, he wasn't about to argue.

This one and only time, he'd follow her lead, his tongue darting into her mouth. One hand cupped her cheek and the other slid down her back and landed on her butt. All he could think of was that tiny little thong.

She pulled back a fraction of an inch. "That better be another snake that slithered down my back and is currently cupping my ass."

"I hate to disappoint you, but it's just me." He'd never appreciated having hands more than he did right now.

CHAPTER 6

CanDee really hadn't expected Cinco to show up for yoga, but here he was standing in her doorway wearing jeans, a T-shirt, and cowboy boots.

"I've never seen anyone do yoga in cowboy boots, but it might work." Probably not, but she'd found that cowboys thought of boots as a necessity like food, water, and cold beer.

"I'm more into spectator sports." One arm leaned on the doorjamb while the other that had been behind his back traveled around front holding a basket. "I brought lunch."

Quick as the snake that thank God hadn't struck her last night, she rolled up on the balls of her feet and kissed him lightly. She took the basket, darted around him, and stepped outside. "Where should we picnic?"

"It's not a picnic." He closed the front door and followed her around the side of the cottage to the backyard.

"All food delivered in a basket is a picnic." She walked up to the large metal trough in the backyard. "What is this? I saw it this morning, but I can't figure out why a cattle trough is in the middle of a fenced-in backyard."

He took the basket from her and shoved his arm through the looped handle. "It's a bathtub with hot water."

"Huh? The one inside wasn't enough? I don't get it." Why have a bathtub outside? Sure, they were out in the middle of nowhere, but privacy was still a concern.

"Carlton Rose built it for his fiancée Prudence so that she would agree to marry him. Prudence was eighteen when she met Carlton, who was thirty-five at the time. He fell madly in love with her, but I don't think the feeling was mutual. She agreed to marry him if he could promise her a hot bath whenever she wanted." He knocked on the huge metal tank at the end of the trough. "He came up with this."

She touched the worn pump handle. "So just pump the water directly into the tank . . ." She bent down and inspected the tank. "I see. Build a fire under the tank to heat the water and then lift the lever so the water spills into the trough."

He nodded. "Personally, I think Prudence didn't want to marry Carlton so she gave him what she thought was an impossible task."

"Poor Prudence, not only did she have an awful name, but she was forced to marry a man she didn't love." A hot bath alfresco might be nice. She looked around. The vines of various vine-growing things covered the field fence in a healthy, lush green. The trough tub was a lot bigger than the itty-bitty claw-foot in the one and only bathroom in the cottage. As long as she bathed late, no one should be the wiser.

"Since we're picnicking, do you have a blanket we can sit on?" Cinco shaded his eyes from the noon sun and pointed to a shady spot under an arbor holding up a massive red rosebush.

"There's a blanket on the bed and I'm sure somewhere else in the house there's another one, but you'd probably know better than I." She nodded in the direction of the house. "Would you mind?"

"There are several in the closet next to the bathroom. I'll be right back." He balanced the picnic basket on the edge of the tub and headed around to the front of the house. The cottage had a back door, but Lucy had told CanDee that the key had been misplaced sometime during World War I and no one had gotten around to replacing the lock.

Because she knew it would make him blush, she called, "And stay out of my underwear drawer. I'll know if anything's missing."

She moved the picnic basket to inside the tub and climbed onto the side so she could look into the tank. After prying the lid up, cautiously, she glanced inside. It was squeaky clean. Wow, whoever cleaned the cottage was very thorough.

"I sincerely hope that my oldest son hasn't started wearing women's underwear." Dr. Lucy Rose stepped into the backyard.

How exactly did CanDee answer that? Picturing him in lacy pink underwear was disturbing.

"So you've found the bathtub." Lucy walked over to the opposite side of the tub from CanDee. "Bear and I used it to warm up after skinny-dipping last week."

The older woman grinned from ear to ear. There wasn't the slightest bit of embarrassment or bragging in her voice. She was just stating the facts. It was good to see a long-married couple that still had an appetite for each other.

"That's why it's so clean." CanDee climbed down. "Cinco showed me how it works. How long does it take the water to heat up?"

"Not as long as you'd think, once the fire gets going. There's wood and kindling on the back porch." The older woman pointed to the piles of cut wood and smaller branches. "When the water is as hot as you'd like, you open the other panel so that the water can circulate out from the tank and back to the tub. Your water will stay hot until the fire dies out."

"It's really ingenious." Oh yeah, tonight she was having a long, hot backyard bath.

"A word to the wise, start the fire first and then pump the water in. It's faster." Lucy smiled up at CanDee. "I'm so glad that you decided to stay. I'm afraid that I would've had to have murdered my oldest child if you'd left, so thanks for saving me the trouble."

"I've already started my research." She didn't know why she felt the need to tell Lucy that, but she did.

"I know." Lucy shook her head. "I'm not worried about that. In fact, you have the family historian wrapped around your little finger. Cinco knows more about this place than anyone. Since the day he was born, he's had an insatiable appetite for history."

So she'd be spending lots of time with Cinco. That worked for her.

She glanced back at the gate to the front yard. "What was his wife like?"

It really wasn't her business, but she wanted to know.

Lucy's perfectly groomed eyebrows bounced off of her forehead. "He told you about Naomi?"

"He mentioned being married and I gather that it didn't end well." CanDee watched the gate like a hawk, not wanting Cinco to find them talking about him. No one liked to be discussed behind his or her back, and usually CanDee wouldn't mind going to the source for information, but talking about his marriage seemed to hurt him.

"I'm surprised that he told you about the divorce since he hasn't really said much to anyone else. I have my suspicions, but you should wait for him to tell you the whole story. All I know for sure was that she's a lying, cheating bitch and I hated her from the moment I met her. Of course I tolerated her because I thought she made Cinco happy, but all she caused was misery. I can say without a doubt that she's the only person that I truly hate." Lucy's voice was mean but level.

"Wow. She sounds like poison." Cinco seemed so no-nonsense that it was hard to think of him with someone like that. Then again, she didn't know him that well.

"Poison, that's exactly what she was. I'm glad that he finally divorced her." Lucy crossed her arms. "Thank God she's out of our lives."

"Mom, are you staying for lunch?" With a blanket tucked under his arm, Cinco opened the gate, stepped into the backyard, and closed the gate.

"No." She smiled at her oldest son. "Just dropped by to see how CanDee was settling in." She walked over to him and patted him on the arm. "I see that you're taking care of our guest. I'm off. I'm meeting your father for lunch and then I have back-to-back surgeries this afternoon."

He leaned down and kissed her on the cheek. "See you later."

There was a lot to be said for a man who still kissed his mother goodbye.

CanDee grabbed the basket and walked to him. "So, what's for lunch?"

He led her to the arbor, spread out the blanket, and sat. She sat next to him. He opened the basket.

"Chicken salad sandwiches, root beer, potato chips, and Reese's Peanut Butter Cups." He pulled out the Ziploc-bagged sandwiches and a small thermal bag that held two cold Abita Root Beers. "The Reese's are in here too, but I'll pull them out later."

CanDee reached into the basket and pulled out two bags of Zapps Sour Cream & Creole Onion chips. "I love these, and chicken salad is one of my favorites."

Well, pretty much anything she didn't have to cook was a favorite, but she did like chicken salad.

He unwrapped one sandwich and handed it to her and then unwrapped the other one and took a bite.

"Did you make this?" She took a small corner bite. It was good. She liked a man who could cook. Since she didn't, it was good to have someone around who did. Well, she supposed it would be nice. Her ex hadn't been able to cook.

"Yes, I like to cook." He opened one bag of chips and laid it in front of her and then opened the other bag and popped a chip in his mouth.

He went out of his way to make sure she was taken care of first before he took anything for himself. It was strange having a man see to her first. It felt nice.

"This is really good. I like the chunky pickle bits." She took another bite, chewed, and swallowed. "What else can you make?"

"Just about anything with a recipe that's not too complicated. I follow directions well." He bit into his sandwich again.

"I like a man who can follow directions." And one who put her first. "This is a nice spot." She pointed to the roses. "Who planted them?"

The way the thick vines wove in and out of the cedar trellis made her think that this rosebush had been here quite a long time.

"My great-grandfather, Deuce, planted this rosebush in atonement for his many sins." One side of Cinco's mouth turned up in a grin and a single dimple popped out on his left cheek. "Somehow the bloodred roses that bloom every year were supposed to cleanse his soul."

"Your great-grandfather sounds like a very religious man." Either that or he was a little bit crazy.

"I don't think religion had anything to do with it. It was the shotgun that his wife was holding on him when she found him in bed with the maid that was more the driving force behind his sudden need to cleanse his soul." He unscrewed the cap on a bottle of root beer and handed it to her. "After that, Deuce had a change of heart. He started going to church and pretty much doing whatever Great-Grandmother Roberta told him to do."

"Religion comes in many forms, and apparently the business end of a shotgun is one." She sipped the root beer. "I love root beer but I never buy it." She saluted him with it. "Thanks for this and for lunch."

He looked very pleased with himself. "You're welcome."

"So, what are some more deep dark family secrets?" She wanted to know his, but it was too soon. She wanted him to tell her everything about Naomi, but if Lucy was any indication, CanDee was lucky that he'd even mentioned his marriage.

"There are many mysterious family secrets surrounding the Texas Rose Ranch. Maybe you'd like to go through the boxes in my attic after we have dinner." He took another bite of his sandwich.

"Are you asking me out on a date?" She put her hand over her heart. "It's so sudden. I didn't see it coming."

His gaze wandered over to hers. "Is that a yes?"

"Are you making dinner?" Two nights in a row where she didn't have to eat yogurt for dinner was cause for a celebration.

"Yes."

"Will there be any fooling around?" She nudged his boot with the toe of her running shoe.

"One-track mind." The blush started at his collar and moved up to his face. "I'm beginning to think that all you want from me is sex."

"That's not true. Now that I know you can cook, I want food and sex." She took another swig of root beer.

"I'm starting to feel a little like your cabana boy." His face was still a glowing red.

"Is that a bad thing?" She'd never thought to have her own cabana boy, but if he was offering, she wasn't going to say no.

"I didn't say that."

"Good. Would you be available to serve me drinks bathtub side later this evening? I plan on using Prudence's tub for a long, hot bath." If she played her cards right, she just might be able to get him to build the fire too.

He stared at her, blinked once, and continued to stare.

"I don't think that's a good idea," he whispered.

She looked around in case he was whispering because someone else had wandered into the backyard. She didn't see anyone. "Why are you whispering again?"

"I don't know." His gaze moved to the grass on either side of his boots. "You shouldn't take a bath out here. Anyone could walk by." He pointed to the fence.

"You really think that someone walking by would take the time to peek through the vine-covered fence in the hopes of catching me naked? Wow, are there really that many Peeping Toms on the ranch?" Was he planning on being one?

"Well, when you put it like that . . . no, but who knows if the tub even works?"

"Your mom told me that she and your dad used it last week after they went skinny-dipping." She took another bite of sandwich.

His face went from red to a sickly shade of oatmeal. "I didn't need to know that."

"Why? I think it's cute that your parents skinny-dip." She'd only ever had her grandmother, so family dynamics including brothers and sisters were intriguing. Come to think of it, none of the men she'd ever dated had been from a big family or had much of a family at all. It must be nice to have all of these people around to support Cinco.

He put his hands over his ears. "Stop talking. I wish I could get the mental image out of my head. How would you like it if your parents went skinny-dipping?"

"That would be awkward since they died when I was a child." She didn't say it because she wanted sympathy, she was just stating the facts. She could barely remember her parents, but she was pretty sure that she would have loved to know that they still wanted each other after decades of marriage.

His mouth fell open and then he closed it. "I'm so sorry."

"Thank you." When she was little and people found out about her parents and told her that they were sorry, she'd always wanted to ask why. They hadn't killed her parents, so why were they sorry? She hated the pity in their eyes. She loved being the center of attention except when someone felt sorry for her. That kind of attention she couldn't handle.

"So we're on for dinner?" He sounded a little unsure of himself.

"Sounds good to me." She leaned over and kissed him on the cheek.

"We can talk about the bath then." He took another sip of root beer.

"Okay." As far as she was concerned, there was nothing to talk about. A long hot bath sounded like heaven and with any luck, she'd talk him into scrubbing her back . . . and maybe her front.

CHAPTER 7

At six-fifteen that evening, Cinco opened the oven door, grabbed two potholders, and pulled out the pot roast, which looked a little too brown. He set it on the stove and tried to convince himself that it was blackened instead of burnt.

A knock sounded on his front door.

He threw the potholders down on the counter next to the stove, walked out of the kitchen, through the dining room, out into the reception hall, around the parlor, and finally to the front door. Nothing in this old house was connected by a central hallway. He opened the door to find CanDee holding two cold Shiner beer bottles. She had great taste.

She held one out to him. "I didn't know what you had planned for dinner and I'm not that into wine, but beer goes with everything."

He took the beer and moved aside to let her in. She'd changed into curve-hugging blue jeans and a light-green shirt that tied on one shoulder, leaving the other creamy shoulder bare. If he yanked on the bow at her right shoulder, would the shirt fall off? His hands itched to try it.

She looked around. "Not what I expected."

"Edith's will only stipulated that the outside remain pink. All bets were off on the inside." He leaned against the ornately carved oak staircase. He'd painted the walls a creamy white so that the fancy woodwork around the door casings and the inlaid wooden floors really stood out.

"Somehow, I thought the inside would be as girly as the outside. I imagined dainty velvet settees and needlepoint throw pillows." She looked into the parlor.

"Sorry to disappoint—nothing dainty here." He liked overstuffed leather furniture and nothing fussy. "How about a tour?"

He was proud of his house. He'd restored it, and based on his lack of haunting, Edith approved. He offered CanDee his elbow and she took it.

"This is the reception hall." He pointed to the staircase. "Not sure why it's named that, but *reception hall* is on the house plans."

"You have the house plans?"

"Edith drew them on a piece of paper that's framed in the kitchen. You'll see in a minute." He pointed to the room across from the staircase. "This is the parlor . . . not to be mistaken with the sitting room, which is over there."

He pointed to the room that was catty-corner to the staircase. "Over here is the dining room and through that door is the kitchen."

He led her to the dining room and on to the kitchen.

"I love the high ceilings, and all of the different rooms. It's weird, I wonder when halls connecting rooms came into fashion?" She reached up and touched the scrollwork surrounding the door casing. "This woodwork must have taken forever to make."

"This house took five years to build. It has six bedrooms and one bathroom."

She looked around his kitchen. He'd kept the original cabinets and sink, but the appliances were commercial stainless steel.

"I like how you've kept the history, but updated the house. It's comfortable and it suits you." She pointed to the marble-covered kitchen island. "Did you add that?"

"It's the old kitchen table. I added the marble, but," "—he leaned down and slapped the solid wood leg—"this is Edith's kitchen table."

"It looks like the counter added a couple of inches, but isn't that table a little taller than usual?" She looked around the kitchen. "Come to think of it, aren't the cabinets a little taller than normal?"

"Good eye. Most kitchen cabinets are thirty-five or so inches high. These are forty-eight inches high. Edith and Mel were tall ladies and liked their world to be their height. God knows, I can understand." He was willing to bet that CanDee would be a fan of the taller cabinets. Most things were made for people six feet and under. Naomi had hated this kitchen because at five feet, she hadn't been able to reach anything.

"I love it." CanDee ran her hands along the marble island. "For once, the world rises to meet me instead of me bending down to meet it." She turned back around to smile at him. "I'm beginning to see that Edith ran the show. Because Mel ran the ranch, I assumed that she was dominant, but now I see that Edith was in charge."

"I'm pretty sure that life was Edith's way or the highway." He covered the pot roast with foil. According to the recipe, it needed to "sit" a while.

"Wait a minute. There are six bedrooms and only one bathroom?" She leaned against the island. "I'm losing faith in Edith."

"Don't rush to judgment too quickly. Edith fought hard for that bathroom." He put the lid on the mashed potatoes to keep them warm. "Indoor toilets were rare and some thought unsanitary. Apparently Mel thought that it was disgusting to use the bathroom indoors. Think about it. At the time, the only way to use the facilities involved a bedpan or a bucket—"

"I got it. So Mel was against it." She cocked her head to the left. "What did Edith do?"

He smiled. He loved this story. "She waited until Mel was out of town on a cattle drive and had the bathroom installed in the seventh bedroom. There was no way for Mel to undo it after everything was installed."

"Way to go, Edith." CanDee's eyes scrunched up. "How do you know this?"

"Edith kept a journal." He pointed to the five rows of leather-bound volumes lining the built-in wooden shelves behind the table.

"Holy crap." She walked to the shelves. "These are all her journals?"

"Yes. She started journaling at the age of ten and didn't stop until she died at seventy. Mel bought her a new journal every year." He turned off the fire under the green beans. "I thought you might like them."

CanDee rubbed her hands together in anticipation. "I can't wait to dive into them."

"I can see that you appreciate history as much as I do." The longer he knew her, the more he found they had in common.

"The thing I love most about history isn't the major events, but the people. I like learning about the lives of everyday people. It seems that no matter the time, people are always the same. There's a book by Noah Smithwick called *The Evolution of a State*—"

"*Or Recollections of Old Texas Days*. It's one of my favorites. Lacy Kendall Lehman—you know, husband to the fair Brunhilda—bought Smithwick's land grant. After Smithwick was convicted of being a 'bad citizen' for helping one of his buddies escape custody while on trial for murder, Stephen F. Austin kicked Smithwick out of the settlement that is now Fredericksburg and the surrounding area. Part of this ranch was Smithwick's."

"Well, that never made it into the book."

"Technically, he was kicked out of the state of Texas, but he never left. I loved that he basically wandered around Texas and wrote about it." He'd never been able to discuss books and history with Naomi because the only thing she'd cared about was collecting whatevers. One day it was silver spoons and the next it was carnival glass bowls. Thank God he'd put an end to it before she'd started collecting Picassos.

"Me too. I love the part where he goes to San Antonio and finds the ladies grinding corn into masa. He can't figure out why anyone would mix water with the masa, roll it out, and grill it. And then he bites into his first corn tortilla and he's like 'Oh yeah, baby, bring it on.'" She pulled a journal out at random and carefully flipped it open. "Edith had amazing penmanship."

"She was a schoolteacher before she ran off with my great-great-aunt. They met in New Orleans when Edith was there with her father, who captained a riverboat on the Mississippi. They were on their last day before they headed back to Keokuk, Iowa, where Edith lived." He pointed to the journals again. "According to her, it was love at first sight and instead of getting on her father's boat, she ran off with Mel. They took a boat from New Orleans to Matagorda Bay and a train up from South Texas."

"That sounds romantic." CanDee scanned a page and then flipped to another one. "See, Mel had a little romance in her." She shook her head. "Maybe. Travel back then must have been a pain in the ass. What happened when Mel brought a lady home and told everyone they were an item?"

"Mel's mother, Prudence, replied, 'Forgive her, Jesus, she fell in love with a Yankee.' Prudence was so unhappy about the match that she told everyone that Edith was from New Orleans." He shrugged. "I guess Edith's being female wasn't as hard to take as her being from the North."

"I take it the Roses were Confederates?" She sat at the kitchen table and crossed her legs.

"Only Prudence. Carlton wanted to stay out of things. According to Edith, since he was the bastard son of Santa Anna and Emily Morgan, he felt like Texas should have stayed independent. I get his point. After all, his mother did basically prostitute herself to Santa Anna so that the Texas troops could get the drop on him and win the Battle of San Jacinto. Texas independence had cost Carlton's family—my family—a lot. He must have been pissed that Texas threw independence away to join the United States."

CanDee brought the diary to her nose and sniffed it. "Is it my imagination or does this journal smell like roses?"

"Good nose. Edith wore a perfume called La France Rose. I don't know if she sprayed it on the pages or if it rubbed off when she was writing, but most of her journals smell like roses." It seemed impossible that Edith's scent had lasted this long, but there it was.

"That's awesome." CanDee burst out laughing. "Listen to this." She held the journal up and read, "*At lunch, Mel walked in through the front door tracking mud and dung all over my freshly polished floors. I have asked her time and time again to please remove her boots and leave them on the porch, but she refuses to comply. Since she prefers the smell of muck and dung to my freshly polished floors, I have moved her things into the barn where she can feel free to track filth wherever she chooses. I hope she finds the smell more to her liking.*"

CanDee grinned. "That's awesome. Edith's feisty. I love it."

"Wait until you read the entry about the new dress." He took two plates out of the cabinet, grabbed a couple of forks and knives, and picked up his beer. He headed to the table and put down his handful on the kitchen table.

"Let me." CanDee stood up. "I'll set the table. Where are the napkins?" She looked around.

"See that roll of paper towels?" He pointed to the roll of Bounty on the island.

She took a deep breath and let it out slowly. "Edith would not approve. I'm betting that she was a proper-cloth-napkin kind of girl. Well, I guess she had to be because paper towels weren't invented until much later."

"As a matter of fact, she was. Apparently Mel liked to use her sleeve to wipe her mouth, so Edith cut off all of the sleeves on Mel's work shirts and refused to sew them back on until Mel learned to use a napkin." That had to be one of his favorite stories.

He set a plate at the place he normally used and one next to it.

"Sit down. I'm setting the table." She tore off two "napkins" from the paper towel roll.

Maybe some actual napkins would be nice. Not the cloth ones, but paper napkins. Then again, they were just thinner paper towels folded a couple of times. It seemed stupid to buy two separate paper products when one did both jobs. Still, CanDee was super girlie. Last night in her frilly peach dress and heels and even now in her jeans, she was ultra feminine. She seemed to favor little fussy earrings and shiny lip gloss. She'd probably like some real cloth napkins. It couldn't hurt to check them out on Amazon.

She walked back to the table, folded the paper towel in half, placed it on the right side of his plate, and set the knife on top of it. She repeated the process with her plate. "So, tell me about the new dress."

He leaned back in his chair, crossed his legs at the ankles, and took a healthy swig of Shiner. "I don't remember what the year was, but Edith wanted to buy a new dress for some party that she was having. Mel told her no, that she already had more dresses than any one person needed. Now, it's not that they couldn't afford a new dress, it's just that Mel thought it was frivolous. Edith asked and asked and asked, but Mel shut her down every time. So . . . Edith being Edith, she went directly to Roseville Furniture where she had a charge account and bought all new furniture for the parlor to go with the old dress she was forced to wear."

"Someone's passive-aggressive." She propped a fist on her hip. "I wonder if Mel knew what she was getting into when she brought Edith home from New Orleans."

"I've wondered that too, but I guess Mel was happy because they were together for forty years. I think everyone needs an Edith in their lives." He admired Edith's spunk and her quirky sense of humor. In her journals, she didn't seem whiny or pouty, she just went after whatever she wanted and found a way to get it. When his ex-wife hadn't gotten her way, she'd thrown things and pouted for days.

"Everyone needs an Edith." CaDee nodded. "I like that."

He watched her moving around his kitchen. She seemed like someone who lived life on her terms, which was very Edith. CanDee wasn't a pouter or a whiner, but at first, Naomi hadn't appeared to be either.

"What did Mel do about the new furniture?"

He had a feeling that her quest for knowledge was just as voracious as his. "She bought Edith five new dresses." He nodded. "Mel knew when to admit defeat."

"I wonder if she ever saw the humor in the situation?"

He'd often wondered that himself. "She must have because she put up with it. Just think how boring Mel's life would have been without Edith."

Now that he thought about it, his life could use a little Edith.

"Is dinner ready?" CanDee glanced back at the stove. "It smells really good."

"It's ready." He uncrossed his ankles.

"No, I can get it. You cooked it, the least I can do is bring it to the table." She picked up the potholders he'd thrown aside earlier, slipped one on her right hand, and picked up the heavy roasting pan. Carefully she walked it over to the table, set the other potholder down, and placed the roasting pan on top of it.

"The trivets are in the drawer to the left of the stove along with the potholders." He was bone tired and it was nice to sit and watch her move around his kitchen. She was graceful in a way that only a tall, lanky girl can be.

"Notice how I'm not commenting on the fact that you know what a trivet is"—she opened the drawer—"and that you own three."

"Chalk that up to Naomi. She was into home decorating. She collected lots of things, trivets being one. She had like fifty hanging on that wall." He pointed to wall above bookshelf. "It took me a year to clear out all of the Naomi, but I kept those three trivets."

"Why?"

"Because I needed something to put hot pans on and those were the least stupid looking." He could remember very clearly opening the credit card bill and finding that she'd spent five thousand dollars on trivets. For Naomi, collecting things had been more than a hobby. It was a sickness.

He waited for her ask about Naomi, but CanDee grabbed the handle of the mashed potato pot in one hand and a trivet in the other.

She looked down at the trivet. "Is that a T. rex?"

"Yep." He sipped his Shiner.

"And that's one of the least stupid-looking ones?" She set the T. rex down on the table next to the roasting pan. "I've never understood collecting things. Who needs two hundred teapots? It's not like you can use more than one at a time." She hunched her shoulders. "I guess you could if you were serving tea to lots of people, but honestly, I don't know enough people I'd like to serve tea to that would necessitate more than one pot."

He felt the same way.

"So you're the practical type?" That label really didn't fit her personality.

"Hell no. I just don't think that collecting stuff makes sense. I'm the queen of impractical." She went back for the green beans.

She picked up the handle of the pot and another trivet. This time it was a stick figure woman that looked like a chalk outline the police used. He'd kept that one because it was funny.

"What exactly do you think is impractical? I need an example." He liked trying to figure out how her mind worked.

She set the trivet down on the table and placed the pot of green beans on top of it. "Take throw pillows, for example. One day I plan on having so many covering my bed that I practically need an extra bedroom to house them. And I'd love to have an extra-long brass bed where my feet don't hang off the end." She popped the lid off of the green beans. "The fact that I don't have these things now is immaterial, I'm planning my impracticality very carefully."

"I have an extra-long brass bed." The words were out before he'd thought about what he was saying. He could feel heat rushing to his face as the image of her riding him played over and over in his head.

"You blush more than a thirteen-year-old girl. It's so much fun to watch. I like it." She removed the lid from the mashed potatoes. "Yum. I loved mashed potatoes."

He'd always hated that he blushed, but it wasn't like he could do anything about it. "I'm glad my humiliation entertains you."

He walked to the kitchen and picked a chef's knife out of the butcher-block knife holder to cut the roast, then grabbed a couple of large spoons from the china pitcher full of cooking utensils next to the stove.

"So are you going to show me your over-sized brass bed?" She arched an eyebrow.

His heel caught on the rug under the kitchen table and he stumbled but righted himself before he fell headlong into the mashed potatoes. "Edith had it made for Mel as a Christmas present. It's long enough that my feet don't hang off. I had to get the mattress and box springs specially made, but it's so nice to fit on the bed."

This was way too much detail, but her question had thrown him.

She put her hand over her heart and leaned back in her chair. "To sleep in a bed where I don't have to curl up into a ball just to fit onto the mattress sounds like heaven." She blew him a kiss. "Now I not only want you for your body, but also for your bed. I don't know about you, but I think we should start sleeping together tonight. And for the promise of an enormous bed, I could break my rule and spend the whole night. Heck, I'll even walk-of-shame it back to the cottage in the morning."

Knowing how outlandish she was, he should have been prepared for the offer, but all he could do was stare at her slack-jawed as the picture of her naked and reclining on a million throw pillows, him kissing his way down her body, made it really hard to pull air into his lungs.

CHAPTER 8

CanDee knew her eyes were the size of Double Stuf Oreos, but she couldn't help it. She held her hands up to the heavens, "Edith, I never should have doubted you."

The one and only bathroom was spectacular. It had to be fourteen feet wide by twenty or so feet long. It was a perfect example of Victorian elegance.

"Did you add any of this or is this all Edith?" She'd never seen anything like it.

From floor to ceiling, white tile encased the walls and flooring. There was a gigantic copper claw-foot tub built for at least two people, and two huge porcelain sinks with spindle legs under two oval mirrors, but the circular shower was the best. It took up the entire bay window. A tangle of copper pipes ran around and under the four windows that jutted out over the first story. Several showerheads sprouted out of the pipes at different heights and angles like sunflowers holding their heads up to the sun. On the ceiling, four giant showerheads would rain water down in what must be a torrential flood.

"Edith was a genius, as she clearly states in her journals. She'd actually planned this when she designed the house so the plumbing was in place." Cinco pointed to the amazing set of levers and dials that operated the shower. "It's a wonderful shower, but it takes lots of water."

"It looks like the multiple showerheads and body sprays that are popular now aren't a new idea." She counted seventeen showerheads. She couldn't fathom how they'd heated enough water to fill the tub or run the shower without electricity. "Where does the hot water come from?"

Swimming in the enormous copper tub would be fun—or even better, a long, hot seventeen-showerhead shower.

Cinco smiled and nodded his head. "That's where Edith's genius truly comes into play."

He walked to the bay windows in the shower and crooked his finger for her to follow. He pointed to a lean-to sort of shack thing about fifty feet from the back of the house. "We have a hot spring and that's why Edith insisted on building the house right here. Under the ground, she had several pipes of increasingly smaller diameter installed to boost the pressure enough for the water to make it to the second floor."

She stared out at the little unassuming building. "Edith really was brilliant. Well, apart from the fact that the shower has four large windows in it."

Clearly, privacy hadn't been an issue for Edith.

"Actually, opening the windows after the shower is a great way to vent the steam, but there is some trade-off on privacy." He hunched his shoulders. "Still, it's not that big of a problem out here. There's really no one else around."

She looked around. "Where's the toilet?"

Gently, he turned her around and pointed. "See that closet to the left of the door? That's the toilet. Edith's one concession to Mel so she could have some privacy."

"What's in the closet on the other side of the door?" She was beginning to think that Edith was possibly a Mensa candidate.

"Just towels and stuff. Nothing spectacular."

CanDee leaned so that her back and butt were against Cinco's chest and thighs. "So, are you going to let me take a swim in your shower?"

"Maybe . . . someday . . . not tonight." His voice was high and scratchy. He cleared his throat. "Not tonight."

He was nervous. If he hadn't been standing behind her, she knew she would have seen him blush. Was it the suggestion that she'd be naked in his shower or the fact that her backside was smashed up against him that made him nervous?

"Stop that." There was a smile in his voice.

"What?" She wriggled her butt against him. "I have no idea what you're talking about."

"The hell you don't." He stepped back and laughed.

"I want to see your bed." She winked at him, all innocence. "I need to see if Edith had another stroke of genius."

"Well, if it's just for informational purposes." He leaned down and kissed her lightly on the lips and then pulled back.

"Are you hitting on me?" She put her hand on her chest. "What would Edith say?"

He grabbed her hand and pulled her out of the bathroom, down the hall, past several bedrooms and to the door at the end. "Edith would have approved of you."

"Are you sure, because I don't know . . . she might have called me a shameless hussy or some other—" She caught sight of the bed. "Oh my God."

It was a beautiful brass and wrought-iron bed with fancy scrollwork and flowers. In width, it appeared to be queen-sized, but the length had to be one and a half times larger than a regular bed.

"I love Edith." CanDee ran to the bed and jumped on it, landing on her back and making a snow angel right in the middle. "My feet don't hang off. I think I might cry."

She glanced back at Cinco, who was hovering in the doorway. It was like he didn't know whether to come in or stay put.

She rolled off the bed. "I can tell that my being in this room makes you antsy so I'll leave before you start whispering again."

She tried to walk past him, but he pulled her into his arms and kissed her hard on the mouth. She slid her arms around his neck and plastered her body to his.

"It looks like this is a very bad time." A deep male voice said from behind CanDee.

Cinco ended the kiss and stepped back, but his arms stayed around her. Annoyance radiated off him. "Then why are you still here?"

She turned around. It was Rowdy.

"Because I'm on very important family business." He grinned.

"What business?" Cinco kept his arm around her. It was possessive, and she kind of liked it. Phillip had never put a possessive arm around her in public . . . or anywhere else, for that matter.

"I heard you took off work early and were making your famous pot roast. I came to taste-test it for you. I'd hate for you to serve it if it sucks." He held a hand up like a traffic cop. "No need to thank me, that's just how I roll."

"Too late. We already ate." Cinco pulled CanDee into him. "And we're on our way to the attic."

"'On our way to the attic?' Is that what you kids are calling it these days? Because it looked like you two were going to go at it right here in the hall." Rowdy wagged a finger at Cinco. "You really should lock your front door. Anyone could walk in. For instance, I could have been giving a Girl Scout troop the ranch tour and then I would have had to answer some very interesting questions."

"The tour doesn't include my house." Cinco worked his jaw back and forth.

"It does now." Rowdy crossed his arms.

"You know that Rancho Red wine you're so proud of?" Cinco's eyebrows bounced off his hairline. "It's about to become a collector's item."

"How do you figure that?" Rowdy's handsome face curved into a smile.

"After I kill you, there won't be anyone to make it anymore. It will become scarce and the price will skyrocket. Maybe I should buy a couple more cases before I feed your body to the pigs."

"Well now . . . that's just mean. And a little gross. Here I am offering my superior gastronomic palate and you go and offer to murder me." He uncrossed his arms. "I'm telling Mom."

"Some things never change." Cinco gave CanDee a peck on the cheek before turning back to his brother. "Leave . . . now."

"What happened to southern hospitality? Maybe I should just leave." Rowdy huffed around sarcastically. "I'm not feeling very welcome."

"What part of *leave now* did you not understand?" Cinco rolled his eyes.

"I can't believe all of this hostility, and from family no less. Honestly, it's enough to make me storm out of here, but thank God, I have better manners than that." Rowdy squared his shoulders in resolve.

"Since when? Don't let the door hit you in the ass on the way out." Cinco cocked his head to the left.

"Here I am checking in on my celibate, old-maidenly older brother—making sure he didn't die in his old-lady house and then not be found for like two weeks because he's a celibate, old-maidenly kind of guy and all I get is anger. Don't be a hater. I'm all about the love. Take a couple of deep breaths and let the love in." Rowdy took two deep, dramatic breaths.

Cinco glanced at his watch. "How much longer is this going to take?"

"It's hard to say, you might want to pull up a chair. Seeing as how I'm still holding that grudge over Charlotte Renfro, this may take hours." Rowdy smiled sweetly.

"Who's Charlotte Renfro?" CanDee knew she was being baited but she couldn't help it.

"Only the love of my life. See, my dear older brother is responsible for destroying what could have been the most significant relationship of my life. When I was a mere babe of fifteen and our dear parents were out of town, I had a small gathering of friends—"

"A party. You had a party complete with half of the varsity football team passed out on the front lawn." Cinco's patience was wearing thin.

"Whatever . . . anyway, after weeks of preparation I talked Charlotte Renfro into going up to my bedroom and was about to seal the deal when my dear older brother walks in, picks me up—naked, mind you—and tosses me across the room. I had to wait a whole three weeks before she was ready to give it up again." Rowdy shook his head. "I thought brothers were supposed to stick together."

"I hate to be the bearer of bad news, but you're adopted. Mom and Dad have been waiting for the right time to tell you." Cinco blew out a frustrated breath.

"So hurtful. Why do you have to be so mean?" Rowdy looked honestly wounded.

"That wasn't as hurtful as this." Cinco, leaned down, picked up the wooden block he'd used for a doorstop, and hurled it at his brother. Rowdy ducked.

"All this animosity . . . it makes me so sad." Rowdy wiped a fake tear away. "I'm sensing that you want me to leave—"

"Finally." Cinco nodded.

"But, I can't just walk out when my brother is in pain and so clearly needs me . . ." Rowdy was a grade-A drama queen.

Off went Cinco's left boot, which then whizzed through the air at Rowdy.

"Maybe we should all hold hands and form a prayer circle to pray for Cinco's anger management issues. Do you need a hug, big bro?" Rowdy held out his arms.

Off went Cinco's other boot and headed for Rowdy's head.

"I'm beginning to see that you're not ready for help." Rowdy backed down the hallway. "You can't help someone who won't help themselves. I'm sorry to do this, but I'm going to have to gather reinforcements. Maybe Mom and Dad will be able to talk you down off the ledge." He shook his head. "I'm sorry that it's come to this, but in your current adversarial mood, I just don't know what else to do."

"Lock the door on your way out." Cinco called to Rowdy as he clomped down the stairs.

"You're welcome, CanDee," Rowdy yelled up from the bottom of the stairs. "I got him to start undressing, the rest is in your hands. Make sure he gets lucky, because clearly he's jealous of my abilities with the ladies and that stress is turning him mean."

The front door slammed closed.

"I'm not sure how to apologize for him." Cinco scratched the back of his neck. "*I'm sorry* doesn't seem like enough."

"I'm an only child, so watching siblings is always interesting. Are the two of you always like this?" It seemed that the Roses laughed a lot, which was nice.

And clearly, Rowdy would be someone's Edith. He needed a tolerant mate.

"Shall we?" Cinco pointed to the door next to the bathroom.

"What?" They weren't going to have sex? "Don't tell me you're playing hard to get?"

Cinco would be an excellent lover. Judging by how he always seemed to put her first, she had no doubt that would extend to the bedroom. A man who valued her comfort above his own was hard to find. Come to think of it, Cinco was the only one she'd ever met.

"No, I agreed to show you the boxes in the attic." He put his hand at the small of her back and urged her toward the door.

"You're not pulling a Charlotte Renfro and making me wait three more weeks before you decide to give it up . . . are you?" She'd never had such a hard time getting a man in her bed.

"You're impossible." He opened the attic door for her, reached around her, and turned on the light.

"No I'm not, I'm just thinking about the amazing shower I'm going to take after sex." She grinned. At least he wasn't whispering when they talked about sex this time. It was progress . . . sort of.

"You're just using my body to get to my shower." He grabbed her hand and gently pulled her up the steep flight of stairs.

"There's a lot of things I'd do for seventeen showerheads, but sex seems like the most pleasant. For example, I'd eat a pound of crickets or babysit triplets, or even spend an evening line dancing. Seventeen showerheads would be worth it." Would it be breaking and entering if all she did after breaking in was shower?

"How flattering. I'm right up there with eating crickets." He looked down his nose at her.

"Well, I could bump you up if, say, you offered me shower sex. Then you'd be right up there with Double Stuf Oreos on my most favorites list." Both he and the shower would be amazing.

"I'll keep that in mind." He pulled her up the last stair and her eyes nearly fell out of her head as she took in the treasure trove before her.

Old furniture that looked like it was from Edith's time was neatly covered in white sheets and stacked in one corner. Perfect columns of boxes were laid out in a grid. Her palms actually itched with the need to run her hands over the things that Edith loved. Mundane artifacts made history real to her. Her heart went pitter-pat as she fairly vibrated with excitement. This was going to be fun.

CHAPTER 9

Seeing CanDee rolling around on his bed had almost cost Cinco the romance he wanted to give her . . . well, both of them. He'd rushed into things with Naomi and he wasn't going to make the same mistake with her. She was special. With CanDee he wanted to savor . . . everything. First kisses, first touches, first dates . . . first everythings.

"I can't believe that this stuff is so well preserved." She went to the furniture stacked in the back. "Is this Edith's parlor furniture?"

"It sure is." He knew she'd love it almost as much as he did. The only reason that it wasn't downstairs was because it was horribly uncomfortable. He didn't have the heart to throw it out, so it just sat up here collecting years.

She whipped one of the white sheets off of a pink velvet high-backed chair and sat. "Wow, this sucks." She moved around, trying to get more comfortable. "It's both lumpy and hard, which is difficult to achieve."

She stood. "What's in the boxes?"

She walked over to the first stack, leaned up on her tippy-toes and tried to peek into the sealed wooden crate, but the top didn't budge.

"Clothes, housewares, you name it. Apparently we Roses are hoarders." He picked up the box for her and set it on the floor by the furniture. "I haven't been through them since I was a kid. I just remember there's lots of stuff."

She bent over with her butt in the air and tried to lift the top off.

He had to admit, she had a nice ass. All he could think of was last night and her tiny underwear.

"Are you staring at my butt?" She wiggled her backside.

"Yep." No use in denying it.

"Maybe you could give me a hand with this?" She wiggled her backside again.

He squatted down in front of her and came face to chest with her gaping-open green shirt. He got a great view of her black, lacy bra and the outline of her breasts.

"I'm beginning to get the idea that you'd rather see me naked." She stood and propped a fist on her hip.

"I'm not going to lie, the idea has merit." His gaze took its sweet time roaming down her body.

"Stop picturing me naked and open the box." She rolled her eyes. "Now you have an attack of the libido? Where was that ten minutes ago after your brother left?"

"You have a nice body and I like looking at it." He grabbed the lid and pulled, but it didn't move. He peered down at it. Tiny squared nails kept it closed tight. "Sorry I didn't think of this sooner—give me a second and I'll get a hammer."

He ran down the stairs to the second floor, bolted down the hall, then down the set of stairs to the first floor. He rocketed into the kitchen, went to the pantry, and grabbed his toolbox. He clomped up the attic stairs two at a time.

CanDee's back was to him. She'd slipped off her shirt and jeans. A tiny strap of black lace was tucked between the round cheeks of her bottom and a black, lacy bra strap wrapped around the middle of her back like a band. The little thing didn't have straps. She was even better in person than in his imagination.

She pulled something over her head. A dress? The shiny gold beads blinked in the light of the three bald light bulbs. He stepped heavily on the top step and it creaked under his weight.

She whipped around. "What do you think?"

She picked up the matching feather headband and slipped it around her head. The feather was a moth-eaten mess, but the gold beads winked in the low light.

She hummed a few bars of "Puttin' on the Ritz" and did the Charleston. "Wasn't Edith a little too old to be a flapper?"

The dress was at least two sizes too wide and two sizes too short. It barely covered her ass. She looked good enough to eat.

"Yes, she was a little too old to be a flapper, but her daughter-in-law wasn't." He loved her energy. CanDee enjoyed life and saw things differently than others. She didn't just see an old dress, but something fun to play dress-up in.

CanDee stopped dancing and her eyes squinted like she was trying to figure out string theory or where the other sock disappeared to in the dryer. "Edith had a daughter-in-law? Er . . . um, that would have meant that she had a child . . . how did that work?"

"She and Mel adopted my grandfather, Tres, after his family died in a fire in 1915. It destroyed the main house and part of the cottage. Tres was the only one to make it out and he was burned very badly. Edith nursed him back to health. He lived here until after he married and a new house was built."

"Well, that's just sad." She climbed onto a chair that she'd pulled over to another stack of boxes and pulled something out. It was a black top hat. "Sir, I believe I found your hat."

She handed it to him.

It was sturdier than it looked and weighed a couple of pounds. He popped it on his head. "How do I look?"

"All you need is a monocle and you can be Mr. Peanut for Halloween." She leaned back and eyed him. "Or that dude from Monopoly."

He turned and the hat banged on the rafter. With the hat, he had to be seven and a half feet, easy. Tall hats weren't meant for tall men. Still, he left it on and went to the crate. He pried it open with the back of the hammer. Inside was a mess of rags.

"Why would anyone want to keep rags?" He looked up at CanDee.

She walked over, knelt down, and sifted through the rags. She pulled out a long length of gauzy off-white material. "It's a wedding veil."

Carefully, she pulled it free and slid the cap part onto her head. She struck a pose. "What do you think?"

His mouth turned dry as the Sahara. She looked so beautiful. In his mind's eye he could see her wearing that as she walked down the aisle toward him. His chest felt like an elephant was sitting on it. He couldn't seem to pull enough air into his lungs.

"That bad?" She whipped off the veil and leaned down to get a better look at him. "You're looking a little gray around the gills. It is a little hot in here. Maybe we should do this another time?"

He'd never thought about getting married again, but he hadn't not thought about it either. His palms began to sweat and blood drummed in his ears. Still holding the veil, she leaned over and rummaged around in the box.

"Look, here's the dress that goes with it." She pulled out a faded blue dress with lots of faded pink and white ribbons. She stood and held it against her. "That is the ugliest wedding dress I've ever seen."

"It's Edith's. She was wearing that in her wedding photo." He had to agree with CanDee. While he wasn't into fashion, he had eyeballs and that dress was making them hurt.

"Thank God those photos were black and white and couldn't capture the poor choice of colors." She glanced skyward. "I'm losing faith in you, Edith."

She rummaged around in the bottom of the box and came out with some pink leather boots with buttons all the way up the sides.

"Dang, she had some big feet. I wear a nine and a half so these have to be twelves at least." She held a shoe up next to her foot. It looked like a giant pink banana next to her creamy white foot. "These are like transvestite big."

She handed him one of the pink shoes and he held it against his socked foot. It was almost as long as his foot. "These are huge."

She set the shoe down and felt around in the box. "I think this is all that's in here."

She tucked both shoes back into the crate, carefully folded the veil and then laid it in the open crate, and did the same with the dress. "These really should be in a museum so that others can see them. Does Roseville have a museum? I think the family museum is too small to house this collection."

"Roseville doesn't, but the next town over, Fredericksburg, does. Let's see what's in the rest of the crates before I call the museum. I'll need to check with the rest of my family, but since I'm really the only one who cares about history, it shouldn't be a problem." He'd never really thought about donating anything to a museum. It wasn't that he didn't want to, it was only that he thought of these things as family history and wasn't sure anyone else cared to see them. Until now, no one had.

"On to the next box." She stood and weaved her way around the stacks to the back. "Holy cow, this is cool."

She'd found the old Victrola. He smiled to himself. He remembered when he'd found it twenty or so years ago. He'd loved it and had it downstairs until Naomi had moved in and moved it back to the attic. Since they were too bulky to collect, she'd had no use for it. He'd forgotten about it and should bring it back downstairs. Maybe he'd do it tonight.

"Does it work?" He could hear the smile in her voice.

"Yes, ma'am." He meandered through the box maze. "Let me pull it out and we can listen to it while we sift through the rest of the boxes."

He liked doing things for CanDee; he had the strangest urge to beat on his chest and drag a brontosaurus home to feed her. In an effort to impress her, he walked right up to the free-standing Victrola, wrapped his arms around it, and lifted it. It only weighed one hundred and fifty or so pounds, but it was bulky and awkward. One of the doors on the front where the records were stored popped open and a few of the records teetered to the side and threatened to fall on the floor.

"Let me help you." CanDee caught the records before they spilled out and shattered. She walked beside him, holding the doors closed until he gingerly lowered it to the floor.

"So you wind this crank to power it?" She touched the lever on the side.

"Yes." He straightened and stretched his back. "Open the lid, choose a record, fit it on the turntable, and place the needle on the first groove in the record."

She opened the door on the front and carefully pulled a record out. "How about Vess Ossman's 'Maple Leaf Rag'?"

"Whatever. I'm sorry to tell you that they all basically sound the same." He liked music, but this was more tinny than acoustically pleasing.

She pulled the record out of its paper sleeve, opened the Victrola's lid, placed the record on the faded green turntable, and applied the needle. She cranked the handle and a fast-paced banjo ragtime tune drifted out. The tune was so fast that it was hard to believe that anyone's—presumably Vess Ossman's—fingers could move so fast.

"It sounds like he's at the bottom of a well." CanDee listened intently. "I guess it's all they had and was probably a major technological advancement in its time. I have to say that it looks better than it sounds."

She kept nodding along with the beat. "I'm getting use to it. Perfect music for attic hunting."

Two hours later, they'd been through every box, stacked them based on contents—clothes in one corner, furniture and housewares in another, documents and photos in another, and a miscellaneous stack for the stuff that didn't fit into the first three categories.

"I'm trying to think of a reason why someone would have a box full of porcelain doll heads, but I have to tell you that serial killer is all

I'm coming up with." She patted the box she'd just stacked in the miscellaneous pile.

"My grandmother painted china as a hobby. I guess she didn't get around to making the bodies before she died." He didn't want the night to end, but it was well after midnight and he needed to be in the saddle no later than six.

CanDee yawned and threw her arms up in a deep stretch. The hem of the too-short flapper dress rode up as he was standing behind her, and he got a nice view of creamy cheeks. He wanted to unwrap her like a present on Christmas morning.

"So, are you going to continue to stare at my butt or are you going to turn your back so I can change back into my jeans?" Slowly, she lowered her arms and turned around. "Don't get me wrong, I'm okay with stripping down in front of you, but I'd hate for you to revert back to whispering."

She grinned.

"You love taunting me." He tried to sound wounded, but he couldn't control his smile.

"I do. I'm thinking of taking it up as a hobby. Sudoku is so boring." Her voice was low and seductive. "Maybe I should take off my clothes and see if it gets your attention. Because if I wait for you to remove them for me, I'll be old enough to join AARP."

"What's the harm in taking our time?" He had his reasons, but when she looked at him like that, he could barely remember his own name.

She ran her hand up her shirt. "I'm only here for six weeks. Wouldn't you rather have five and a half weeks of amazing sex over, say, four weeks of amazing sex?"

He'd forgotten that she was only here for a short while. Maybe he could convince her to prolong her stay. He had a feeling that she wouldn't leave until she'd had her fill of him and he aimed to make sure that never happened.

"Dusty up here." He reached up and ran a finger along one of the overhead beams, then showed her his dust-covered finger. "Aren't you worried about getting dusty?"

"Nope. I plan on being on top." She stepped back, picked up her clothes, and sauntered down the attic stairs.

CHAPTER 10

Early the next morning, CanDee flopped onto her back. A mattress spring poked her in the lower back, so she turned onto her side, which felt even worse. No matter how she positioned herself on her bed, she couldn't get comfortable and her feet hung off the end. She glanced at the clock—six-fifteen. Another night of little to no sleep in the lumpiest bed ever. She rolled onto her stomach and closed her eyes, willing her body to relax and fall asleep. A minute later, she gave up and got out of bed. She yawned and stretched.

A thought struck. Not a mile away, there was a soft, cozy, empty bed that was more than long enough to fit her body. And, probably some leftovers to fill her belly. In her book, that was a win-win situation. Cinco had said that she could stop by anytime . . . well, now, for instance, seemed like a great time. She could work at Cinco's house, putting the documents they'd found last night in chronological order. And then there was that shower.

She glanced down at the wrinkled tee she used as a sleep shirt. A long, hot, seventeen-showerhead shower—the thought made her weak in the knees.

She pulled on a pair of yoga pants, a bra, and a clean T-shirt, threw a dress and her toiletries in a large canvas bag along with her notes on the Rose family and her laptop, slid her feet into some gold flip-flops, and headed to the door. She had put her hand on the knob to open it when she remembered her shampoo and conditioner. Men weren't known for their great selection of hair products, so she ran back into the bathroom and grabbed those and stuffed them in her bag.

She flip-flopped her way across the yard and to the barn motor pool in search of a golf cart. Last night, hoping for a little high school car-date groping, she'd walked all that way to Cinco's house so he'd have to drive her home, but all she'd gotten was a chaste peck on the mouth. It was like he was going out of his way not to fool around with her. He was attracted to her—last night's kissus-interuptus had proven that.

Maybe his equipment didn't work. She stopped in her tracks and shuddered. Holy crap, that would suck. How did she bring that up? She searched her brain and absolutely nothing came to mind. For now, she was ruling out that possibility until she had further evidence.

She pulled the barn door open. A short man with an eye patch over his right eye looked up from under the hood of a truck he was working on. He reminded her Popeye—all muscular forearms and a squinty face.

"Don't just stand out there, girl, come on in and close the door. You're letting out all the air conditioning." His deep gravelly voice fit him perfectly. "Were you raised in a barn?"

He laughed at his own joke.

"Are you Lefty?" She tried not to look at the eye patch, but it was hard. Clearly he'd gotten his name from the missing or injured right eye. She stepped into the barn and closed the door. She shivered. It was freezing in here. He really liked his air conditioning.

"Who's asking?" His one eye sized her up.

"I'm CanDee McCain." She held out her hand as she walked to him. "I'm here writing the family genealogy."

His eye narrowed as he watched her hand like it was an unwelcome houseguest who'd stayed too long. "Uh huh. I heard you was coming."

He turned back to the engine. Okay then, introduction over. She dropped her hand.

"I'd like to borrow one of the golf carts." She pointed to the closest one.

"Nope." He didn't even turn his head, he just kept working on the engine.

What did he mean, *nope*?

"I'm sorry, I don't understand. I can't borrow a golf cart? I was told that I could." She wasn't sure what to do.

"Have to take the test first. There's a written portion of a hundred questions, the oral portion, the driving portion, and finally a vision test. You'll need to make an appointment." One hand shot out from under the hood and pointed to a clipboard hanging on a nail by the office door. She remembered the clipboard from the other day.

Okay, she could take a test. She walked over to the clipboard and picked up the pencil tied to the metal ring. She leaned in closer to get a better look at the calendar. "This says that the next appointment for a driving test is two years away. I can't wait that long."

"Then you'll have to walk. I'm a very busy man." He slapped one tool down hard on the side of the truck and picked up another. "Rules is rules."

"But—" She jumped when a telephone rang in the office. It was startling because it sounded like the kind that hung on the wall. It had been ages since she'd seen anything but a cell phone.

"Excuse me for a minute." Lefty straightened to his full height of five feet two and strutted to his office. Napoleon couldn't have had this much self-importance. He closed the door so he could take his call in private.

She glanced down at the closest golf cart. The keys were in it. Without thinking about it, she rolled the barn door open, jumped in the golf cart, turned the key, and backed out. She knew it was wrong, but she didn't have two years to wait for a driving test. Lefty would have to get over it.

She stomped on the gas petal, taking the golf cart to its top speed in case he was chasing her. She wouldn't put it past him. Lefty suffered from a textbook Napoleon complex and she was just the person to be his Waterloo. After all, one man's barn was this man's castle. Now she sounded like Grammie.

She glanced over her shoulder but didn't see anyone. This was Texas—he might have a gun. She hunched down in her seat, not sure how it was helpful, but that's what people did in the movies. She took the turn to Cinco's house and kept looking over her shoulder. Stealing the golf cart was kind of exciting. When she finally got to Cinco's driveway, she decided to park the golf cart in his barn. It was best to hide the evidence.

Now for the breaking-and-entering portion of her morning. She was on a regular crime spree.

She took the front steps two at a time and walked to the door. She tried the knob and it was unlocked, which was kind of a letdown. Surely breaking and entering should have been more exciting.

"Hello," she called in case Cinco was there. It really didn't matter if he was, she just wanted to know.

There was no answer.

She walked in and closed the front door. She parked her canvas bag in the parlor. With its huge window seat in the bay window letting in natural light, it would be a great place to work. Next stop, the kitchen. She opened the Frigidaire, found the leftover pot roast, pulled it out, and set it on the counter. She went back to the fridge, found a head of bib lettuce, some mayo, and an open carton of orange juice. With the remaining four slices of white bread she found in a bag on the counter, she made two sandwiches—one for her and one for Cinco. She wrapped his in the bread bag and put it in the fridge and put hers on a plate. She poured herself a large glass of orange juice and returned the carton to the fridge. She took her sandwich and her OJ to the kitchen table and pulled out several of Edith's journals.

After she'd eaten the sandwich and drank her OJ, she went journal by journal and put them in chronological order. She took her dishes and glass to the sink, washed them, and put them in the rack to dry.

She climbed the stairs and meant to go to the attic and pull the boxes with photos and documents down so she could sort them, but she was drawn to the over-sized brass bed. She yawned deeply as she stared down at it. Just a small nap . . . an hour at most.

She stepped out of her shoes and yoga pants, and curled up on his delicious bed.

Four hours later, Cinco hosed the cow dung off of his boots with the garden hose by his front door before shucking out of them, leaving them on the porch to dry, and opening his front door. He had just enough time for lunch and then he had a mountain of paperwork to wade through before he'd planned on stopping by the cottage to see if CanDee wanted to have dinner with him. Truth was, he'd stopped by there on the way here and she'd been nowhere to be found. Maybe she'd run to town to make her getaway after she'd stolen the golf cart.

He laughed to himself. He'd had to talk Lefty out of calling the Texas Rangers, the Sheriff's Department, and the Highway Patrol. It took spunk to cross Lefty. As it stood, CanDee was banned for life from using any mechanical vehicle owned by Texas Rose Ranch.

He walked past the parlor and noticed a pink canvas bag that he didn't remember owning. He walked into the kitchen and found a plate and cup that he hadn't used drying in the rack. He was starting to feel like he was in a scene from *Goldilocks and the Three Bears*.

His kitchen table held stacks of Edith's journals. CanDee was here somewhere.

"Hello," he called as he walked through the house. When she didn't answer, his heart kicked up a notch. What if she tried to lift some boxes in the attic and hurt herself? He took the stairs three at a time. The light wasn't on in the attic. On his way to the attic, he glanced past the open door to his bedroom and stopped. She was asleep on his bed, her head on his pillow, her body facing him.

At that moment, he wanted nothing more than to lie beside her and pull her into him. He missed that—spooning. He missed it a lot. There was something primal and comforting about snuggling up to a woman . . . to CanDee. Not only did he want to keep her safe, but he wanted that feeling for himself.

"Are you going to stare at me all day?" She yawned. "Or are you going to join me?"

It was tempting.

All he had to do was take off his clothes, slide in, and peel off her shirt and whatever else she had on, and they'd be skin to skin.

"I can't now, I'm on the clock." He bit his upper lip and told himself he had a million things to do, but he couldn't think of a single one. He turned to go.

"Suit yourself." She yawned again. "I made you a sandwich, it's in the refrigerator."

He stopped and turned back around. She'd made him a sandwich. She'd thought of him. She'd made it and put it in the fridge for him for later. A sandwich was something so small and seemingly insignificant, but it was thoughtful. Kindness shouldn't have caught him off guard, but it did. In the four years that he'd been married to Naomi, he couldn't remember her making him anything. In truth, all she'd done was spend his money and sleep with his friends. Kindness wasn't in her nature.

CanDee had made him a sandwich, which meant more to him than she could have known.

He unbuckled his belt, flipped the button open on his jeans, and unzipped them. They fell to the floor in a heap at his feet. The paperwork could wait. He could take an hour or so, he was the boss. He shrugged out of his T-shirt and tossed it on the floor.

"I wouldn't have taken you for a boxer-brief kind of guy, but they suit you." Her voice was low and sleep-mussed. "You have an amazing body."

Did he? He glanced down. He'd always thought of himself as kind of skinny. But CanDee thought it was nice. Her opinion was all that mattered.

He walked around the bed, slipped in behind her, and snuggled up to her back. "We're just napping."

"Okeydokey." She wriggled in closer to him and pulled his arm around her. Apparently her shirt had ridden up, so his hand rested on a warm expanse of her stomach.

She yawned and stretched, her warm backside rubbing the front of his boxers.

"Sleeping only . . . remember?" He eased his hips back from her, putting a few inches between their lower bodies.

"Right." Her backside wiggled over until it found him. The hard-on he'd had since pretty much the first time he saw her pounded painfully against his shorts. This was a bad idea.

He pulled away, but she held his hand on her stomach in place. He hesitated. "On second thought, I don't have time—"

She rolled over and covered his mouth with hers. Her tongue roamed the inside of his mouth as she leaned into him.

He should set her on the other side of the bed and leave her, but her body felt so good against his and it had been a long time since Naomi. He wanted this . . . he needed this.

He rolled her on her back and his knee slid between her legs. His hands snaked under her shirt, one hand at her lower back pressing her hips to his, and the other finding her breast. With his index finger and thumb, he rolled her nipple and then cupped her breast.

She moaned softly against his lips as her legs opened wider. He kissed his way down her neck and nudged the spot right below her ear. She moaned again and he sucked that spot hard. His mouth found her nipple. He licked and sucked playfully.

One of her hands tunneled through his hair holding his mouth to her while the other slid down his chest to his boxers. She circled him hard and worked his cock. Her thumb massaged the tender tip as she stroked him.

Her nipple wasn't nearly enough, he had to taste her. His hand slid down her belly and found the tiny scrap of lace covering her. He slipped a finger under the lace and into her warm wetness. She was so fucking wet for him. He slid another finger in and used his thumb to draw tiny circles above her opening. Her hips moved against his hand. As he worked her nipple with his mouth, her breathing turned heavy and her hand stroked him faster.

She felt so good against him, under him. Gently, he unwrapped her hand from him, and kissed his way down to her sex. He spread her legs wide . . . he wanted to see her . . . to taste her.

There was a thin line of short red curls pointing the way to heaven. With his fingers still stroking her from the inside, he set his mouth on her. Slowly, he made circular movements, lightly licking. Her hips bucked against his mouth and she turned sweeter—like tangy strawberries warmed by the sun. Her hips picked up his rhythm and with every lick his cock strained to get to her. Her breathing got faster as her hips bucked harder against his mouth. He increased the pressure to finish her off. Her muscles tensed and then she moaned as the orgasm washed over her.

When she lay back boneless against the pillow, he wanted to roar like a lion. He'd put that rosy-flush on her body and he could still taste her sweetness. He eased up and kissed his way up to her face. He wanted to be gentle, but his body wouldn't let him. He needed her . . . needed the release.

He made to roll off of her, but her legs clamped around him, holding him on top of her.

"Condom." His voice was rusty.

She reached over to the nightstand, pulled the top drawer open, and grabbed the box of Trojans.

"I moved them in here from the bathroom medicine cabinet." She grinned.

He snagged the box, tore it open. In a flash, he had it on and was ready. As gently as he could, he slid into all of that warm heat.

She sighed contently and lifted her hips to take him deeper. She wrapped her legs tighter around him and rolled him on his back.

"You've done the work so far, it's my turn." She leaned forward, placing her hands on either side of his head. He took her nipple into his mouth as she rode him hard, each thrust taking him closer to the edge. Her hips built to a frantic pace, stroking him. Every muscle in his body tensed. He bit his bottom lip so hard he tasted blood trying to hold the orgasm back.

"Oh . . . oh." CanDee moaned as she tightened around him.

He pumped harder and harder as the first wave of orgasm crashed through him. She rode him until he'd almost forgotten his own name and then she rolled off and lay beside him.

He curled into her, surrounding her with his body.

"So you went through my medicine cabinet?" He smoothed her long, coppery hair down and buried his face in it. It smelled like coconuts and lemons.

"Yes. I'm a girl, which means that I've snooped in every cabinet, drawer, and closet you have." She reached back, found his hand, and wrapped it around her.

"Did you find anything interesting?" He loved that she was honest.

"You have an alarming array of antacids. I've never seen so many." She slid his hand up to cover her breast. He could get behind that plan. "Do you have some stomach ailment I should know about?"

"No, just a love of spicy chili." He nuzzled her neck.

"Speaking of chili . . . does your spicy chili involve beans?" She stilled, waiting for his answer.

"No, ma'am, this is Texas. It's all meat, all the time. Only Yankees or Californians put beans in their chili." Absently, he ran his thumb over her nipple.

"Thank God. Beans in chili are a deal breaker for me. I'd hate for whatever we have to be over before it really started." She relaxed into him.

He grinned. They'd just had sex and discussed chili. He could get used to this.

CHAPTER 11

Three hours later, CanDee was hard at work. On the floor of the parlor, she had documents and pictures laid out in a huge timeline. Starting with the original land deed titling the first thousand acres to Colonel Lacy Kendall Lehman all the way to the marriage license of Lacy Kendall Rose IV and Lucy Anne Braxton in 1975.

She was halfway through the boxes and the timeline was starting to take shape. Carefully, she pulled another piece of browned-with-age paper out of a box. This was the land deed for the additional acres purchased by Lacy Kendall Lehman that had belonged to Noah Smithwick. She scanned the deed and laughed.

"What's so funny?" Cinco asked from the chaise-lounge end of the brown leather sectional sofa. He'd brought a stack of paperwork and his laptop in there to hang out with CanDee.

The company was nice.

"This is the deed for Noah Smithwick's acres. The language is a little different. It states, '*Lacy Kendall Lehman, a man with impeccable morals, kindness toward his family and livestock, and his unwavering Christian generosity . . .*' and then there are lots of heretofores and thuses and hences." She held the document up for him to see. "And there are no less than five official seals. They really wanted to make sure that your three-times-great-grandfather was the owner of these acres."

"I guess they felt like they needed to make up for Noah Smithwick." He typed something on his laptop and moved a paper from one pile to the next.

She walked the paper over to the beginning of the timeline and gently stacked it on top of the original deed. On the way back to the box she was currently sorting, she noticed a stack of photos on top of yet another box. "Where did these come from?"

Cinco looked up from his computer. "I found those photos in a shoebox in the barn. I thought they might be useful."

Gingerly, she held the top photo up and then turned it over. *Tres, age 14* was written on the back. The black and white was of a tall skinny boy, unsmiling, and with his hands to his sides. She moved that one to the bottom of the pile. The next one was a wedding photo of a stiff groom with scars on his face and hands standing next to an even stiffer-looking bride. She turned it over. *Tres Rose and Suzette McCloud Rose, 1942.* She pulled out the other photo and set the remaining photos on the box. She went to the window and held the two photos up. "That's odd."

She compared the photos again.

"What?" Cinco banged away on the laptop.

"Tres started out tall and skinny with freckles and ended up as short and dark skinned. I guess the fire and working outside did that to him."

That had to be it, or maybe the perspective of the photo was off. Perhaps—she turned the wedding photo over and looked at the name—Suzette had been tall.

"Probably just a trick of lighting or something." Cinco rustled through his paperwork, picked up one, typed something in the computer, and then put the paper in the other stack.

"You're probably right." She set the pictures down on the sofa, "I'm surprised that you don't have people to do that for you."

He looked up from the laptop. "What?"

"Don't you have an assistant or someone who can handle the paperwork? That would give you more time to concentrate on running the ranch instead of running the paperwork." No one who ran anything did their own paperwork. It was the American way.

"I did." He glanced down at his lap. "Naomi was my assistant."

"Oh." She smiled and hoped that it made him less uncomfortable. "Somebody had an office romance."

"It was less romance and more of a pursuit. She saw dollar signs and I was the easiest way to get to the money. She lured me in, faked a pregnancy, spent my money, and slept with everyone but me. Only after the ink dried on the marriage certificate did she start to show her true colors. When we were dating she'd been into the same music I like and we seemed to follow the same sports teams, but it was all an act." He sounded so matter-of-fact—that was the worst part.

"Whoa, wait a minute. Faked a pregnancy? How did that work?" She moved the stack of papers on his right and sat. Naomi seemed like a class-A bitch.

"Well, I was about to end things because she'd run up thousands of dollars on my American Express—"

"What? Why did you give her your credit card?" It didn't make sense.

"I didn't. She was my assistant and once she became my girlfriend, she thought she was entitled to my personal assets." He sounded disgusted with himself. "After we started sleeping together, she went shopping."

"Why didn't you call the police? Identity theft is a crime." Then again, she hadn't called the police when her ex had run up her credit cards. Life was never that black and white.

"I almost did, but she promised to return everything and then she turned up pregnant." He shook his head. "Part of me knew it was a lie, but another part of me wanted it to be true so badly. I grew up in a big, rowdy family. I guess I wanted one for myself. And, I felt like a fool for having been played."

He took a deep breath and let it out slowly, like he'd just pushed through a hard task. "Now, it's your turn to tell me something personal."

Anxiety rolled around in her stomach. She'd never signed up for a game of tit for tat.

"I'm not wearing any underwear." It was hard to get any more personal than that.

He cocked an eyebrow in her direction. "While that's interesting, that's not what I meant and you know it."

Everything in her screamed to keep things light, and her palms started to sweat. Light and funny were her fall-back plan, light and funny meant things weren't getting too deep, but light and funny wouldn't work for Cinco. He wanted more. It was written all over his face. As long as things didn't get too personal, she was all in, but the minute she started attaching feelings to whatever it was that they had, she wouldn't be able to stay. She just couldn't take any more hurt. Years of being taken advantage of had made her the queen of wanting less. Less was more in her book.

She opened her mouth to throw out another great one-liner, but it stuck in her throat. "I was with Phillip for six years. I worked two full-time jobs while he wrote the great American novel and pursued several other careers that he was interested in for about five minutes each. While we were together, he managed to pay off his credit cards and charge up mine . . ."

All the light and funny faded into the background. The anxiety turned to nausea, but she needed to tell him the rest. She needed to say it out loud. "In my spare bits of time, I wrote my first murder mystery. It was something I'd been dying to write since, well . . . forever. When I left to write the King Ranch genealogy, he cleaned out my checking account, took my novel, and left. He must have done it the second my car pulled out of my apartment parking lot because when I got back eight weeks later, I found that I'd been evicted for nonpayment of my rent and my things had been sold at auction."

The auction had been the worst part. The possessions that had been her parents'—her only link to them—were gone.

"He called me every single night at nine sharp while I was at the King Ranch and not once did he mention that he'd moved out." Her voice was hollow, like she was recounting details from someone else's life. "I didn't figure out until I got home why he'd insisted that I take his laptop and leave mine behind. He'd told me to take his because it was newer and nicer, and at the time, I'd thought how wonderful it was that he wanted the best for me."

She nodded. "I completely understand your feelings of humiliation. Mine involved sleeping in my car until I worked up the courage to tell my grandmother what happened and move back in with her. It's funny, the hurt feelings from a breakup are never as bad as disappointing family."

Every muscle in his body tensed like a caged lion waiting for the door to spring open.

"You should have gone after the son of a bitch. Hell, I want to go after him myself." His voice was a low growl. In a move that was more possessive than consoling, his arm came around her and he pulled her to him. "I don't suppose you'd give me his last name. I got the Phillip part."

She shook her head. "I appreciate the bravado, but it wouldn't do any good. My parents' things are gone and if I ever saw him again, I'd probably rip him limb from limb. Since I can't rock prison-jumpsuit orange, I'll wait for karma to kick his butt."

She wasn't a roll-over-and-take-it kind of girl, but she didn't have money for a legal battle and thanks to her missing laptop, she also didn't have any evidence that she wrote *Murder, Mayhem, and Madness*. Sometimes life sucked, and all she could do was wait on the kindness of the Universe.

"Are you sure? I could find him for you." His offer sounded a lot like *I could kill him for you.*

"No, I'm good. I'm happy to never see him again." She put her head on Cinco's shoulder. It was nice to be comforted by someone and it was good to have gotten the Phillip mess off her chest. She'd never really spoken of it to anyone. She'd only told her grandmother part of the story. "I imagine it's the same with Naomi."

"If I never see her again, it will be too soon." Absently, he massaged her shoulder.

"How did your parents feel about Naomi?" She remembered Lucy mentioning his ex-wife. Lucy hadn't seemed sorry to see Naomi go.

"My parents hated her, but they didn't tell me that until she was gone." Cinco kissed the top of CanDee's head. "They tolerated her because they thought she made me happy. They don't know about the credit card bills." His tone suggested that they never would.

"What did she buy?" CanDee didn't want to ask how much money his ex had run up in debt, but it seemed like a lot. Apart from the occasional splurge on shoes at an upscale resale shop, she couldn't think of anything worth buying.

"Lots of things. For example, crosses. Once she bought ten thousand dollars' worth of crosses at a store in Marble Falls. I almost had a heart attack when I opened the bill." He shook his head. "Crazy."

"I don't understand. Crosses, like the kind with Jesus hanging on the front?" She couldn't comprehend spending ten thousand dollars on anything. Her gaze went to his face. "Were they encrusted with rubies and made of gold?"

"I wish. At least I could have seen them as an investment." Laughter rumbled up and made his chest shake. "That would have made sense. She bought one hundred and twenty-four crosses to hang on that wall." He pointed to the wall across from them. "She claimed to have started collecting them."

"Was she overly religious?" She tried to imagine a bunch of crosses crammed on that wall and shuddered. "That makes me claustrophobic just thinking about it."

"Tell me about it. Every day I walked into my house, there was another collection of things hanging on the wall. Birdhouses, teapots, clocks, china plates, plastic flowers, baskets, you name it and she collected it. And then there was all the crap she displayed on every available surface—carnival glass, crystal ink wells, imported porcelain egg cups, cake stands, snuff boxes, silver spoons."

"Damn, I don't even know what most of that stuff is." She looked around at his large comfy furniture and tried to imagine his house cram-packed with things. "How did you manage to get around amongst all of that crap? I would have been afraid that I'd break something."

"That's exactly how I felt. She had these baskets hanging down from the kitchen ceiling. I bumped them all the time. I hated coming home." His face screwed up. "I just realized that. When you hate to come home, it's time to move on."

"Come to think of it, I was so excited to get away from Phillip for the eight weeks at the King Ranch. I should have known then that it was over." She remembered the huge sigh of relief she'd felt as she'd pulled away from the curb of her apartment.

"Hindsight is always twenty-twenty. We're both better off without them." He chewed on his upper lip—an action she was beginning to realize meant he was mulling things over. "I don't suppose you'd reconsider giving me Phillip's last name. I have a few choice words for him."

"Nope, I'm good. Thanks for wanting to fight my battles, but I'm perfectly happy to fight them myself. I can stand on my own two feet even if the shoes I'm wearing aren't that comfortable." Even when it meant crawling back to her grandmother's house because she hadn't eaten in two days and had hit rock bottom. Finding a job without a permanent address was impossible and she'd experienced firsthand the desperation of homelessness.

"What about you? What did your family think about Phillip?" Every time he said *Phillip* it sound a lot like *asshole*.

"My grandmother hated him. She swears she didn't poison him that one time, but he spent the night in the ER with food poisoning." Now it was funny, back then it wasn't. She remembered that her grandmother had made a batch of blueberry muffins—Phillip's favorite—and practically forced them down his throat. When CanDee'd tried to take one, her grandmother had batted her hand away and told her that they were all for Phillip. Luckily, he'd never put two and two together and come up with poisoning.

"Your grandmother sounds like good people." He grinned. "I'd love to meet her."

"Maybe someday you will." It wasn't that she didn't think they would get along, it was that recently Grammie had gone from weird to downright odd. Since her grandmother had joined that Wicca coven, all her Christian friends had hit the road. Then again, dancing naked in her backyard on sun and moon feast days had probably alienated the neighbors. If CanDee ever made it big in publishing, she was definitely fencing in her grandmother's backyard. "Just don't take food from her."

"Why? Don't you think she'll like me?" He shot her the little-boy sad eyes. "I'm good with grandmothers."

"I'm sure she'll love you, but now she's vegan. I don't think there's any risk of her poisoning you, but she could tofu you to death." CanDee loved meat and couldn't think why anyone would give it up. "You can't throw a rock in Austin without hitting a vegan."

"That's funny since I'm pretty sure they only eat rocks." He laughed.

She nodded. "Not all rocks. I don't think they can eat fossils since they used to be animals."

"I hadn't thought of that. I bet you're right. I dated a vegan once . . . she hated the Brazilian steakhouse I took her to. I knew right then, there wouldn't be a second date." He closed his laptop, moved it to the side, and pulled her into his lap. "So what's this I hear about you not wearing any underpants?"

"I forgot to throw some clean ones in my bag." She pulled at the hem of her dress. "After that fantastic shower, I didn't want to put on the ones I wore over."

"That shower was pretty fantastic." His grin was drop-dead sexy. "It's hard to pinpoint the highlight. I enjoyed watching you wash your hard-to-reach places almost as much as I liked backing you up against the window and experiencing your hard-to-reach places."

One of his hands inched the hem of her dress up while the other dug in his front jeans pocket. "You know . . . I've never had sex in this parlor."

"Really?" She looked around inspecting the parlor. "So, what's your plan?"

She repositioned herself so that she was straddling him. His free hand slipped under the hem of her cotton summer dress and found nothing but her.

"I like you bare-assed." One finger dipped inside her. "Nice."

The other hand came out of his pocket with a palm full of condoms.

"Planning ahead?" She sat up on her knees, giving him better access.

"More like wishful thinking." He dipped another finger in and her hips picked up the rhythm of his hand. "You like this?"

She licked her lips. "Very much."

"Why don't you let down those tiny excuses for straps and pull down the front of that dress so I can get to you. Then I want you to lie back and watch me play with your body." His gaze fastened on the outline of her hard nipples through the dress.

"You like giving direction, don't you?" she cooed. She was fine taking direction—some of the time.

She pulled one strap over her shoulder and then the other and eased the elastic-backed dress down to her waist. Since the dress had a shelf bra, there was nothing between her chest and him.

"I see that you follow directions well." He stared at her breasts like a hungry man eyeing up his next meal.

"Sometimes." She grabbed the condom from him, backed off his lap, and knelt in front of him. She ripped the condom open and smiled up at him.

"W-w-what are you doing?" His stammer was charming.

"Not following your directions. Safety first." She took the condom in her mouth and went for his belt.

His eyes turned huge. "I like the rebellious side of you that doesn't follow instructions. As long as you understand that I'm in charge."

She was willing to let him believe that he was in charge . . . some of the time.

CHAPTER 12

Covertly Cinco watched CanDee sort through the boxes as he pretended to work on his laptop. The sex break they'd taken an hour or so ago had been incredible. She still wasn't wearing any underpants, so keeping his mind on the massive amount of busywork that went with running the cattle portion of the Texas Rose was impossible. Maybe it was time to hire an assistant.

Who was this Phillip and how could he find out the asshole's last name? He'd taken everything from CanDee and there had to be something that Cinco could do to help her. She'd lived in her car. The thought made him physically ill. She'd been alone and homeless and probably scared. Acid rolled around in his stomach. It felt like he'd eaten a gallon of extra-spicy chili.

All because of Phillip.

Cinco's hands fisted at his sides and more than anything he wanted to beat the shit out of her ex. What kind of self-centered asshole treated a woman—especially one as funny and kind and intelligent and beautiful as CanDee—or anyone—that way? Since Cinco had no idea what Phillip looked like, he imagined that he was some weasel-faced, pansy-assed, weak-chinned motherfucker with soft hands and zero testosterone.

He closed his laptop and gave up the pretense of work in favor of just watching CanDee. He liked having her in his house. She filled it with energy and life. Maybe he could get her to stay a while . . . move some of her things over? It wasn't like she was moving in, just spending the nights she was here with him. How did he get her to think that it was her idea?

"Oh my God." She held a brownish picture up for him to see. "It's Mel and Edith on their wedding day. I recognize the dress."

She brought it over to him. "Why is Mel dressed as a man?"

He took the picture from her. "The last time I saw this, I was a child. It never registered then."

"I wonder if Mel was always dressed as a man." CanDee sat next to him and folded her long legs under her. "When I was researching something—I don't remember what—I found a story about a stagecoach driver who was known for his hard drinking and bad temper. When he died, the coroner found out that he was actually a she. Apparently, she was the first woman to vote for president."

"That's interesting." He'd have to google that. "I don't know if Mel always dressed like a man or just for that day so she could get married to Edith."

"Cross-dressing was probably more common in the Old West than we think." She took the picture and analyzed it.

"Cross-dressing? Wait a minute." He remembered Edith had written in her journal that Mel was just more comfortable in men's clothes. It was kind of cross-dressing. "I don't think Mel was a cross-dresser, I think she was just more comfortable dressed as a man."

"Isn't that the same thing?" CanDee quirked an eyebrow.

He thought about it. "I guess you're right."

He draped his arm around the back of the sofa. "Interesting. We have a cross-dresser in the family."

"Is that hard for you? How do you think your parents will feel when it comes out?" CanDee's gold-brown eyes held nothing but concern.

"Are you kidding? My mother will be so happy. We're all pretty sure that Rowdy is gay. He's a big flirt but he doesn't date but once a year when he goes out of town for a"—he threw up some air quotes—"wine festival, but there isn't one. Mom's convinced that he's so in the closet that he only sets himself free one week a year. Short of coming out and asking him if he's gay, we've all bent over backwards to let him know that he's loved and all we want is for him to be happy."

"That's very progressive of you." CanDee didn't sound judgmental, but a little shocked.

He shrugged. "Family is family. I love all of my brothers for who they are and I want the best for them."

"I feel the same way." She nestled into him. "I hope when I have kids, they feel comfortable enough with me and themselves to tell me anything."

"You want kids?" It was an odd question that felt strange on his lips, but it was better to get those things out in the open at the beginning of a relationship because he'd been down this road before.

"Of course. I want a whole house full. Being an only child was kind of lonely." Her stomach rumbled and she put her hand over it. "Sorry, it's been a long time since I ate that roast beef sandwich."

The more he found out about her, the more he liked her.

"How do you feel about chili?" He was content to snuggle with her on the sofa for the next two weeks, but his woman was hungry, so he needed to feed her.

"That all depends. Does it involve crackers?" Her stomach rumbled again.

"Absolutely. Although, I hope you're not talking about those sissified butter crackers because out here in the country we eat saltines." He stood and gently pulled her up next to him.

"You're a good man. Chili requires saltines. Now, if we could just get you back on track with the Double Stuf Oreos, you'd be the perfect man." She threw a hand up. "Wait, I spoke too soon. Do you snore? It's not a deal breaker because it can be fixed, but I'm going to have to stand firm on the Double Stuf Oreos."

"Nope, no snoring . . . at least that I know of, and trust me, Naomi would have let me know." It was hard to keep the hatred out of his voice.

"We should put your ex and my ex in a cage and see who comes out alive." She smiled broadly. "My money's on Naomi."

"Me too. Especially since I picture Phillip as a Shakespeare-spouting, hipster wannabe with too much self-importance who spends his free time at poetry slams and debating correct comma usage." He realized that he actually hated the little shit more than he hated his ex-wife.

"You nailed it . . . that's him, down to the grammar nazi. Once I tried to tell him that grammar wasn't what made a book good and he didn't talk to me for a week." She kissed him on the cheek. "Nice call."

Settling his hand on the small of her back, he led her to the kitchen.

"How about a beer while I put together the chili?" He nodded to the fridge as he dropped his hand and headed to the pantry.

He grabbed three cans of tomatoes, a couple of onions, a head of garlic, chili powder, and cumin. He dumped his armload down on the kitchen island. He walked to the summer kitchen off to the left, flipped up the top of the chest freezer and pulled out three pounds of ground meat.

"That's a crap load of meat." She handed him a Shiner. "That's got to be, like, a side of beef." She did the math. "I guess you don't cattle ranch for fun."

"There's always meat around here." He reached into the freezer for the container of his secret ingredient.

"And that's just one of the many things I like about you." She held her Shiner bottle up to clink with his.

He obliged.

"What's that?" She pointed to the container as she took the meat from him.

"Secret ingredient." He led her back into the kitchen and set the plastic container on the island.

She dumped the frozen meat down next to it. "What do I win if I guess what the secret ingredient is?"

"I don't know. What do you want?" He popped the frozen meat into the microwave and hit defrost.

Her lips pursed as she mulled over her prize. "Reese's Peanut Butter Cups moved to the fridge permanently."

He held out his beer bottle again. "Done."

He set it down, pulled a chef's knife from the butcher block, grabbed a cutting board, and headed back to the island. "What do I get if you lose?"

"What do you want?" Gently, she took the knife and the cutting board from him. She laid the cutting board on the island, picked up an onion, sliced off the top, and peeled away the skin. "How do you want these cut?"

She was helping? The thought never occurred to him that she would help him. It was more than nice. "Finely diced."

"You got it." She moved the onion skin to the side and sliced the onion.

He sipped his beer and watched her work. He'd watched her a lot today and he still hadn't gotten his fill. Especially since she was wearing a short skirt and now that he knew she was minus those underpants, he waited for that skirt to ride up.

"Did you decide?" She peeled the second onion.

"Decide on what?" What had they been talking about before?

"What you win if I can't guess the secret ingredient." She diced the onion.

He opened the fridge, picked up a couple of bell peppers, and closed the door. "If I win, your underpants are gone . . . while you're under my roof."

"You're kind of pervy . . . I like that about you." She set down the knife and picked up her beer. She held it out. "Done."

He clinked her bottle.

"You're never going to guess." He set the bell peppers next to the diced onions. "Feel like dicing those too?"

"Absolutely." She picked up the knife. "And I have excellent deductive powers. Those Reese's are as good as refrigerated."

"Stretch, let's not get ahead of ourselves." He opened the cabinet next to the commercial stove and pulled out a large cast-iron Dutch oven. He set it on the front left burner and turned on the gas to high.

CanDee finished dicing the peppers, set the knife down, and picked up the plastic container. "I can tell from the packaging that this is a container used for restaurant takeout."

She popped the lid off, smelled it, and then scraped her thumbnail across the surface and licked her thumb. "Is this what I think it is?"

"That all depends . . . what do you think it is?" He grinned. She was never going to guess . . . not in a million years.

"Do you have the chips that go with it?" She smiled it again. "It's salsa and I know exactly where you got it from."

"How is that possible?" There was no way.

"Does your family know that you drive to Austin for your salsa?" She looked like the cat who'd eaten the canary.

His mouth fell open and he realized that the arm holding his beer that had been on its way to his mouth hung in midair. "How did you know?"

"This is Vivo's salsa. Do you have the extra crispy chips that go with it?" She looked around.

"Unfortunately, I don't. This is the last of the salsa I bought before they closed down. How in the hell did you know that it's Vivo's salsa?" It was the best salsa in Texas, but the restaurant had closed down, so his supply was at an end.

"It has a distinctive color and odor." She set the salsa down and picked up her beer. "They opened back up."

The microwave dinged so he opened it, carefully took out the meat, and dumped it into the hot pan. "Don't toy with me, woman."

He picked up the cutting board and dumped the diced veggies in with the meat. Then he picked up a spatula and mixed everything together.

"I'm not toying with you. They reopened a couple of months ago. New owners, but everything tastes the very same. Best chicken tortilla soup." She closed her eyes like she was imagining a bowl.

"And the nachos . . . don't forget the nachos." His mouth watered. "I don't suppose you'd be up for a road trip sometime soon?"

He could practically taste the crispy chips, picadillo, beans, and cheese on his tongue.

"Absolutely. I'm always up for a road trip. Hell, I'm in just for the chips and salsa. I almost cried when they reopened." She picked up the veggie trimmings and tossed them in the garbage can under the sink and then picked up the cleaning wipes next to the trash can, plucked one out, and wiped down the island. "Oh wait, did you need the garlic chopped?"

She tossed the cleaning wipe in the trash and went back to the island.

"Yes, three cloves, please." He stirred the chili. It was nice cooking with her. She didn't wait to be asked to do something, she just jumped right on in there and did it.

"Does your family know that you regularly go to Austin?" With her thumbnail, she peeled off three cloves of garlic, placed that large chef's knife on top of the garlic, and brought her fist down hard on the flat of the knife, crushing the garlic.

"Yes, in fact the whole state knows that I regularly go to Austin." He pulled himself up to his full height and held out his hand. "I'd like to introduce myself. I'm your local state representative for district seventy-three, Lacy Kendall Rose V."

"No way." She minced the garlic.

"Really. The fine citizens of district seventy-three voted me into office last year. I have an office at the Capitol and everything."

"So I'm sleeping with a politician." Using the knife, she scooped up the garlic and brought it to the stove. "That sounds so sleazy. I draw the line at getting on my knees under your desk. A woman's got to have a moral compass."

He laughed. "Don't be silly. That's what interns are for."

Her eyes turned huge and her hand went to her mouth.

"Wait . . . no. I don't have any interns. I was kidding."

She grinned. "Sucker. You're such an easy mark."

"You are a pain in the ass." He pulled her to him and kissed her lightly.

He had a feeling that he would never get enough of her. The more time he spent with her, the more time he wanted. His father had told him that a lifetime wasn't enough with his mother. Now he understood what that meant.

CHAPTER 13

So what if she'd spent the night and woken up next to Cinco? CanDee wasn't happy with herself. This was the beginning of attachment, which might lead to moving in together, which could lead to happiness and then a load of heartache.

She was tired of telling herself that this time would be different. Before Phillip had been Markus—the poet. She'd been in college full time and still managed to pay off his car by borrowing money against her car. Prior to Markus had been Rob—the Pilates instructor who'd been taking a break from Pilates to find himself. Apparently his voyage of self-discovery had involved backpacking through Europe on her dime. There was only one explanation: she was a sap. Well, that, and her picker was broken. She'd never really thought of herself as a doormat, but she had footprints on her forehead that said otherwise.

Cinco was different. He hadn't asked to borrow money or her car. Then again, her ten-year-old Toyota Corolla looked like toy next to his enormous Chevy 2500. And he wasn't likely to want to backpack through Europe or have her pay off his credit cards, or steal her novel.

So, okay, she'd spent the night and woken up next to him. It wasn't a big deal.

Cinco had a better bed and a shower directly from heaven, so she was only being practical. This wasn't a relationship, but it kind of was . . . so what . . . it would never lead to anything permanent.

With her fork, she scooped up the last of her scrambled eggs from her plate. He'd left hours ago, before the sun even thought about waking up. She sipped a cup of hot, fresh coffee. He'd set a timer on the coffeemaker so she'd have some fresh when she woke up. How had he known what time that would be?

On a frustrated sigh, she glanced at the refrigerator, where he'd left her a note apologizing for leaving so early, but that he'd cooked her breakfast and left it in the fridge. And, he wanted her to feel free to work here and maybe he'd be able to sneak away for some lunch with her. Damn it if her heart didn't flip-flop at the thought of seeing him again.

CanDee's palms began to sweat, so she rubbed them on her pajama bottoms. This was familiar—a little too familiar. Her relationships always started out this way. Everything was all shiny and new and the sex was fantastic, and they spent every waking moment together.

And then a new toothbrush would appear in her bathroom. She shook her head. It would all start with a toothbrush and then some underwear and a clean shirt. Pretty soon an overnight bag would show up, and then she would give up a little drawer space and start stocking the fridge with his favorite foods.

And then someone—usually her—would have the great idea that they should move in together. Somehow, she would end up footing the bill for his student loans and credit cards and his car payment. She rubbed her slick palms on her pants again.

Only . . . this time, it would be different. Cinco would never move in with her and he sure as hell wouldn't ever let her pay for a damn thing. She nodded to herself as she picked up her dirty plate and mug and took them to the sink. She washed them and placed them in the rack to dry.

Grabbing a cleaning wipe from under the sink, she wiped down the kitchen table and then tossed it in the trash can.

She straightened.

Holy crap. Her toothbrush was lined up next to Cinco's on the bathroom sink. She remembered placing it there last night. She leaned on against the counter, closed her eyes, and pinched the bridge of her nose. For the love of God, she'd packed an overnight bag that was sitting next to her side of the bed.

Hold on a minute, she didn't have a side of the bed, it merely was the side that Cinco didn't sleep on. It could belong to anyone . . . it wasn't hers.

One thing was for sure, she was firm on the drawer space. She absolutely was not putting any of her things in any drawers in this house. It was final and that was nonnegotiable.

But her shampoo, conditioner, and shower gel were lined up next to Cinco's in the shower. Still, that wasn't a sign of commitment, it was only a smart choice. His selection of shampoo was one of those all-in-one shampoo-conditioner things. He didn't even have shower gel. No, no, it made sense to leave her toiletries here because no matter where she slept, she was only showering here.

It was only efficiency and a deep love affair with his shower that kept her things here. And proximity to research tools that she needed to do her job. Wasting time running back and forth between the cottage and Cinco's house didn't make sense. She nodded. This was a much better arrangement. Plus, she got lots of free food. The smart choice was to stay here some of the time and maybe leave her toothbrush here and possibly some clean clothes—not in a drawer or hanging in the closet or anything, just in a bag or something, maybe even downstairs and not anywhere near her side . . . um, the other side of Cinco's bed.

Whatever was between her and Cinco was different and in no way would lead to heartache. They were both consenting adults who happened to enjoy each other's company, so why shouldn't they spend time together?

Since she was leaving in a few weeks, they really didn't have time for anything serious. Just a few laughs while she got her work done and then she was back to Austin and her novel. That was the way things were. End of story.

The thought that she would only be here for a short time should have made her happy. It would suck to not see Cinco every day, but she loved Austin and missed her friends. She shrugged. Well, she hadn't really thought much about them, but she would miss them probably very soon. Although, she couldn't bring a single name to mind.

Well, she missed the food in Austin and the shopping. She glanced at the fridge. The food was pretty good here and she really didn't have any extra money to use to go shopping. That was beside the point. She loved her life in Austin.

Her little apartment was all her own. No one had a key to it but her. She'd been down that road and had had the bare mattress on the floor and no furniture to prove it. Life was better when she controlled how much of it she shared with someone instead of the other way around.

Maybe as payback for the hard work she'd been putting in on the Texas Rose genealogy, she'd reward herself with a couple of hours on her mystery. She marched into the parlor, picked up her laptop, settled into a comfy spot on the sofa, and got to work.

Several hours later, there were footsteps on the front porch. She leaned over and peeped between the slats of the wooden blinds. Cinco was washing off his dirty boots with the garden hose. She glanced at the clock on her computer and was shocked to find that four hours had passed.

It was lunchtime already? That was the fun of writing for pleasure, time just melted away. She closed her laptop and controlled the urge to meet him at the door with a kiss. It was stupid and sappy and needy and, oh hell, she went to the door anyway.

It opened just as she made it into the reception hall.

Cinco stepped inside as a barrage of sunlight nearly blinded her. Thankfully, he closed the door behind him, shutting out the light that practically burned her retinas.

He leaned down and kissed her. "I'm so glad you're still here."

That made her smile. He hadn't taken for granted that she would still be here.

"Where else would I be?" Damn, that came out wrong. "I mean, I've been here murdering people."

That was even worse.

Four very pronounced lines dented his forehead.

"Lefty wasn't one of them, was he? I couldn't find him this morning." He glanced around. "Do I need to help you bury the bodies?"

"Nah, I used your pig idea." She swiped her hand toward the kitchen. "The kitchen's a mess. It turns out that chopping up bodies is messier than I thought."

"You're kidding, right?" He glanced at the kitchen. "I'm not going to find anything in there that might require me to call my attorney?"

"You have an attorney?" She thought about for a second. "Oh, yeah . . . you're a politician. The state of Texas probably gave you one at your swearing-in ceremony. Was that before or after they brainwashed you into thinking that it's okay to spend ten thousand dollars on a hammer?"

"I could tell you, but then I'd have to kill you. Since my pigs are all full up from your murders, I'd have to resort to plan B, which involves dumping your body in the fallen-in dugout. I've had a busy morning and that just sounds like way too much work, so let's just skip the hammer question." He hugged her tight and then smacked her playfully on the bottom. "Your legs look a mile long in this miniskirt."

His arm went around her shoulders and they headed toward the kitchen.

Compliments from him made her feel so good. Although she reminded herself that at the beginning of a relationship, compliments were plentiful, but at the end they were nonexistent. "I forgot to ask you last night, since you're a state representative, am I supposed to call you Your Highness or something?"

"Only in the bedroom, sweetheart." He grinned. "Stud will do for everyday and maybe Stallion for special occasions."

"Spend some time with the horses this morning?" She hip-bumped him.

"As a matter of fact, I did." He hip-bumped her back. "So do you want chili with crackers or crackers with chili?"

Slowly, his arm worked its way down her back and ended up on her butt. From there it was a short trip to the bottom of her miniskirt. He inched the denim up. "What do you have on under this thing?"

"I've never known anyone so fascinated with my underwear." She batted his hand away. "Lunch first and then sex."

"So you're using me for my food and then my body." He smacked her on the butt again and then his hand slid away. He went to the fridge and pulled out the giant pot of chili.

"You have a problem with that?" She leaned on the counter and watched him. He was comfortable in the kitchen and didn't mind eating what he cooked, which in her book was the hallmark of a great chef.

"No, I don't mind a bit. Just wanted to put it into words." He grabbed two bowls out of the cabinet, scooped chili into them, and popped them into the microwave.

He walked right up to her, wrapped his hands around her hips, and lifted her onto the counter. It was cold against the backs of her thighs. His mouth came down on hers in a hot kiss. His tongue darted inside her mouth and leisurely explored.

Her hand went to the front of his Wranglers and popped his belt buckle open.

He drew back. "I thought it was lunch first and then sex."

"That's right." She unbuttoned his jeans. "It's your turn to go commando."

"But . . ."

"Let me show you how it's done." She leaned back, slipped her hands under her skirt, looped her thumbs in the silk straps at her hips, and yanked her panties down. She rolled on one hip and then the other, pulling them down to her knees. With her right toe, she snagged them and flipped them off.

"Th-th-that's s-s-s-so hot."

"Stammering, that's about the cutest thing ever." She wrapped her legs around his hips and pulled him to her. Her hands went to the waistband of his boxer briefs. "Your turn."

"What about the chili?" He nuzzled the spot right behind her ear. Goosebumps broke out all over her body. "What about it?"

"I'm not hungry for it anymore." He kissed his way down her neck and nipped at her nipple through the cotton of her T-shirt.

"Oh yeah? What did you have in mind?" She planted her hands on the counter and leaned back to give him access to her.

"I'm thinking something sweet that tastes like summer strawberries." His mouth moved to the other nipple.

"Really? What would that be? It's not summer." She rocked her hips forward. She wanted him to say it. She liked when he told her what he wanted to do to her body.

"You. I'm having you for lunch." His mouth sucked on the inside of her thigh.

She popped the snap on her skirt and went for the zipper when he stayed her hand.

"Leave it on." He fisted her skirt and yanked it up over her hips.

The cold counter bit into her backside and made her shiver. "Why?"

"It turns me on. There's just something about mussing you up that gets my blood pumping. Don't get me wrong, I like seeing you naked, but right now, there's just something downright naughty about mussing you up." With his tongue, he traced a path to her opening. "You're always so put together and girly. I like seeing your clothes wrinkled and knowing that my hands rumpled your clothes. Later, when I look over at you and see the mess that I've made of you, it's going to turn me the hell on all over again."

"That works for me." She slid her legs onto his shoulders. "Feel free to wad up my clothes all you want. Anything else you need from me?"

He held her hips tight. "Some moaning would be nice and keep your eyes on mine. I want you to watch me as I make you come."

His warm tongue licked at her and she rolled her hips up to give him better access. She held his gaze as she lifted up her shirt and pulled down the cups of her bra. His eyes turned to liquid aqua as he growled against her sex.

This was safe . . . this was easy. When it was just sex, she knew the rules.

Sex she understood, that she could handle—it was the waking up beside someone every day that made life complicated. She wasn't ready for complicated.

CHAPTER 14

After lunch, Cinco found it hard to leave CanDee. He just wanted to hang out with her and see what wacky thing would come out of her mouth next. But work was work. It had to be done. This afternoon, they were cutting and baling hay. He'd almost asked her to come help, but she had her own work and she'd probably distract the cowboys. She'd sure as hell distract his brothers, who'd also showed up to help.

He glanced over at Rowdy. His younger brother crossed the field and walked toward him. For the love of God, Rowdy's jeans were pressed with a crease down each leg sharp enough to slice a tomato.

"I went by the cottage last night to apologize to CanDee for interrupting, but she wasn't there. I went by again this morning, but she still wasn't there." Rowdy grinned. "Tell her that I said I'm sorry."

Cinco sniffed the air. "Are you wearing cologne . . . to cut hay?"

"I wear cologne every day. Being well groomed is the mark of a gentleman." He straightened his cuff links.

"You wore cuff links to cut hay?" Cinco was tired of beating around the bush. "Are you gay? Mom thinks so, but I've got my money on serial killer. You don't have someone chained to the wall in your basement waiting for you to lower the bucket with the lotion . . . do you?"

"Don't be ridiculous. I don't have a basement. And, I'm not gay. What makes you think I am?" He didn't look mad, only curious.

"We know that you're not really going to a wine festival the first week of September every year. Mom thinks you're meeting up with your gay lover but, I think you're hunting for your next victim." Cinco held his hands out palms up. "Don't get me wrong, we love you no matter what, but if you'd just tell me where you've buried the bodies, I'm sure their loved ones would like some closure."

Rowdy looked horrified for a moment and then he wiped his face clean. "I'm not gay or a serial killer, although I did eat a bowl of Frosted Flakes this morning. Where I go for one week a year is none of your business." He looked anywhere but at Cinco. "Does everyone have an opinion about where I spend that week?"

"It's gone way beyond opinions, we have pool going. The pot's up to five grand. The twins think you're having an affair with a married woman who can only get away one week a year. T-Bone thinks you're a spy, Lefty thinks you're a cat burglar, and most of the ranch hands think you're a contract killer." Cinco doubted that Rowdy would tell him or anyone where he went. Clearly he was very tight lipped about it. He wasn't sensing shame, just secrecy. "Do you have community service or something?"

"No. I'm not a spy, contract killer, gay, or a cat burglar, and I don't have a secret family. Where I go is my business." Rowdy folded his arms. "Are you sleeping with CanDee?"

"None of your business."

"Now you know how I feel." Rowdy sighed like the weight of the world was on his shoulders. "You can tell everyone that I'm not doing anything illegal and that they need to mind their own business."

"Is there a woman involved?" Cinco just wanted to make sure that his pain-in-the-ass brother wasn't going to get hurt.

"Yes and it's complicated so don't ask."

"Mom's going to be so disappointed. You know how she secretly wants one of us to be gay." He clapped a hand on his brother's shoulder. "You were her best shot."

"Don't make me kick your ass again." Rowdy cocked his head to the left.

"Like that would ever happen. Besides, I'd hate for you to mess up those sissy jeans. How long did it take you to iron them into submission?" He glanced at the jeans.

"There's this place called a dry cleaners that washes and irons your clothes. Maybe if you'd buy your clothes from somewhere other than Walmart, you'd have heard of it." Rowdy wiggled his hips. "Stop staring at my butt, I know it's fabulous, but it's embarrassing."

"Boy, stop shaking your booty around all these men, you're going to get them excited." Lefty yelled from behind them.

Cinco turned around to find Lefty walking toward them.

"They can look, but they can't touch." Rowdy waggled an index finger at Lefty. "Have you tarred and feathered CanDee yet?"

"That little hellcat is on my list." Anger flashed in Lefty's eye. "You know I'm partial to gingers, but this one's a pain in my ass."

"You hate redheads." Cinco wasn't about to tell him that the stolen golf cart was parked nicely in his barn. "Your third ex-wife was a redhead."

"Yep, Fancy was a ginger, but that's not why I hate her." Lefty shifted to the right and let loose a big wad of brown tobacco spit. "She took off in my 1978 Cadillac Eldorado with my favorite set of longhorns on the front. Your granddaddy give me them horns. They was huge."

He shook his head and mourned anew the loss of the steer horns. "I ain't never seen another set that big."

As if to pour salt in Lefty's open wound, off in the distance, CanDee drove the golf cart through the edge of the field, her coppery hair blowing like a flag in the wind.

Lefty's eye latched onto CanDee like he was judging the distance and length of time it would take to catch her. His top lip snarled. "I'll get her . . . you mark my words."

"Why didn't you just let her take the golf cart?" Rowdy shaded his eyes as he watched CanDee dart across the landscape.

"She ain't taken the test. Rules is rules." Lefty let out another dirty, brown stream of tobacco juice. "Besides, she reminds me of my fourth ex-wife, Lulu. I hate Lulu."

"Was she the opera singer or the Vegas showgirl?" Cinco had a hard time keeping up with Lefty's ex-wives because the number of them varied by the day. Sometimes the older man had five and sometimes it was closer to ten. Since he'd known Lefty forever and never remembered him being married, either the wives didn't exist or he'd married them all before coming to work for the Texas Rose. Since he'd been here for well over fifty years, Cinco's money was on fiction.

"Showgirl. Son, I ain't never married no opera singer. Their voices is too loud. A man can't have no peace if he's with a woman with a loud voice." Lefty's tone suggested that every man should know that.

"What did Lulu do to piss you off?" Cinco knew it was a bad idea to bring up the ex-wives because Lefty would be in a pissy mood the rest of the day, but it took his mind off of CanDee.

"She wrecked my '71 Ford F-250 custom sport. That truck had the best air conditioning. One dial to turn it on or off, not like today where everything's got to have some fancy microchip dual-zone crap." He glanced heavenward like he was sending up a prayer to his old truck. "I miss Gladys."

"I thought her name was Lulu." Rowdy folded his arms across his chest.

"The truck, son, the truck. Keep up. Her name was Gladys and she was my girl. Her clutch was a little sluggish, but I never held that against her." His eye went all misty like he might actually cry.

"Maybe if you'd have treated your wives with half as much affection as your vehicles, some of them would have stayed around." Rowdy grinned as he stepped back, no doubt getting out of the way of whatever retribution Lefty had in mind. Lefty didn't take constructive criticism or any criticism at all. He was more of a my-way-and-don't-think-of-there-being-a-highway kind of guy.

"Because I love your momma and daddy, I'm going to forget that you said that." Lefty gave Rowdy the snake eye as he let loose another stream of tobacco spit. "But you're on my list. No golf cart for a month."

"Now, that's just plain mean." Rowdy's nostrils flared. "And here I was thinking that I'd let you drive my new truck."

Lefty's eye turned huge. "Your Chevy 3500 with the comfort package finally come in?"

"Yesterday. The dealership is delivering it this afternoon." Rowdy sweetened the pot. "Electronic fold-in mirrors, towing package, power running boards, and air-conditioned seats. It can tow a house without a struggle while pumping out music on the crazy good sound system."

"You know you're my favorite out of all you boys. I'm always saying that. Just ask anyone." Lefty nodded.

"I thought I was your favorite." Worth stepped up behind Lefty. "Now my feelings are hurt."

"Who hurt your tender little feelings now?" Dallas walked up to join the party.

"Lefty says that Rowdy's his favorite." He turned to his twin.

"Now that's a lie. Everyone knows that I'm his favorite." Dallas pulled a pair of worn leather gloves out of the back pocket of his overalls and worked his giant hands into the them.

"Are those my gloves?" Worth's gaze zeroed in on Dallas. "Wait a minute. Are those my overalls?"

"What? Mom says that I'm a grown-ass man now so I need to do my own laundry. She won't do it and she won't let Mary do it anymore. Since I don't have any clean clothes, I had to do something." Dallas stepped a little funny and pretended to pull his underwear out of his butt crack. "I don't like your tighty-whities. They crunch everything together. I don't know how you stand it."

"You're wearing my underwear? I'm locking my room from now on." Worth's fist reared back for the nice solid blow to the chin, but Rowdy caught his hand.

"Y'all can kill each other later—right now we need to get this hay in." Rowdy held Worth's hand until he was sure the urge to kill his twin had passed.

"Where's T-Bone?" Lefty scanned the horizon.

"Back at school. He left this morning. Classes start soon." Cinco was proud of his baby brother. "I still can't believe we're about to have a PhD in the family."

"That kid's smarter than all of us put together." Lefty nodded. "He got all the book smarts."

Worth leaned into Rowdy and sniffed. "Are you wearing cologne?"

"What is the big deal?" Rowdy looked around. "I always wear cologne."

Dallas looked him up and down. "A man only wears cologne if he wants to get laid."

Everyone took a step back from Rowdy.

"'Cause I'm the only one out here who ain't related to you, I feel like I should just tell you that I ain't into dudes." Lefty blew Rowdy a kiss. "Although it has been a while, so maybe I need to keep my options open."

Lefty walked over to a patch of mud made by a small hole in the irrigation pipe, scooped up an handful of the mud, walked back over to Rowdy, and smeared it down the left leg of his pressed jeans.

"What the hell?" Rowdy looked down in shock.

"I can't stand to look at them spotless sissy pants one minute longer." Lefty nodded to himself. "If I were you, I'd hop up in the cab of that work truck before I take some good, honest mud to that clean white shirt."

Rowdy hightailed it to the front of the truck. "I'm surrounded by philistines."

"Don't go around calling people weird Bible names. That don't make no sense." Lefty called after him. "Call me an asshole or son of a bitch, but leave the Bible out of it. You can't go around throwing out Bible curse names. It's disrespectful." He punctuated that last sentence with a big glob of tobacco spit.

"It looks like we're stuck stacking." Dallas's lip curled. "I hate stacking."

"Why can't we get a real hay baler instead of this old piece of shit?" Worth shook his head. "Large round bales of hay would be so much easier to distribute than these tiny-assed rectangular ones. We'd only need to put out one of those instead of five of these."

Lefty's one eye glared at Worth. "Did you just called my sweet Betsy here"—he patted the hay baler—"an old piece of shit?" He whispered the last part like he didn't want the machine to hear it.

"Yes." Worth wasn't backing down and Cinco didn't blame him. His brother had borrowed his underwear and those crappy little rectangular bales were a pain in the ass—there was just so much one man could take.

"Son, I'll have you know that Betsy here has been a trusted member of this family since your granddaddy was in charge. You need to treat her with some respect." Lefty climbed up into the metal seat. "We don't need no stupid, turd-looking hay bales. Rectangular ones have worked for a hundred years and they'll work for a hundred more."

He fired up the engine and Betsy purred like a kitten.

Cinco didn't have the heart to tell the older man that he'd already ordered a brand-new hay baler and was awaiting delivery. He wasn't looking forward to the day he would have that conversation with Lefty, but it was coming.

Lefty put Betsy in gear and eased her down the field in a straight line. The machine scooped up the cut hay, bundled it into a rectangle, wrapped wire around it, and spit it out the back like a chicken laying an egg. Rowdy followed Betsy slowly in the pickup while Cinco, Dallas, and Worth tossed the bales in the back of the truck. It was hot, messy work, but it was part of ranching.

Four hours later, Cinco was bone tired as he pulled up to his house and parked next to the barn. All he wanted was to see CanDee and drink an ice-cold beer. He liked having her in his house. She made coming home a lot more appealing.

CHAPTER 15

CanDee was not waiting by the door for Cinco to come home; she was merely standing there by accident. The fact that she'd been accidentally watching out the windows by the front door for the last thirty minutes was in no way an admission that she'd missed him this afternoon.

A guitar riff trilled from the parlor. Grammie's ringtone. She walked into the parlor and picked up her phone. After sliding her finger over the screen to answer the call, she said, "Hello."

She walked back to her post by the front door.

"Did I catch you at a bad time?" Grammie yelled over what sounded like a leaf blower. Her grandmother thought it was frivolous to only do one thing at a time, so her life was about multitasking even when it didn't make any sense. Like calling someone while blowing leaves or eating a sandwich while taking a shower.

CanDee held the phone in front of her mouth and screamed, "I can barely hear you!"

"I'm working on my Harley. Hold on." Grammie turned off the engine.

"Harley?" CanDee shook her head. "Since when do you own a motorcycle? And why are you working on it? You can barely put gas in the car. The last time you worked on the car, you tried to air up the tires and ended up letting all of the air out of them."

It was too far for CanDee to drive over and rescue Grammie if the motorcycle fell on her and broke every bone in her eighty-pound body. While CanDee was an Amazonian, Grammie was a pigmy. Even though they had the same eyes, people still didn't understand how they were related.

"Me and the girls from the coven have started up a motorcycle club. We're the Westside Witches. Unfortunately we spent all of our money on these cool black leather jackets, so we had to pool what was left and buy one Harley. We trade off weeks." There was a clicking noise on the other end of the phone that sounded like one of those wrenches with ball bearings used by mechanics.

When it came to Grammie, nothing shocked her anymore.

CanDee knew she was going to regret asking, but she couldn't help herself. "What exactly are you doing to the motorcycle?"

"Customizing. This new muffler will increase the horsepower and torque and make her roar like a lion." Grammie banged on something.

"Do you remember the time you bought that build-your-own-helicopter kit off the Internet?" CanDee took a deep breath and let it out slowly. "You were going to start a tour-Austin-by-air business?"

"That wasn't my fault. Some parts were missing." More banging from Grammie's end. "Besides, I sold that kit for a nice price at my last garage sale."

CanDee rolled her eyes. There was a sucker born every minute and Grammie had garage sales to prove it.

"I got the muffler from Walmart—how hard can it be?" The banging stopped. "You don't happen to know what a rectifier bracket is . . . do you?"

"Sorry." Grammie might be a strong and independent woman but sometimes, CanDee thought she may need a keeper. Sometimes structure would be nice, but Grammie didn't do structure, which was why she'd changed careers like other people changed socks.

"Well, that's not why I called. Just wanted to remind you about tomorrow." The banging started up again. "It's the twenty-fifth anniversary of your parents' death."

CanDee sucked on her top lip. She'd lost track of time. She really should go back to Austin and spend the day with her grandmother. She'd lost her parents when she was four and had only vague memories of them. They'd been out on a date night to the movies and been killed by a drunk driver. Remembering their death day was more about grieving for Grammie than it was for her. There were times when she felt sad that she didn't know them well enough to grieve for them. Growing up, she'd often felt bad that she didn't feel worse.

It was only about a two-and-a-half-hour drive to Grammie's from here. "I can leave in an hour or so and be there—"

"No, stay put. The Westside Witches are coming over for a campout in the backyard and then tomorrow we're taking a Hill Country ride in your parents' honor." Grammie heaved a sigh like she'd just picked up something heavy.

"How does that work with only one Harley?" CanDee watched out the front window for Cinco.

"Well . . . between the five of us, we have one motorcycle, a skateboard, three bicycles, and two cars. Marybeth is going to see if she can borrow her granddaughter's Vespa but her granddaughter might need it for her pizza delivery job. I'm thinking we take turns on the Harley and maybe change every ten miles or so. Haven't worked all of the kinks out yet." Grammie heaved another sigh. "If we make it to Fredericksburg, I'll give you a call. Maybe we can meet for lunch or something."

"Sounds like a plan." CanDee continued to watch out the front window.

"Listen, honey, I need to go." The engine cranked on. "It looks like I need to run to the auto parts store."

"Okay, I love you." CanDee should mention Cinco. "I've met—"

"I love you too, baby doll. Talk to you soon." Grammie hung up before CanDee had a chance to tell her about Cinco.

What did it mean that she'd wanted to tell her grandmother about the new man in her life? She straightened and leaned against the wall. It meant about as much as her not waiting by the front door for Cinco.

She glanced up and walked over to the painting of a field covered in bluebonnets that was hung next to the front door. She tilted it to the right so that it was off balance and stepped back in satisfaction. Cinco's truck pulled into the yard and then parked next to the barn. She busied herself fixing the painting.

Five minutes later the front door opened.

"I'm just fixing this crooked painting." She turned around.

Cinco was shirtless and sweaty. She drank him in. Nice pecs melted into luscious abs.

"This is a good look for you." She leaned against the now very straight painting. "You should come home like this more often."

By home, she meant his home, which was not in any way hers.

He ran a hand over his abs. "You think?"

"Oh yeah." She reached out, dipped her index finger underneath his belt buckle, and pulled him to her.

"Don't, I'm all sweaty and gross. I'll get you dirty." He braced his arms on the wall on either side of her head.

"No, you won't." She ducked under his arm. "Race you to the shower."

If she kept things light and sexy then maybe her mind wouldn't realize that she was falling in love with him. At that thought, her right big toe got caught on the first stair and she went down like a sack of potatoes.

"Are you okay?" Cinco knelt at her feet and checked her toe. "I don't think it's broken."

No, that's not what would end up breaking. Maybe a broken toe was better than a broken heart.

She plastered a fake smile on her face. "I'm fine. Go on up. I'll be there in a minute. I'm just going to get some ice for my toe."

She needed a moment to just sit here and figure out when she'd actually started falling for Cinco. Hell, she'd only known him for, like, ten minutes. But wasn't that just her modus operandi—jumping headfirst into things? No one loved a whirlwind romance more than CanDee, only hers tended to be more hurricanes than whirlwinds. The heartache and devastation in the wake of her other romances should have been enough of a deterrent, but here she was, making the same old mistakes.

"Stay here. I'll get you some ice." Cinco sounded concerned.

Well, he wasn't the only one. She was starting to think of them as a couple. For the love of God, she had an overnight bag here. Why couldn't she just sit back and enjoy the ride like a normal person? Instead she was obsessing over a stupid bag and maybe some feelings. She needed to stop living in the future and start living in the moment. Trouble was, those moments she'd lived in before had taught her to finally look ahead.

"Here." Gently he set a small plastic bag of ice directly on her toe. "I think you just stubbed it. That usually hurts like hell."

The cold bit into her toe, which did hurt like hell.

"Really, I'm fine." She stood. "I'd call another race to the bathroom, but clearly, my coordination is off."

Cinco wasn't like Phillip. Then again, Phillip hadn't started out as an asshole—that came later and seemed to be her effect on him. What would her effect on Cinco end up being?

"After the shower, how about we go out to dinner? You know, on a real date, like, at a restaurant." There was a slight hitch in his voice like he was a little bit nervous.

"Sounds wonderful and I like that you asked instead of assumed." It was her turn to be nervous. "Mind if I sleep here again tonight?"

Here she was, talking herself out of having a relationship with him, and she went and did this? "It's okay if you don't want me to, it's just that you have a wonderful bed."

"Always using me for my bed. Pretty soon, I'm going to get a complex." He leaned down and kissed her lightly on the lips. "Stay as long as you like. I like coming home to you in my house."

Damn if that didn't make her heart go pitter-pat. She tried to convince herself that his comment was more about loneliness instead of sentiment, but rational thinking was new to her. Until recently, she'd led with the heart. Now she was leading with her head.

She had to admit that having someone to talk to instead of herself was nice. For the most part, writing was a solitary profession. She worked from home and if she didn't make the effort to get out, she'd never see another living soul.

"What is the dress for this date?" They had a date. She had to squelch her inner teenager from jumping up and down.

"Casual. I'm taking you to my favorite barbeque restaurant." His brow furrowed. "Unless you'd like to go somewhere fancier."

"Nope. I love meat." She glanced up at him as they walked. He was watching her with the oddest expression on his face. "What?"

"Nothing." He continued to watch her.

"Why are you staring at me? Do I have something on my face?" She swiped a hand across her mouth in case there was some chocolate residue from the Reese's Peanut Butter Cup she'd eaten a couple of hours earlier.

"I didn't realize that I was staring." He looked away. "It's just . . . well, you love meat and you're really good in bed. I feel like I won the lottery."

She felt her smile all the way down to her toes and then her rational brain kicked in, looking for signs that he was lying. She hated that her second reaction was all about finding the motive behind his comment, but unfortunately, he was paying for the many sins of others.

She didn't detect anything but sincerity.

"Ditto, Cowboy. You can cook, have a fantastic body, your shower is straight from heaven, and your bed is long enough that I don't hang off the end. There's really not much more a girl can ask for." She smiled up at him.

He liked her, at least in bed. That was more complimentary than any other ex had been.

He waited by the bathroom door for her to walk in first. "So, when do I get to read your novel?"

Her stomach dropped to her knees as her toe caught on the doorjamb and she did a face plant into the white- and black-tiled room. "Damn, I'm clumsy tonight."

Cinco was at her side and pulling her up before she could get her knees under her. He sat her in his lap.

"Is something wrong?" He tucked a lock of her hair behind her ear.

"No." She was not discussing him with . . . well . . . him. He hadn't noticed the subject change, that was good. It wasn't that she didn't want him reading her novel—she didn't want anyone to read it until it was published.

"You seem a little distracted." His blue eyes held concern.

"I'm good. Sometimes I get lost in work. And my grandmother called." She shook her head like she was clearing it. "Tomorrow is the twenty-fifth anniversary of my parents' death."

He pulled her in for a hug. "I'm so sorry. Why don't we take tomorrow off? We could go into San Antonio and play tourist." He patted her back.

Now she felt like an ass. She'd thrown her dead parents under the bus all because she didn't want to talk about or analyze her feelings for him. Her eyes rolled heavenward in case they wanted to throw some lightning bolts her way for doing something so coldhearted.

"No, I'm good. It's better for me to stay here and keep my mind busy with work." The least she could do was not mess up his schedule for tomorrow. "Besides, my grandmother and her coven might take a ride out here. Maybe we could meet them for lunch or something?"

Holy crap, she actually wanted to introduce him to her grandmother. That was long-term-relationship territory.

"I would love that." He leaned back. "Wait a minute . . . coven?"

"Yeah, Grammie sort of joined a Wicca coven." It was always so much easier if people knew little to nothing about Grammie before meeting her.

"Cool. Can't wait to meet her." His smile was genuine. Her palms began to sweat. She really wanted him to meet Grammie too.

Now she really needed a subject change. "Maybe I should watch you shower?"

One eyebrow rose. "That sounds like a wonderful idea. It is only fair. You let me watch you."

As long as she kept everything light, everything would be okay.

"I'm going to need some mood music." From his back pocket, he pulled out his iPhone, tapped an icon, and Meghan Trainor belted out "Lips Are Movin."

"We need to talk about your choice in music." He seemed like a perfectly sane person until he picked a playlist.

"Music is a reflection of who I am."

"Exactly, and you're not a twelve-year-old girl. Since music is so personal, I'm not going to suggest that you pick something more age appropriate, I'm merely pointing out that if you went to a concert for one of your favorite singers, you'd be the creepy guy in the hoody driving the sketchy panel van." She shrugged. "Sorry, I gotta call them as I see them."

"What can I say? I have layers." He turned the master shower lever on and water poured out of all seventeen showerheads.

She sat cross-legged on the floor. From this angle, the shower looked like a car wash for human bodies. "Aren't you supposed to be removing those layers?"

He moved his hips to some imaginary beat that clearly had nothing to do with the music playing. "How about these moves?"

She leaned closer to get a better look. "Are you milking a cow or flipping me off? I can't tell."

He spun around on the ball of one foot and then swayed a little. "Sorry, that spin was a little too fast. I'm a little dizzy."

"Thank God, I thought you might be having a seizure." She reached up to the counter and turned off Meghan. "I think you need to unbutton and unzip and show me your goods. Maybe if you do a good job, I'll join you."

She could separate sex from love. Men did it every single day. Today, she was going to think like a man. Then again, all they thought about was food, boobs, and sex, so what should she think about the other twenty-three and a half hours of the day?

CHAPTER 16

An hour later, Cinco opened the door to his tiny closet and looked for something nice to wear. He was just taking CanDee to Cranky Frank's in Fredericksburg, but he still wanted to look nice. Nothing but a sea of blue jeans and T-shirts. It looked like he was wearing blue jeans and a T-shirt.

She had gone back to the cottage to get ready and he was picking her up.

He pulled out a pair of jeans that looked less worn out than the others. Should he iron and starch the jeans like Rowdy? He shook his head. His brother's jeans had looked ridiculous and besides, he wasn't sure if he had an iron. Vaguely, he remembered seeing one somewhere downstairs a couple of years ago, or that might have been at his parents' house. Naomi had a collection of antique irons, but he'd eBayed those puppies years ago.

No, these jeans would do just the way they were. He returned to the closet and pulled out a nice and fairly new red Ralph Lauren T-shirt and laid it on the bed next to the jeans.

He glanced back at the closet. It was overstuffed with clothes. Maybe it was time to clear out some of the old stuff that he didn't wear. Who knew, after everything was sorted out, maybe there would be some extra room for CanDee. It sure would be easier if she moved a few things over here. That way, she wouldn't have to waste so much time driving back and forth.

He looked at the dresser. He could probably carve out a little space in there too. Women had lots of stuff and needed lots of storage space. Later, he'd get to work on cleaning things out.

Fifteen minutes later, he was dressed and parking his truck in front of the cottage. The sun was setting, creating quite a show of colors.

Out of the corner of his eye, he caught motion. A small man appeared to be sneaking around to the back of the cottage. Someone was after CanDee. He jumped out of the truck and ran after the man, tackling him.

"Son, get off me." Lefty rolled out from beneath him. "What the hell?"

"What are you doing?" Cinco sat back on his haunches and brushed grass and dirt from his shirt. So much for looking good for CanDee.

"I'm looking for the key to the golf cart. She hid it. It ain't in the cottage, I checked. She's got to have hidden it outside." Lefty got on all fours and crawled around the grass looking for the key.

"You'll never find it." CanDee stood tall on the front porch with her arms crossed. "You shouldn't have given me the runaround."

Lefty's mouth twisted in a snarl. "Rules is rules." He rolled back on his knees and slowly stood. "It don't matter, I just remembered I got a second set of keys."

"You mean this?" CanDee held up a key ring with one solitary key on it.

Lefty's eye got huge and he drew in a deep, slow breath. "You broke into my office?"

"I did not, the door was open. You happened to not be there. I intended to leave you a note, but I saw the spare keys and thought that sent the message just fine." CanDee grinned as she waggled the key back and forth.

"You . . . I'm of a mind to . . . oh." Lefty stomped around trying to find the right words. He turned back to CanDee and pointed to his left eye. "I've got my eye on you."

CanDee blew him an air kiss.

Lefty growled in return.

Cinco stepped in front of Lefty and put a hand on the older man's shoulder. "Why not just give her permission to use the golf cart?"

"I'd sooner eat my own kidneys for breakfast." Lefty squared his shoulders. "Stay out of this, son, it's between me and the hellcat."

"I think Gina"—she pointed to the golf cart—"is looking a little too white. She needs some color, maybe something in a pink racing stripe?"

Cinco turned Lefty around. "CanDee, stay on the porch while I walk Lefty back to the barn." Cinco dropped his voice to a whisper. "Just remember that she's a guest at our ranch. Mom invited her."

"She's a demon from hell," Lefty yelled.

"He started it," CanDee yelled back.

"Now, children, let's play nice." Cinco practically pulled Lefty toward the barn. He knew exactly how his mother felt every time he got into a fight with one of his brothers.

"She's crazy." Lefty growled out. "Rules is rules. All she had to do was take the driving test."

"Two years from now?" Cinco understood her frustration. He kind of liked that CanDee wasn't a rule follower.

"What? I'm a very busy man." Lefty's tone sounded a little less angry.

"She's a guest and needed transportation. Try to think of it from her side." Cinco knew the old man wouldn't, but it was worth a try.

"She doesn't have a side. Rules is rules." Lefty's hands fisted at his side. "It's on now."

"Bring it." CanDee yelled. Clearly she'd overheard Lefty.

Cinco shot her a dirty look and she smiled and waved like she hadn't seen it.

They walked in silence the rest of the way to the barn. Cinco slid the door open and let Lefty go in first.

"Son, just because I'm going after your girlfriend don't mean I don't like her. She's a hellcat and every man needs a woman with a little hellcat in her." Lefty sighed long and hard. "It might be best if you stay out of this."

"Okay, but no bodily harm or property damage." Cinco wagged his index finger at Lefty. "Promise me."

"I promise." He grinned. "Just some good, clean fun between two worthy adversaries."

He hadn't seen Lefty this excited about anything in a long time, and Cinco had a feeling that CanDee could give as good as she got. Still, he just might give her a heads-up.

"Go get her, but don't cross any lines because I plan on keeping her around for a very long time." That's not exactly what he'd meant to say, but it was true. He liked who he was around CanDee, and what they had together was what he'd thought love was supposed to be.

Lefty rocked back on his heels and studied Cinco. "You're sweet on her. I mean, I know you've got the hots for her, who wouldn't, but it's more than that." He cocked his head to one side and nodded. "I like you with her. Y'all complement each other. You're starting to act more like yourself—well, how you acted before Naomi." The way he said *Naomi* sounded a lot like *crack whore*.

The older man held out his hands like a traffic cop. "Don't get me wrong, CanDee's still going down, but I'm glad you'll be there to pick her up."

Cinco's eyes narrowed. "Just so long as it doesn't go beyond good, clean fun. I don't want to have to step in."

If he chose sides, he'd have to take the one against the man who'd been like a grandfather to him.

Lefty grinned. "I'm harmless."

"Yeah, which one of your ex-wives would agree?" Cinco turned on his heel, walked out the open door, and pulled it closed. Maybe he'd warn CanDee about Lefty, but part of him wanted to see what she'd do. It was going to be one hell of a ride, seeing what kind of trouble those two could get into.

He walked over to the cottage where CanDee was still waiting on the porch.

"What's Lefty's net worth?" CanDee stepped into his favorite high heels.

"Why, you thinking about extortion?" Even though he'd told her tonight was casual, she'd worn a light-blue short cotton dress. He liked that she was girly. Her hair was curled and her lips looked like shiny peaches.

"Nope. I was just wondering if he could afford a contract killer." She leaned down and grabbed a brown purse that was the same color as her shoes.

"He promised me that no blood will be shed." He hopped up the two steps to meet her and offered her his arm. "What about you?"

She took his arm. "What about me what?"

"Do you agree to no bloodshed?" He opened the passenger-side door for her and helped her up. He closed the door and walked around the hood to the driver side and climbed up.

"There are many levels of civil. I'm sure that I can find one of them that works for me." She pulled her seat belt around her and clicked it. "No promises on the bloodshed, but I'll try to keep it Band-Aid-sized."

"I guess that's as good as I'm going to get." He could practically see the mischievous wheels turning in her head. "Just remember, he's an old man."

"And I'm a helpless female." She grinned. "So, after dinner, are we going to make out in the backseat?"

"I swear you have a one-track mind." He liked that she was so into him. Every time she came on to him or even looked across the room and undressed him with her eyes, she made him feel spectacular and sexy and wanted. Naomi had never made him feel this wanted, even in the beginning. There was something satisfying knowing that CanDee wanted him as much as he wanted her.

"I'm only here five more weeks. I have to work in all the sex that I can since I can't seem to find a man in Austin worth dating." She adjusted the air conditioning vents to her liking.

She was so matter-of-fact. For some reason, that hurt. Knowing that she already had one foot out the door didn't sit right with him. Naomi had hated living at the ranch. She'd claimed she wanted them to move to the big city so she could have culture, but all she'd wanted was to be closer to her boyfriend.

"Ranch life a little too slow for you?" The words had come out harsher than he'd wanted.

"No, I love the ranch. The air is clean, no traffic, and"—she rolled down the window—"the stars go on and on."

She leaned back in and hit the button that rolled the window up.

"Then why are you in such a hurry to leave it?" Why was he mad? He knew she wasn't going to stay forever, but it pissed him the hell off that possibly staying hadn't even occurred to her.

"I'm not, but this isn't my home. I have a life in Austin and commitments that I have to keep. Virgil and Virginia Stanley of Bullard, Texas, want me to write their genealogy." She watched the stars from the windshield.

He knew she had a life that didn't include him, but he wanted her to include him. "I know old Virgil. Nice man, great cattleman."

"Good to know. He's anxious for me to get there." Slowly, she turned her head. "Where is Bullard?"

"Between Tyler and Jacksonville. East Texas." It was a beautiful part of Texas.

"I need to meet with him sometime soon. He doesn't do video chatting and according to his wife, he believes that cell phones are evil."

"I could go with you. We could make a long weekend of it. I'd love to see old Virgil again." His voice sounded slightly desperate. "I've got some business I'd like to discuss with him and East Texas is beautiful in spring."

He'd have to make up some business to discuss with Virgil.

"Sounds like a plan. Now . . ." She reached down on the floorboard for her purse and pulled out a book. It was one of Edith's journals. She'd marked a page with a piece of paper. "I have some questions about your grandfather."

She opened the journal. "Okay, so there was a fire in 1915 that killed everyone except Edith, Mel, and your grandfather, who they called Tres. I'm assuming because he was Lacy Kendall Rose III?"

"That's right. Don't call my father Cuatro because he hates it." He liked watching her work, especially when she was on to something.

"Bear fits him so much better." She scanned the journal page. "Here's what is strange. The night of the fire was a little over a week after Tres turned fifteen. He was badly scarred on his face and hands. Edith was very meticulous in her journal entries, but on the summer kitchen doorjamb where she measured and recorded everyone's height, she must have made a mistake. On his fifteenth birthday when she measured him, he was three inches taller than he was two weeks later when she talks about making him some new clothes. I guess his burned up in the fire."

"Edith was meticulous all right, but it sounds like she got things mixed up." He flicked on his blinker to turn onto the county road. "Tres moved in with her and Mel after the fire. They nursed him back to health."

"I know." CanDee held up the journal. "Edith spends a lot of time on it. Apparently his burns were pretty severe and they thought he wasn't going to make it. I get the impression that Edith would have liked to have a child and she thought of Tres as her own."

"PawPaw Tres died when I was little, but I remember the faded scars. They covered his face and his arms, but I wasn't frightened of them. He always wore denim overalls and a pearl-buttoned work shirt. He was fun. Always had candy in his pockets and loved to talk about

World War II." His grandfather made him smile. He'd loved doing anything with PawPaw.

"I wish I could have met him. I bet he had great stories to tell." Her eyes lit up. "I would have loved to ask him about Mel and Edith."

"He said once that Mel was rough and tough and cussed like a man unless she was around Edith, who didn't tolerate bad language. Also, there was something about him getting drunk or coming home drunk." Cinco searched his memory. "Oh yes, for his seventeenth birthday, some of the ranch hands gave him his first taste of whiskey and he came home drunk. Well, Edith didn't like that one bit, so she marched over to the bunkhouse, took the bottle of whiskey the men were drinking, turned on her heel, and marched right back to the house. Since Tres had told her that he liked the way being drunk felt, she encouraged him to drink some more. Long story short, he drank most of the rest of the bottle and passed out. The next morning he had the hangover from hell, so of course Edith set him behind the push lawn mower and made him cut acres of grass in the hot, blazing summer sun. When the vomiting started, she had no pity. From that moment on, my grandfather never touched another drop of alcohol. He couldn't even stomach beer."

"Edith was devious. I love that about her." She closed the journal. "The more I read about her, the more I wish that I could have met her. She was definitely a woman before her time. I wonder what she would have been if she'd been born a little later. Not that being a housewife isn't a noble profession, it's just I don't think it would have been her choice. Even though it wasn't that long ago, it's hard to imagine a world where women can't do whatever we want."

"I've always thought that she would have been an excellent architect. She designed the house and oversaw the building of it. I'm pretty sure that she got exactly what she wanted and wouldn't take anything less. I've always wanted to meet her too." As a boy, he'd always hoped that he'd inherited a little bit of Edith's spirit. It wasn't until he was older that he realized that was genetically impossible.

"It had to be hard, don't you think? I'm sure their unconventional relationship wasn't well received everywhere. I know that your family has clout, but it couldn't have been easy. And according to these"—she held up the journal—"Edith entertained clients, held dinner parties, and was president of the garden club. Essentially, she was the wife of a cattle baron. I think that it would have been both impressive to see and heartbreaking to watch. She talks extensively about the local Lutheran minister's wife. Edith does not have good things to say about her."

"Yes, dear sweet Myrna Crabtree." He glanced over at CanDee. "How far have you gotten? I don't want to spoil the suspense in case you don't know what happened to Pastor Crabtree and his lovely wife."

"I haven't made it there, but I can't wait. Tell me what happened. Did they find Myrna's body at the bottom of a well or did she simply disappear without a trace?" Excitement glowed all over her face. She was really into this and clearly loved history as much as he did.

"Perhaps you noticed the old white abandoned church building on the road as you turned in to the ranch?" He loved stories where people got what was coming to them.

"Yes, I did."

"That was Redeemer Lutheran. It's funny how funding suddenly dried up after Myrna called Edith the spawn of Satan and told her that she was going straight to hell. The next morning Pastor Crabtree was out of a job and the ladies' garden club had a building exclusively for their use." He shook his head. "You don't bite the hand that feeds you."

"What happened to the Crabtrees?" CanDee chewed on her bottom lip in anticipation.

"The pastor died of syphilis and Myrna faded off into the sunset. Some said that she was forced into prostitution and others say she became a housemaid for a family in Ohio." He grinned.

"You made that up."

He put one hand over his heart. "Swear."

"I'm totally going to research it." CanDee turned serious. "I hate that she made Edith sad, but I hope that Myrna didn't have to turn to prostitution just to get by."

"I love that you see the people behind the history."

"Most of the time, history only records the major events. I like the everyday. Seeing people act the same way a hundred years ago as they do now is interesting. It seems that no matter when, we are all just trying to provide for our families and live our lives." She held up Edith's journal again. "Even when she writes about the tedious details of her life, I'm fascinated."

He was fascinated too.

CanDee had become important to him and he was going to miss the hell out of her when she was gone. He bit his top lip. There was only one thing to do . . . make sure she never wanted to leave.

CHAPTER 17

Cranky Frank's was exactly what CanDee was expecting. The red cinderblock building on the outskirts of Fredericksburg looked like a Texas barbeque joint.

"Are you sure they're open?" CanDee glanced at Cinco as he pulled into the empty parking lot. It was completely empty and the lights were off. He didn't seem like a man who would make a date and not make sure that the restaurant was open.

"No. They close at three or whenever they run out of food, whichever comes first." He parked and turned off the engine.

"Are you planning on breaking in?" She loved barbeque as much as the next girl, but going to jail for it seemed a little extreme.

He walked around, opened her door, and helped her out.

"I don't need to break in." He walked to a potted geranium by the front door, gently nudged it to the side with his boot, and picked up something. "I have a key. The owner buys their meat directly from us for a very good price. He was more than happy to do me a favor."

He unlocked the door, reached around the doorjamb, and flicked on the lights. Cinco moved aside and let her go in first.

Inside, neon beer signs were sprinkled between pictures of famous people who'd eaten there, and enough NFL memorabilia hung on the walls to make sure the public at large understood that this was a meat-made man cave where women were welcome, but only if they could eat their weight in brisket. There was an order window in the back left corner, and the right held a counter with a drink machine and a small buffet table that was completely empty.

Tables with mismatched chairs and a couple of full-length wooden picnic tables were close enough together to provide adequate seating without feeling cluttered. The picnic table in the back was set with a plastic tablecloth, some silverware, and napkins that were tucked into two plastic cups. A Shiner beer bottle had an unlit candle sticking out of the top. Romance barbeque style. It was perfect. This place was perfect. Exactly the place she would have chosen for a first date. Nothing pretentious or complicated.

"I believe that our table is ready." She pointed to the picnic table.

"I think you're right." Cinco put his hand at the small of her back and led her to the picnic table. He pulled out the bench for her.

She smoothed her skirt down and sat.

"I'll get the food. Frank told me where everything is." He pocketed the key and went to the little window ordering area. Several pots banged around and the sound of lids being opened and closed followed.

"Need some help?" She picked up the plastic cigarette lighter next to the candle and lit it.

"No, I have things under control." More pots banged. "Aha, here we go."

He backed out of the small kitchen area carrying a huge aluminum-foil-covered pan.

"Holy cow. You did tell Cranky Frank that there were only two of us, right?" The pan was one of those giant metal serving dish things commonly used for cooking large turkeys.

"I told him that I didn't know what you liked, so I guess he gave us some of everything." He set the pan down on the table and unwrapped the foil.

"Wow, that's some serious meat." Brisket, beef ribs, short ribs, sausage, and chicken were piled high. She reached for the white Styrofoam containers and pulled them out one at a time. "Looks like we have coleslaw, potato salad, green beans, and"—she opened the last container and sniffed—"chocolate pudding. Nice."

She glanced over at a small plaque across from their table. "This is one of the best barbeque places in the world?"

"Yes, as judged by *Texas Monthly*." Cinco slid onto the bench opposite hers.

"I can't wait to dig in. Where should we start?" Her fork was poised over the meat. "What's your favorite?"

He eyed the meat. "Everything is good, but I have to say that the brisket is the best."

She stabbed a couple of pieces of brisket and flopped them on his plate and then popped some onto her plate. "It smells really good." She picked up the coleslaw. "Want some?"

His brow dented. "Thanks, but I should be serving you."

"Why?" She opened the slaw, spooned some out onto his plate.

"Because I'm trying to impress you." He grinned. "Is it working?"

"I don't know. Let me try the food and I'll tell you." She liked that he was a little bit nervous and seemed to be trying really hard. It made her feel wanted and important. She couldn't remember a time—especially after she'd started sleeping with her previous boyfriends—that she'd been made to feel special by a man.

She cut a sliver of brisket and popped it in her mouth. It was moist without being greasy and the bark had just enough spice to complement the meat. She stood, leaned across the table, and kissed him lightly on the mouth. "Fantastic. Consider me very impressed."

His smile was bright and genuine. "Wait until you see what I have planned for dessert."

"I hope it's me." She winked.

A deep blush started at his neck and worked its way up to his face. "Believe me, I've spent a good deal of time today thinking about that."

"At least you're not whispering. That's progress." She leaned over and kissed him again. "Your blush is so sweet. I love it."

She sat back down, picked up her napkin, and set it in her lap. "So, tell me about dessert."

He rubbed a hand over his face. "I've never blushed this much . . . ever." He sounded embarrassed.

"It's adorable." She cut another piece of meat and popped it in her mouth. "Can I ask you something?"

He swallowed and then wiped his mouth. "Anything."

"I'm not sure how to put this nicely but . . . what's wrong with you?" She shook her head. "I mean, why are you single? You're wonderful. I can't find anything wrong with you."

His face lit up which was even sweeter than the blush. "I was kind of wondering the same thing about you."

It was stupid that he could make her smile this much, but here she was, smiling from ear to ear. "I'm single because my grandmother says that my picker is broken."

Plus, CanDee couldn't afford to support anyone else because she was barely supporting herself. When she looked back on her relationships, they all involved her money being spent on other people.

"What about you?" There had to be a reason he was single. The good ones were always married.

"No one's caught my eye until now. My mom says that I don't get out much." He scooped a spoonful of coleslaw into his mouth but kept his gaze on her. After he swallowed, he slid his hand over to cover hers. "Tell me about Phillip."

Her smile froze on her lips. She didn't want to talk about Phillip or any other of her failures. She picked up one of the white Styrofoam containers in front of her. "Potato salad?"

"You don't like to talk about your past. I get that, but I'd like to know more about Phillip." His hand was on hers, reassuring her that it was okay.

"I don't understand." Why couldn't they just keep things casual?

"I want to know everything about you. He's a part of your past and I want to be a part of your future." Clearly, he wasn't going to drop this.

"Why do we need to talk about this now?" Here they were, having a lovely dinner, and he dropped the past-relationship bomb. It was like he was rubbing her face in her mistakes. "Can't we just enjoy each other's company and not worry about things that don't matter?"

He sighed heavily. "One day, you're going to trust me enough to tell me what he did that hurt you so much."

"It's not that he hurt me . . . well, he did, but I just don't think it's relevant to our"—she didn't want to say *relationship*—"situation."

"See, this is what grown-up people do. After small talk, they tell each other about themselves. That's how they get to know one another." He hacked off a piece of brisket and stuffed it into his mouth.

"Are you sure—I mean, you don't get out much, so how would you know?" She forced her facial muscles into a grin. She wasn't purposefully being evasive; she'd just like a bit more time before Cinco realized that she was nothing more than a doormat. Right now he saw her as strong, and she hated that one day that would change.

"Yes, I've read many articles on the Internet." He hid his frustration behind his grin. He picked up his napkin, wiped his face, refolded it like he needed a moment, and then placed it back in his lap. Every move was deliberate and controlled. So he went quiet when he was frustrated. Good to know.

"Okay, but I don't recall making small talk. We'll need to discuss the weather, how black is the new black, and the rift between Caitlin and Kris over his becoming a woman." She pointed at Cinco with her fork. "And we haven't even started talking about sex. Trust me, I can talk about that for hours."

Maybe distracting him would change the subject.

His frustrated smiled turned into a full-fledged frown. "Is it just me you have trouble confiding in or is it everyone?"

She told herself that she had no idea what he was talking about. After all, she was an extrovert, so over-sharing went with the territory, but just because she tended toward being a chatterbox didn't mean that the information she was spouting was of a personal nature.

She ground out a breath and wiped her mouth. "Fine. Phillip, in addition to being the asshole who left me homeless, also screwed around on me while I worked my ass off keeping him in designer clothes and expensive mocha lattes. He, of course, couldn't be bothered with anything as mundane as work while he was writing the great American novel or any of the other careers I paid for. The loss of my things—well, except for the few items that had belonged to my parents—was nothing compared to the humiliation of betrayal and the loss of dignity that went along with it. I don't like to talk about it because I hate being reminded that I'm a gullible idiot who should have known better. The boyfriend before Phillip cheated on me, as did the one before him. My grandmother is right. I only pick the wrong men."

Revealing her past made her feel like she'd ripped the bandage off an open wound and then taken a knife and stabbed herself a couple hundred more times. He'd wanted honesty and he'd gotten it. Now she just wanted to go home, lie in bed, and stare up at the ceiling until her mind went numb and she could put the heartache away so she didn't have to feel it anymore. Life was messy and she needed some alone time to block out the mess.

Every time Phillip had looked at other women in restaurants while having dinner with her had hacked away at her self-esteem until she'd told herself that there must be something wrong with her because she wasn't enough to keep his attention. Every time Phillip had turned an argument around on her and had her apologizing for suspecting him of cheating cut away at what little pride she'd had in herself until she'd stopped bringing it up. In the beginning of their relationship, she'd been excited to see him, but at the end, anxiety filled her every time she'd walked through the front door. Love worked for everyone but her. She so desperately wanted the happily-ever-after that everyone else had, but she wasn't sure how to go about getting it.

"I know how it feels to have the person you think that you love sleep around." His voice was rusty, like he hadn't meant to say it. "Naomi slept her way through most of the ranch hands and propositioned every one of my brothers, who all declined and came straight to me. I know the humiliation and heartache and hatred of watching yourself do and say things that turn you into someone you don't like."

CanDee watched him. His eyes held the hurt that she'd seen in the mirror too many times. He got it . . . he really understood. She took a breath. "Slowly, I turned into a version of myself that I didn't recognize. I was going through his phone while he was in the shower and checking his wallet for receipts that would confirm my suspicions. Every time I'd find another piece of damning evidence, I'd mean to confront him about it, but would talk myself out of it . . ."

"Because you didn't want to know. Deep down you knew, but as long as it was just a suspicion, it wasn't real." He reached across the table and covered her hand with his. "The night I came home a day early from a business trip and found her in bed with my best friend, I nearly lost it."

There was shame on his face.

"What happened?" She knew the shame and would have spared him the telling, but he was right, they needed nothing between them.

"Trent Slattery had been my closest friend since childhood. And when I found her on top of him, I pulled her off." He looked down at his hands. "That it's in me to hurt a woman makes me sick."

Slattery—why did that name sound familiar?

"Did you hurt her?" She just didn't see violence in him. He might be the strong, silent type, but there was a quiet gentleness about him.

"No, but I was rough." His face held nothing but shame and regret.

She took both of his hands and kissed the palms of each. "You were angry and upset, and your restraint is admirable. I'd have belted the bitch. I was saved the indignity of finding Phillip with another woman, but I would've still belted him and the bitch."

"That's different. You're a girl—"

"So my theoretical violence is okay? I'll have you know that I took two semesters of kickboxing in college. I have a mean right hook." She smiled.

"So you don't fight like a girl?" The shame was fading from his face.

"I wouldn't go that far. There would still be lots of hair pulling and stupid slap fighting, but I'd get in a few jabs to the body first." She continued to hold his hands. "You are a good person, and whoever Naomi drove you to become isn't the real you. Don't beat yourself up . . . for something that didn't happen."

He kissed the backs of her hands. "I like the way you see me."

She'd never thought of things that way. "I like the way you see me too."

CHAPTER 18

Early the next morning, Cinco—freshly showered, shaved, and clothed—quietly made his way downstairs and into the kitchen. He was exhausted, but man, was he ever happy.

CanDee had finally opened up about Phillip, though he still hadn't found out the man's last name.

Last night, after they'd gotten home, she'd insisted that they take a bath together, which had led to some hot, soapy, bubbly fooling around. Sex had never been this good with anyone else.

He took the last stair, turned the corner, and found the kitchen full of light.

CanDee, wearing nothing but his red T-shirt from the night before, stood behind the stove and flipped a pancake. If he weren't half in love with her already, this would have been the start.

"I didn't know you could cook." He inhaled the sweet perfume of fresh coffee as it ran in a steady stream from the maker into the pot.

"Don't tell anyone, people might start asking me to cook." She turned around.

She was wearing the rhinestone glasses she'd worn her first day here. "I like the glasses. How come you don't wear them more often?"

"Usually I wear contacts, but I can't find my bag this morning. I know I brought one over yesterday. Have you seen it?" She scooped up the pancake from the cast-iron pan and placed it on top of the pile that had been warming under a bowl. "Here." She held the plate with the butter-covered pancake stack on it out to him.

"Thanks." He took the plate and went to the table. "I unpacked your bag."

She poured more batter into the sizzling hot pan. "I don't understand. You took it back to the cottage and unpacked it?"

"No." He picked up the maple syrup she'd put out on the table and poured a good bit over his pancakes. "Why would I unpack it at the cottage? I moved some of my stuff around and put your clothes in the top dresser drawer."

She turned around and her mouth fell open.

"Now you have a place to store your things." With his fork, he cut a triangular piece of pancake. "You're welcome."

"But . . . but . . . I didn't ask you to do that." She looked a little shell-shocked. "I don't need drawer space. My clothes need to stay in my bag on the side of the bed that isn't yours."

"Too late. They're already put away." He slid the spoonful of pancake in his mouth and chewed. "These are pretty good."

"But . . ." She turned back to the pancakes.

"I can repack your stuff, but then I'll have an empty drawer. It just makes sense having your things in it." He hacked off another chunk of pancake.

"Fine, but that's it. I'm not bringing anything else over. The rest of my things are staying at the cottage." She ground the spatula into the bottom of the pan and flipped the pancake over with a loud splat.

"If you say so. Personally, I think you should probably rotate your clothes a little bit or maybe do your laundry here." He slid in another bite.

"No thanks. I can manage there." She pulled another plate down from the cabinet and practically slammed it against the counter.

What was wrong? Clearly, CanDee wasn't a morning person.

"Okay, but doing your laundry in the kitchen sink sounds a little old fashioned while I have a perfectly good washer and dryer right over here." He smiled to himself. He was beginning to see that she had a problem with moving in with him. Well, they'd just see about who won that argument.

"Crap." She exhaled loudly as she scooped the pancake out and slapped it on the plate. "If it's okay, I guess I can do my laundry here."

She made it sound like she was doing him a favor.

"If you think that's best. There's plenty of hangers and space in the closet in my room in case you need to hang anything up to dry." He'd moved a few things to the closet across the hall last night after she'd fallen asleep.

She opened her mouth to say something and then closed it.

"Thanks for making breakfast." He sniffed the air. "Is something burning?"

"Damn." She practically ripped off the oven door opening it. "I have bacon in the oven."

She pulled out a baking sheet with several slivers of black ash lined up across the top.

"Damn it. I don't seem to be able to multitask when it comes to cooking." She set the pan on top of the stove. "Sorry."

"The pancakes are enough for me and they're really good." He pushed back from the table and went to the coffeepot. "You made coffee and pancakes. That counts as multitasking."

He poured her a cup and then one for himself. She flipped another pancake onto the waiting plate.

"Why don't you sit down and eat? I'll finish the pancakes." He took the spatula from her and handed her the cup of coffee. With his index finger, he pulled the collar of the T-shirt she was wearing and looked down. "You don't have anything on under this."

She clamped a hand over her mouth in mock surprise. "Oops."

"Woman, you're causing me to have some seriously impure thoughts."

He wrapped an arm around her waist and pulled her to him. "Seriously impure."

She ran her hand down his lower back and landed it squarely on his butt and squeezed. "To my way of thinking, you're wearing way too many clothes."

He flipped the last pancake onto the plate and turned off the heat. With his free hand, he handed her the plate. "You need to eat."

"If you insist." She dropped her hand, took the plate, and headed to the table.

He followed her and managed to sit down before she could pull out a chair. Gently, he pulled her onto his lap and settled her on his left knee. She put her plate on the table next to his. With his right hand, he picked up the syrup and doused her pancakes in sweet goodness. With his left hand, he inched up the hem of her T-shirt—*his* T-shirt—and drew light circles on the inside of her thigh with his thumb.

"What are you doing?" She jumped when he dipped a finger between her thighs.

"Multitasking." He cut off a hunk of pancake, scooped it up with her fork, and brought the fork to her mouth. "Open for me."

He dipped another finger inside her as she opened her mouth and he slid the forkful in. She chewed and swallowed as her hips found the rhythm of his hand. In nothing but his T-shirt, she was extraordinary. He cut off another piece and tried to lift the fork, but she stilled his hand. She took the fork from him, grabbed his hand, and guided it under the T-shirt to her left breast. He tweaked her nipple as her hands fell to her sides. She sat back against him with her head on his shoulder as her thighs opened.

Her hand cupped the front of his jeans.

"No, love, this is just for you," he whispered close to her ear. He wanted her hot and liquid under his hands for no other reason than to capture this memory in his head for the hours today that he'd be away from her.

"Oh . . . faster." She moaned as he increased the pressure and the pace.

Her hips bucked against his hand and then her muscles tightened around him. She arched her back and then relaxed back against him.

Her breathing slowed to normal. "Nice."

Her hand went to the front of his jeans again and she tried to unbuckle his belt.

Reluctantly he released her breast and tried to bat her hand away.

"I don't have time." He stood her up and made to get up himself, but she leaned down and kissed him hard, her tongue exploring the inside of his mouth. Her hands undid his buckle, popped the button on his jeans, and ripped the zipper down. She straddled him and worked him with her hands.

"What are you doing?" He closed his eyes and enjoyed the feel of her.

"Finishing breakfast." She stroked him until he lost the battle for sanity.

He couldn't wait for lunch.

CanDee put the last breakfast dish in the dish drainer to dry.

Cinco had put her things away. They were no longer in her overnight bag. How had she let that happen?

And then somehow, he'd bamboozled her into agreeing to bring her laundry over and wash it here. What if she left her clean laundry unattended and he put that away too?

Holy crap. She leaned against the kitchen counter. Somewhere along the way, she'd become the deadbeat in the relationship. She was sleeping in his bed, eating his food, and her clothes now resided in his drawer. Wait, no . . . not resided, they were merely hanging out in his drawer until she moved them out. See, she still had the ability to move them out. Nothing was set in stone . . . she was free to leave at any moment.

She sucked on her top lip. She kind of wanted to stay. His house was old and homey and she could feel the history around her everywhere. If she were ever to buy a home, it would be just like this . . . well, with more bathrooms and minus the pink paint.

That kind of felt like a slap to Edith's face.

She glanced heavenward and mouthed, "Sorry."

Crap, now she was talking to a dead woman . . . again.

Anxiety made the pancakes and syrup roll around in her stomach. Cinco hadn't asked her for anything or made her feel anything but welcome, but staying here came with strings. Only he hadn't put them there, she had. Well, if she'd added the strings, she could cut them at anytime . . . but she kind of liked them. She liked the idea of something tying her to Cinco. He understood her possibly better than she understood herself. He made her feel wanted and beautiful and safe. And he had a fantastic ass and shoulders and chest. Come to think of it, he had a really fine everything—inside and out. She and Cinco had so much in common.

She rolled her eyes. Phillip had also claimed to like the same books and music. They'd bonded over George R.R. Martin and debated Harry Potter versus the Lord of the Rings. Early in their relationship, Phillip had pretended to be on Team Harry but as the years droned on, his true J.R.R. Tolkien self came out.

Cinco had no motivation to lie to her. All he wanted from her was her. That was a new one. All he wanted was her.

What did it say about her that she was suspicious of a man who'd taken nothing from her, but only given?

It hit her. He was taking care of her instead of the other way around. It was nice to have someone else looking out for her. Maybe she would just let him for as long as he was willing, but she wouldn't only take. He needed to be taken care of too. Breakfast had been a great start and lunch wasn't a bad idea either.

She'd go into Roseville or maybe a little farther to Fredericksburg and hit the grocery store. It was her turn to provide dinner. God knew she was no cook, but she did have one dinner that she made reasonably well . . . meatloaf with mashed potatoes and a salad. Maybe she'd even pick up a brownie mix for dessert.

She started opening cabinets and taking stock of what he had and what she would need. Her phone was on the table, so she picked it up and texted Cinco asking if he needed anything from the grocery store. A few seconds later, a text came through telling her that there was a list on the fridge.

She tore it off the magnetic pad and set it and her phone on the table. The fact that she was going to the grocery store to buy food for the house that she sort of shared with her boyfriend-type person was a little much, but she wasn't that anxious. Okay, she was anxious and her palms were beginning to sweat. Cinco had unpacked her bag. Right now, her things were tucked away in a drawer. She took a couple of deep cleansing breaths and wiped her hands on the T-shirt. This wasn't a big deal. She could handle it. Cinco wasn't Phillip and she should enjoy the time she had left on the ranch.

She made her way upstairs and into his bedroom. While she wasn't entirely comfortable with her clothes nestled in his drawer, she was willing to give it a try.

It wasn't forever, but she could handle it for right now.

She yawned and stretched. The clock on the bedside read five fifty-two. No one in their right mind was up this early. She yawned again. Stores wouldn't be open for another few hours. She glanced at the bed. It was probably still warm.

She flipped off the overhead light, waited for her eyes to adjust to the darkness, and felt her way around to the bed.

Cinco really needed a dog. This big old house was too lonely for just one person. She crawled back into the side of the bed that wasn't Cinco's. Maybe she'd bring it up to him over dinner. She yawned again. Yep, this place needed a dog or two.

CHAPTER 19

Four hours later, CanDee grabbed her purse and headed out to her golf cart. Since she had both sets of keys, she no longer needed to hide it in the barn. It was neatly parallel parked under a tree in the front yard. As soon as she closed the front door of the house, she knew there was a problem.

"Son of a bitch." She stared at the golf cart, which was up on blocks and missing four tires. "Lefty, I give you points for trying, but you've met your match, old man. This means war."

Like hell she was going to walk over a mile to her car. She glanced around and her gaze landed on a perfectly good alternative. On the side of the barn, there seemed to be some sort of farming machine hooked up to the oldest tractor she'd ever seen. She was pretty sure that Teddy Roosevelt had ridden that very tractor on his charge up San Juan Hill.

At the back of the tractor, she climbed up onto the metal seat, which seemed to be suspended in air. Based on the amount of metal and the design, the tractor was old, but the bright green and yellow paint looked showroom ready. It was a John Deere Model "D," according to writing painted on the side. There were lots of levers but no key. Since it didn't have a key, how was she supposed to turn it on? Not to be deterred, she pulled out her smartphone and googled *starting and driving a John Deere Model "D."* Five videos came up. God bless YouTube.

After watching a video, she hopped down from the seat, walked around to the front, opened the compression caps on either side of the engine, leaned over and pushed the throttle lever a tiny bit forward, and then walked around to the flywheel and cranked it around until the engine shushed to life. She could actually see the gears turning and hear the motor running. It sounded like a Harley with a head cold. After closing the compression caps, she climbed back into the seat, eased off the brake, and gently pushed the throttle forward. She bounced along at a whopping two miles an hour, but at least she wasn't walking. Carefully, she gave it more throttle. What the tractor lacked in springs to cushion the ride, it made up for in style. This bright and shiny piece of American ingenuity should have been pulling a float in the Founder's Day parade or roped off in a museum. She felt like waving to the imaginary masses of people not lining the path she was taking to the cottage, but she didn't. Waving to imaginary people was probably a bad idea.

She made it to the cottage in record-ish time. True, it would have been easier and faster to walk, but she wouldn't have gotten to ride on a parade-worthy piece of farm equipment. She parked the tractor and whatever it was pulling between two large oak trees, then jumped down onto the grass.

"Just what in the holy hell do you think you're doing to my poor Betsy?" Lefty's eye was squinty and mean.

"Her name is Betsy?" She looked at the tractor. "She's really more of a Bertha or maybe Edna."

She hadn't thought it was possible for his eye to turn meaner, but it had. "Her name's Betsy and no one rides her but me."

"Apparently not. And Betsy really isn't a stout enough name for her." She patted the flywheel. "She sure is pretty."

CanDee walked around him to Connie, her Corolla. Because the driver-side door no longer locked—which was good because the only key had broken off in the ignition—she opened the door and climbed in.

Lefty followed her to her car and pointed an index finger at her. "You stay away from Betsy—"

"Put the tires back on my golf cart or Betsy and I are going to become best friends. I'm thinking of painting *Edna* on both sides of her engine just so everyone knows her real name." CanDee slammed the door and hand-cranked the window down. "I'm running into town. Need anything?"

Just because they hated each other didn't mean they couldn't be friends.

His top lip snarled. "Some WD-40 and a bag of Peanut M&M's."

"Okay, I'll be back later." It was her turn to point at him. "Wheels back or the tractor gets it."

She rolled up the window and backed up enough to turn around. Lefty reminded her a lot of her grandmother's ex-fiancé. CanDee had thought he was going to have a heart attack when Grammie used one of his fancy screwdrivers to plant flowers in her front yard, and then there was the time she'd used a hammer to tenderize meat. Now that CanDee thought about it, that's what caused the breakup. After the meat incident, he'd packed up his tools and moved out. Since Milford was kind of an ass, he wasn't hard to get over. It looked like Grammie's picker was broken too.

Since poor Connie was tired of having to drive over these bumpy dirt roads, she was particularly finicky today. On a good day, she did zero to sixty in seven and a half hours, but today wasn't a good day.

Four hours later, CanDee pulled up to Cinco's house with a trunk full of groceries. The golf cart was still up on blocks. As she stepped out of the car, she shook her head. Lefty didn't take directions very well. After she unloaded everything, she was going to pay him a visit.

"What do we have here?"

She turned around. It was Rowdy.

"Nice timing. I could use a helper." She placed two canvas bags full of groceries in each of his hands.

"I see that you and Lefty haven't resolved your differences." He nodded to the golf cart.

"He'll come around. Wait and see." She picked up the remaining three bags and closed the trunk. "I brought him Peanut M&M's and some WD-40. If he wants them, he has to return my tires."

"I wouldn't hold your breath. Although, he does love Peanut M&M's . . . especially the yellow ones. He says they taste better." Rowdy opened the front door and let her go in first.

Information noted. She'd remove the yellow ones before handing over the bag.

"Your mother did a great job on manners." She walked in and waited for him to shut the door.

"My mother might be small, but she's mighty." He grinned. "Plus, being a doctor, she can kill us fifty different ways and make it look like an accident. Not that she's threatened it, but it's sort of implied."

They headed to the kitchen. She set her bags on the island and he set his on the counter by the sink.

He reached into one of the bags and pulled out a box of saltines. "So, are you in love with my brother or what?"

She nearly dropped her purse. "What? No . . . that's . . . not . . . we're . . . what?"

"I'm going to take that as a yes." He ducked into the pantry and put the saltines away.

"I am . . ." She couldn't get the *not* out and finally decided on, "It's too soon to tell."

"He's falling hard for you. Please don't break his heart. Naomi was an evil bitch and she nearly destroyed him. I may want to kill him from time to time, but no one else gets to hurt him." He reached into the bag and pulled out two cartons of eggs, opened the fridge, and slid them in.

"I understand. I don't want to hurt him and would never do it intentionally." She'd end up leaving him and that would devastate both of them.

"I guess that's the best I can hope for." He pulled out two whole cut-up chickens. "Why did you buy these? And come to think of it, the eggs?"

"I don't know." She shrugged. "I guess I was hungry for chicken and I thought we . . . um, Cinco might like some scrambled eggs for breakfast."

She sure as hell hadn't meant to say *we*.

"No, I get the whole food part, but we have our own chickens who produce eggs and great meat. Bobby Don's in charge of meat processing. I'm surprised Cinco hasn't given you the ranch tour." His eyes narrowed. "Too busy doing other things?"

She grinned. "You have no idea."

"I like you with him. Cinco actually talks now and laughs. I thought that was gone until you waltzed into his life." He pointed to the chicken. "How about fried chicken for lunch?"

She pulled a plastic sack full of russet potatoes out of her bag. "I didn't see a Kentucky Fried Chicken anywhere around here. That's where my fried chicken comes from. I hope you weren't expecting homemade."

She headed to the pantry to put the potatoes away.

"I happen to make excellent fried chicken. I have a secret recipe and if you're nice to me, I'll even share it with you as long as you don't tell Cinco. What he doesn't know won't hurt him." He pointed to the bag of potatoes in her hand. "Why don't you put some of those on to boil while I get the chicken in some buttermilk."

"Aren't you worried about messing up your fancy Armani suit?" She'd never seen a man in a suit do anything but sit at a desk. "Why are you wearing a suit?" It wasn't like he was a stockbroker or a lawyer.

"It's a workday. I always wear a suit." He slid off the suit jacket, carefully folded it, and laid it across the back of a kitchen chair.

"You are very high maintenance. Anyone ever told you that?" She liked him in what she supposed was an older-sister sort of way.

"More than one woman has mentioned it. Hey, I emailed your friend Justus. I love the name of her business—Justus Flor-All. That's funny." He unhooked his cuff links and rolled up his sleeves. She'd never met a man who actually wore cuff links. "I sent her some pictures and she sent me back some drawings. She's very talented. Usually, I don't hire people without meeting them first, but she's pretty amazing."

"I know. In addition to being a fantastic landscape designer, she's also a pretty incredible human being." She'd spent many a night on Justus's sofa after Phillip. If Justus had known how bad things were, she would have insisted that CanDee move in, but Justus's one-bedroom was already crowded between her and her five-year-old son.

"She'll be here in a little over five weeks. I can't thank you enough. Mom's going to love it." He pulled a large, flat bowl out of the cabinet next to the fridge and then opened the fridge and pulled out a carton of buttermilk.

"How do you know where everything is?" Maybe he had some kitchen intuition? She'd never been able to intuit much, especially in the kitchen.

"I used to live here. After Cinco and I graduated from Texas A&M and moved back, we took over this place." He peeled back the plastic from the cut-up chicken and dumped the pieces in the flat bowl.

She shook her head trying to picture it. "I can't quite see the pink Victorian as a frat-daddy bachelor pad. I bet y'all were very popular with the ladies." She pulled a five-pound bag of flour out of one of the canvas bags and headed to the pantry.

"Yeah, well, we tried. Didn't always work, but . . ." He shrugged. "You win some and you lose some."

"Where do you live now?" After putting the flour on the shelf, she walked out to unload more groceries.

"I built a house at the old mill. I started with the old stone mill and added to it. You should come by. I'm about two miles north." He pointed to the back door like she would know which direction that was.

Silly man, everyone knew north was up, south was down, east was right and left was west. It was the way of the world.

"I'd love to see it." She pulled out two cartons of ripe red strawberries and went to the fridge. Cinco had told her how much he liked strawberries.

"You'd love to see what?" Cinco filled the doorframe leading into the kitchen from the hall. "Well, isn't this cozy?"

His tone was controlled.

"My house. I was telling her about my house." Rowdy washed his hands and wiped them on the towel hanging from the peg next to the sink.

"It's weird . . . the house. He took a lovely old stone building and added a lot of glass and angles. Now it looks like some modern art museum." Cinco watched her.

Why was he acting this way? He was tense and his movements were deliberate. He was upset about something.

Oh. His ex-wife had hit on his brothers. Seen through his eyes, this little domestic scene must have brought back some bad memories.

She walked over to him and kissed him loudly on the mouth. She pulled back and slipped her arm around him. She could feel his muscles relaxing under her hand.

"Rowdy is making us his famous fried chicken." She reached down and squeezed Cinco's butt. He removed her hand, brought it to his lips, and kissed her palm. She smiled up at him. "I'm making mashed potatoes . . . after I put the groceries away."

"You work on the potatoes and I'll finish the groceries." He dropped her hand.

She could tell that the awkward moment had passed. She was willing to admit that if she'd been in his shoes, she'd have been a little taken aback too.

"Works for me." She picked up the bag of potatoes, grabbed a pairing knife from the butcher's block, and opened three cabinets before she found a bowl big enough. On the way to the kitchen table, she grabbed a handful of paper towels. She sat, opened the bag, and started peeling, the skin falling onto the paper towels.

"So, I hear Edith's house was the bachelor pad after college?" She grinned at Cinco. "I'm having trouble picturing it."

"We had some good times here." Rowdy walked out of the pantry with a canister of flour and an armload of seasonings. "There was this one time when we ran out of condoms—"

"Do you have to bring that up?" Cinco's eyes were huge and the blush started at his collar and was headed north.

"We're all adults here." Rowdy pulled a plate down, dumped some flour on it, and added a shake or two from the spices he'd pulled out. "Anyway, we kept the condoms in the bathroom for some reason, I don't know why, it's not like people have lots of sex in the bathroom—"

"Speak for yourself." Cinco surprised everyone, including himself. "She really likes my shower."

"He has a point, but I wondered that same thing so I moved them into the nightstand." CanDee scraped her knife around the potato until it was naked and then she tossed it in the bowl.

Rowdy put his hands over his ears. "Stop talking about your sex life. I'm right here and it's gross. I don't need to know these things about you two."

"Such a prude. Wait until you meet Justus. She's going to yank the prude right out of you." She laughed to herself. Justus was very open and honest about everything.

"Anyway, before people started interrupting me, I was about to tell you that one night we both needed a condom and there was only one left. It started with rock, paper, scissors, and ended with punches. By the time we'd hashed out who'd won—"

"It was me. I won." Cinco called from the pantry.

"Anyway, both of our . . . um . . . dates . . . were sound asleep." Rowdy sighed long and hard. "All I got that night was a black eye, a split lip, and some bruised ribs."

"Y'all fight a lot. Is that normal?" She picked up another potato and peeled it.

"Normal for who?" Cinco emptied the last canvas bag. "It's normal for us."

"You don't have any brothers or sisters, do you?" Rowdy reached in the cabinet next to the stove and pulled out a huge cast-iron skillet.

"No, I'm an only child." She finished that potato and moved on to the next one.

"Would that I'd been an only child." Rowdy picked up a bottle of canola oil and poured most of the bottle into the pan. He turned the knob and a ring of fire lit under the pan.

"Please, you'd be a wimpy, old lush gulping down wine in your weird museum house with twenty-five cats if it weren't for me. I made a man out of you." Cinco stowed the canvas shopping bags in the pantry.

"No, I believe that was Jenny Dennison." Rowdy grinned. "She taught me many things none of which, thank God, I learned from you. And I sip my wine, thank you very much."

"It must be nice to have history like the two of you. I mean having grown up together. All I had was my grandmother." Not that she was complaining.

"What's Grandma like?" Rowdy flicked a drop of water into the oil, testing it for temperature. Since he didn't add any chicken, it probably wasn't hot enough. "We never had a grandmother. They both died before we were born."

"Grammie is . . ." How did she make *bat-shit crazy* not sound, well, bat-shit crazy? "She lives by her own set of rules and doesn't care if they make sense to anyone else."

"Like how?" Cinco grabbed a paring knife on his way to the table. He sat down and picked up a potato.

"There was the combination-lock incident." She set another naked potato down and picked up a new one. "In middle school, they issued me a combination lock for my locker so the school would have a copy of the combination. My grandmother threw a fit. Said it violated my right to privacy. I was eleven so I really didn't have much privacy. She went around and around with the principal, who wouldn't relent, so Grammie took it to the school board and threatened to sue."

"What happened?" Cinco scraped the last piece of skin off of a potato and set it on top of the ones she'd peeled.

"I got to have my very own lock." At the time CanDee had been mortified, but now she saw that her grandmother had been sticking up for her. "She called them communists for wanting control over my life."

"I like Grammie. She sounds like good people." Rowdy tested the oil again and got a sizzle. "I can't wait to meet her. I'm great with grandmothers."

"That's because you ply them with wine until they're so buzzed they actually think you're nice." Cinco rolled his eyes and then leaned in close to CanDee. "Really, the best part about him is the wine."

She loved watching them verbally poke and prod each other. Despite their teasing, their love for one another was evident. She couldn't wait to spend more time with the family and see if they all treated each other this way. She was getting a crash course in the Rose family and she had to admit, she liked it.

CHAPTER 20

Cinco liked that CanDee was easy with Rowdy. At first, seeing them together had brought back shades of Naomi, but CanDee wasn't flirting, just talking to him. It was more of a brother-sister kind of thing. Rowdy liked her. She fit into Cinco's life so easily and filled a hole in his heart that he hadn't wanted to admit was there.

Cinco drained the boiled potatoes. He'd taken over cooking the mashed potatoes so that CanDee could ask them some questions about the genealogy.

She sat at the table, legs crossed at the knee. "Okay, I think I have the family tree down. So in 1830 Colonel Lacy Kendall Lehman bought the original plot of land and he and his lovely wife who looks like a man, Brunhilda, moved here and set up housekeeping in a tent."

"She is rather masculine." Rowdy nodded as he pulled a piece of fried chicken out and set it to drain on a paper-towel-covered plate.

"Brunhilda gave birth to Prudence Althea Lehman and Lacy Kendall Lehman Jr., who died at the age of ten. Prudence married Carlton Rose and had Lacy Kendall Rose Jr. Why was he junior again, since his father was Carlton Rose?"

"Prudence was honoring her brother and named her son after him, and they called him Deuce." Cinco pulled a stick of butter out of the fridge. He plopped it into the pan where he'd boiled the potatoes.

"I guess you can call your kid whatever you want." CanDee yawned. "George Foreman named all of his sons after him."

Cinco watched her. She looked tired. He pressed his lips together to hide his grin. He'd kept her up late and gotten her up early this morning. Tonight, they'd go to bed early. They both needed it. Maybe they'd actually go to asleep early too.

She stretched. "Prudence also had Carlton Rose Jr., who I'm assuming they called Junior..."

"They called him CJ, for Carlton Junior." Cinco dumped the drained potatoes back into the pan and grabbed the masher from the crock of kitchen tools next to the stove.

"I know it's important to document all of this, but I don't see the value." Rowdy hunched his shoulders. "I'm just not into this stuff like the two of you. They're dead, who cares?"

"It's important to know where you came from. It's our history." Cinco would have gotten up and thumped his brother on the back of the head, but that would have started a fight and Rowdy was manning a pan full of boiling oil.

"Prudence also had Thaddeus Bartor Rose and Mellifluous Lehman Rose. If my name was Mellifluous, I'd change it to Mel too." She made some notes on the purple legal pad where she'd drawn the boxes and lines of the genealogy. "At the age of fifty, Deuce married Roberta Myrtle Tensdale in 1900 and they had Lacy Kendall Rose III, called Tres. I know about Mel and Edith, but how come CJ and Thaddeus never married?"

Rowdy smiled at Cinco. "You didn't tell her? That's the only part of this whole story that's interesting." He turned to CanDee. "They were Texas Rangers. Some people said they were more outlaws than Rangers, but who knows?"

"That is interesting." She made more notes.

"I mentioned it. I'm sure I did." Hadn't he? His great-great-uncles didn't have much of a presence in Edith's house because she didn't like them. Their things had burned up in the fire.

"For a time, they rode with Lone Wolf Gonzaullas." Rowdy's face lit up. He'd always loved the fanciful tales of his great-great-uncles.

"Are they in the Texas Ranger Hall of Fame and Museum in Waco?" CanDee sat forward, excited. "I love that place."

"Me too." Cinco nodded. Maybe he'd take her there on the way to Bullard. "Yes, last time I went to the museum, there was an exhibit on them. Very interesting."

"You two are made for each other." Rowdy shook his head. "I can't think of anything worse than the Texas Ranger museum."

"I can. The symphony or an art gallery or a poetry reading." Cinco mashed the potatoes.

"That's because you're a Neanderthal." Rowdy pulled the last piece of chicken out of the pan. "Trust me, the symphony doesn't want your knuckle-dragging self there disrupting those of us with taste."

Cinco turned to CanDee. "We tried to return him to the gypsy family who'd left him on our doorstep, but they wouldn't take him back."

"Now, that's just mean. And here I was, sort of interested in this whole family history thing, and you go and say something hurtful." Rowdy was all mock offended. "Sometimes I feel that you just don't love me, big bro."

"Don't fight that feeling." He smiled at his younger brother. He and his brothers might get angry with each other, but they were always there when he needed them. And he was never lonely even when he wanted to be. He had a feeling that CanDee had been a lonely child.

"What did I do to make you hate me so much?" Rowdy shot Cinco the big puppy-dog eyes.

"Do you want that list in chronological or alphabetical order?" He walked to the fridge, pulled out the milk, and poured some in the mashed potatoes. Once he added salt, they'd be ready to eat.

"See." Rowdy put his hand over his heart. "I'm all about the love and he's all about the hate."

"Yes, you've lived such a wounded and misunderstood life. It's so sad." Cinco rolled his eyes.

Rowdy reached into the cabinet on his right and pulled out the slightly smaller cast-iron skillet, and with a potholder moved the chicken-frying skillet to the back burner.

Looked like he was making gravy. He made excellent gravy.

"Big bro, can you chop up a jalapeño for me?" Rowdy spooned some of the oil the chicken was fried in and the browned bits into the smaller skillet.

"Only if you're making jalapeño cream gravy." Cinco covered the mashed potatoes with the pot lid and pulled a jalapeño out of the fridge. "Minced?"

"Yes, sir, on both accounts." Rowdy turned the heat up on the pan.

CanDee finished her notes. "So after the fire, Tres moved in with Mel and Edith and then in 1942 he married Suzette Analisa McCloud, who gave birth to Lacy Kendall Rose IV, aka Bear, who married Lucy Anne Braxton, who gave birth to Lacy Kendall V, Houston Harris, Dallas Collin, Fort Worth Tarrant, and San Antonio Bexar Rose. Why are most of you named after Texas towns and their counties?"

"With the exception of the heir apparent over here, those were the towns where we were most likely conceived. Luckily the twins were twins because Mom and Dad couldn't decide whether they were created in Dallas or Fort Worth. According to them, it was a hell of a weekend." Rowdy grinned. "I'm just happy not to have been named College Station or Alice."

"I think Niederwald or Marfa would have also been terrible names. *Niederwald, go clean your room. Marfa, no, you can't borrow the car.* Neither roll off the tongue." She made more notes and then gathered her things into a pile and slipped them into a leather tote bag she'd hooked over the back of the chair. She pulled out a two-pound bag of Peanut M&M's. "Do you have any gallon-sized plastic bags?"

She stood and stretched.

Cinco pointed to the left-hand drawer in the island. "There."

Was she that hungry that she was going to dig into candy right before dinner? He was about to point that out, but she was a grown woman and it wasn't his place.

She opened the drawer, pulled out two bags, and then sat back down at the table. She opened the M&M's bag and poured the whole thing in one of the plastic bags. One by one, she pulled out only the yellow candies and put them in the other bag.

"Oh, I see. Those are for Lefty. Rowdy must have told you that he likes the yellow ones because they taste better. Smart, and guaranteed to piss him off." Cinco was beginning to see that CanDee was wily. He smiled to himself. Intelligent, beautiful, and devious—what a combination.

"There are still no tires on my golf cart. Until there are, Lefty's life may become slightly uncomfortable." She sifted through the M&M's.

"What else do you have planned?" He arched an eyebrow.

"I don't know if I can trust the two of you. You might be spies for Team Lefty." She matched his arched eyebrow.

"Wow, she's taking this way too seriously." Rowdy added the minced jalapeño to the pan and it sizzled.

"Vengeance is very serious. Plus, I feel that he's slighted not only me, but all women." She pulled out more yellow ones.

"No, I'd say he's an equal-opportunity hater. It's not just women. He hates Yankees, people under twenty-five, people over twenty-four, anyone who's bald, anyone who has hair, and anything with a pulse, and most of all, he hates brown M&M's." Rowdy glanced at Cinco. "Did I miss anything?"

"Nope, I think you covered it all." Cinco took the knife and chopping board to the sink and washed it. He set it in the drainer to dry along with the knife and bowl CanDee had used for peeling the potatoes. He liked that she cleaned up after herself.

"So I need to go heavy on the brown M&M's." She started pulling out everything that wasn't brown. "Got it."

"If we promise not to tell, will you tell us your plan for Lefty?" Cinco just wanted to make sure that everything stayed congenial.

"Well, I take it he wasn't pleased that I drove Betsy to the cottage this morning." She moved colored candies from one bag to the other.

Cinco looked at Rowdy and they both turned to her.

"That was ballsy." Cinco was proud of her. "How did you know that Betsy is his most prized possession?"

She looked up. "I didn't. She just happened to be in the right place at the right time. Total crime of opportunity."

"How did you start the engine? There's no key." Rowdy was in awe of her bravado.

"YouTube video. You can find out how to do almost anything on YouTube." She reached behind her and pulled something out of a plastic Walmart bag. "If both of you promise to keep quiet, I'll tell you the next step in my reign of Lefty terror."

She held up a box. "I bought a bedazzler at Walmart. I think Lefty's eye patch could use some rhinestones. Perhaps something in a smiley face or some pouty pink lips?"

Rowdy laughed. "You're good. Remind me to never piss you off."

"That's really funny." Cinco walked to the kitchen table and sat beside her. "You know that payback's going to be bad."

"Absolutely. I'm waiting to see what he comes up with next. Really, the missing tires were amateur at best." She was all excitement. She enjoyed the sparring. "Who knows? Maybe I'll bedazzle his jeans. Nothing says 'I'm a rough and tough cowboy' like some sparkly angel's wings on the back pockets."

"I like her." Rowdy sprinkled flour over the pan drippings and jalapeño. He stirred and stirred.

"Me too." Cinco leaned over and kissed her on the cheek. "I think I'll keep her."

CanDee winked at him and that was it. He stopped falling and landed smack dab in love with CanDee McCain. He should have been nervous or anxious, but all he felt was peace. It was like coming home after a long trip and finally getting to sit in his favorite chair and sleep in his bed. She was his comfort . . . his home. That's what had been missing with Naomi. She'd never felt like his reward at the end of a long, hard day. CanDee was both a reward and a guilty pleasure.

She was the one for him. The only person who made his life complete. It was so clear. The life they would have together would be full of silly pranks, laughter, and happiness. Along the way, there would be disagreements and heartache, but they would weather it together . . . a partnership based on mutual love and respect. This was the life he wanted . . . this was the life he was meant to have. He had a feeling that he'd remember this moment for the rest of his life and he hoped that he would.

His father had told him that he'd know when the right woman came along, and the right woman was sitting next to Cinco. Did he tell her that he loved her right now? Did she feel the same way about him? Anxiety punched him in the stomach.

CanDee deserved a ring and marriage . . . nothing less. Just because he'd gotten married quickly the first time didn't mean that getting married quickly this time wouldn't work . . . did it?

When should he propose? Was it too soon? What if she didn't feel the same way?

"Are you okay?" CanDee placed her hand over his. "You look a little shell-shocked. Is something wrong?"

He just stared at her. His mouth turned as dry as sandpaper.

"Can you slap him or something before he retreats too far into his head?" Rowdy poured milk into the pan in a steady stream. "Cinco, use your words. Talking is good."

"What's the matter?" CanDee's golden-brown eyes were full of concern.

"Nothing." He shook his head. "A work thing I forgot to do. I just remembered. No big deal."

He shook it off. He needed to find out how CanDee felt pretty damn quick because one-sided love didn't work for him. This time he wanted it all and he aimed to get it. This time, he wanted forever, and his forever was centered around CanDee.

CHAPTER 21

Hours later CanDee rinsed the last dirty dish she'd used to make the meatloaf for dinner and set it in the drainer. She glanced at the oven. The meatloaf had a little over an hour left to cook and she could make the salad later.

She wiped her hands on a dish towel and then set it back on the peg to dry. Having spent a good portion of the afternoon working on the genealogy, she could give herself an hour—just until the meatloaf was ready—to work on her mystery.

The first draft was almost finished and story was taking shape. She rubbed her hands together; she couldn't wait for revisions. That's when she added the sparkle. Right now, *Murder, Mayhem, and Sadness* was just a shell, like a new house in the framing stages. Wait until she added the walls, flooring, and appliances. This was going to bury *Murder, Mayhem, and Madness*.

She sat back. Only now did she realize the name was so close to the first one. She'd plotted the series before Phillip had stolen it, so it never occurred to her to change the name of the second book.

Since it was so close to the name of her first, she doubted she could keep it, but she didn't have to worry about that right now.

She pulled up the Word file and read over her last chapter.

An hour later, the oven timer buzzed. She finished her sentence and fought the urge to ignore the timer and keep going. She was in the zone, the words practically writing themselves. The buzzer went off again. Forcing herself to get up, she stretched out the kinks in her back from sitting in the hard wooden kitchen chair and walked to the oven. With a potholder, she pulled out the meatloaf. It smelled good, which was not usually how things she pulled out of the oven smelled. She set it on the stovetop to cool a bit.

She glanced at the clock on the microwave. Cinco would be home in a half hour or so. Surely fifteen minutes more working on her book wouldn't hurt or put her behind.

Her phone vibrated on the kitchen table. She picked up the phone and didn't recognize the number. Maybe it was another client in need of a genealogy.

She hit answer. "Hello."

"Hey, babe."

Her heart dropped to her knees and she sat down hard in the kitchen chair.

It was Phillip.

"You have a lot of nerve calling me." Her hands started shaking with rage. She did her best to control it. Around him, it was best to keep the chatting to a minimum. Somehow he'd always been able to twist things around so that everything he did was her fault. For someone who prided herself on her wit and sarcasm, she could feel herself wilting into the old pattern of saying "I'm sorry" when he was in the wrong.

That just pissed her off even more. This time, she had nothing to lose—least of all him—so letting loose with the stream of curses that burned inside of her would be fantastic . . . empowering . . . cathartic. She opened her mouth and . . . nothing came out. Her hands shook and her teeth gritted but she'd been struck dumb and didn't have a single good one-liner. One hour from now, a million of them would pop into her head, but for now, all she could do was sit there picturing four different ways to kill him and hide the body where it would never be found.

"I know you're mad. What can I do to make it up to you?" He made it sound like all he'd done was accidentally throw a red sock into a load of whites. "We're stronger than this. Come on, let me make it up to you."

With her free hand, she slapped herself hard on the cheek just to make sure she was dreaming. *Surreal* wasn't a surreal-enough word.

"Short of running over yourself with your own car, I can't think of anything that would remotely make up for your behavior. You can't replace my parents' things. You're a bastard and I never want to hear from you again." She hung up and then blocked his number.

No communication was good communication. The last thing she wanted was to see that son of a bitch again. Part of her was afraid that she'd scratch his eyes out and the other part was afraid that she'd let him belittle and break her down until she nodded and gave him whatever he wanted. The last few months with Phillip, he'd more than walked all over her. And she'd let him. That was the kicker. She'd let him manipulate her.

After not hearing from him for almost a year, why now?

She sat up. He needed something. Her gaze landed on the chapter she was working on for her next book. The dumb bastard needed a sequel and here it was. Over her dead body was he getting near enough to her computer to even read, much less steal, her current work in progress. One book wasn't enough for the asshole, now he wanted her new one.

She was back to wanting to kill him again. Vengeance and rage were the things she needed to hold onto. She wanted to go back in time and tell herself not to go to the party where she'd met Phillip, but that only happened in fiction. Life would be so much better with a time machine. She could go back in time and kill Hitler and possibly the man who invented pantyhose—because it had to be a man; no woman would have been that stupid—and she could have saved her parents' things from having been auctioned off to pay the rent. For that matter, she could have saved her parents.

She scrubbed her face with her hands and then they fisted and she pounded on the table a couple of times.

"What's wrong?" Cinco walked through the kitchen doorway and went straight to her.

"Nothing." She ground the word out. She didn't want to talk about it because then he'd know how stupid and sappy she really was.

He flinched. "Hopefully, one day you're going to trust me enough to talk to me about things that really matter."

Why was he angry? She was the one with ex drama.

Like he was doing something against his will, he sat down next to her and pulled her in for a hug. He just held her and didn't press her for information. The silence droned on and on and she could feel the weight of his wanting to know, but holding back.

Cinco was right. She did have a problem sharing her feelings, but only because she was tired of having them trampled to death. He stroked her back and the strings that she was beginning to attach to him pulled at her heart.

"Phillip called." Those two words sounded like a bomb going off in the silent kitchen.

"And?" His tactic of pressing without pressing was working more than she'd like to admit. He had her wanting to fill the angry silence between them.

"He called out of the blue, like we were two old friends who hadn't seen each other in years and he was just calling to catch up. No big deal." Tears of rage stung her eyes. She wasn't usually a crier, but ex-boyfriends who were assholes tended to be her trigger.

He patted her back and rocked her gently from side to side. "Don't cry. He isn't worth it."

"I know," she said as the first sob croaked out. Tears streamed down her face and snot poured out of her nose creating a sloppy wet spot on the shoulder of his T-shirt.

He just held her and let her cry it out. As the tears began to subside, so did some of the burning desire to remove Phillip's spleen with a dirty spoon.

"I'm so sorry that he hurt you." Cinco stroked her hair.

She pulled back and looked at him. "Phillip didn't hurt me, he pissed me off. I'm not a sad crier, I'm a mad crier."

His eyes narrowed like he was filing that piece of information away for future reference.

"Okay, so what did he want?" Gently, he wrapped his hands around her waist, guided her out of her chair, and settled her on his lap. His arms circled her.

It occurred to her that he liked touching her and was always doing it. Her hair, her hands, her shoulder—it was like he wanted her to know that he was always there for her.

"I don't know. I hung up on him." With the back of her hand, she wiped the remaining wetness from her cheeks. "But I'm pretty sure he wanted the book I'm working on now."

Cinco's brow squenched up. "Why would he care about my family history?"

"My mystery. He wants *Murder, Mayhem, and Sadness. Murder, Mayhem, and Madness*, my first book, is really popular." How come she hadn't been able to see Phillip for who he really was until after they'd stopped dating?

"Wait a minute." Carefully, he stood her up and then did the same. He walked out of the kitchen and came back a couple of minutes later carrying a book. "This book. You wrote this book?"

He handed her a copy of *Murder, Mayhem, and Madness*.

Cinco had no idea that he was rubbing her nose in her mistakes, but it felt like he was. She glanced down at the book. The cover with its giant red cross and the knife sticking through it had never made sense to her. There were no crosses in the book. Since she'd refused to buy, much less read, Phillip's version, she had no idea where the cross came from.

"Phillip Harcourt is your ex." It wasn't a question so much as verification.

"Yes." She pushed the book away. "Unfortunately."

Anger turned his eyes reptilian. "That bastard. He's made millions off of your book while you lived in your car. I want to break him in half and punch him square in his butt chin."

"Butt chin?" Oh, the deep cleft in Phillip's chin. Now that she thought about it, it did look like a butt. "You've met him?"

"I waited two damn hours at BookPeople for him to sign my copy. Bastard." He fisted and unfisted his hands. "He stole from you."

Cinco turned on his heel, walked to the island, opened a drawer, and pulled out a black Sharpie. He opened the book, ripped out a page at the front, and handed her the pen. "Would you sign it for me?"

She blinked once and then twice. It was her first book signing. Something so small meant so much. "I'd love to."

She flipped the book open to where the title page should be but was now missing. On the dedication page, which she couldn't help but notice didn't mention her, she wrote, "Cinco, thanks for being my very first fan. I like knowing that you enjoy my work. I love being with you. CanDee McCain."

She handed it back to him. "Wow, that felt good."

He read the inscription. "I love being with you too."

He traced the uneven edge that remained of the ripped-out page. "That bastard."

She had the distinct impression that he wanted to kill Phillip on her behalf. She kissed him on the cheek. "Usually, violence doesn't turn me on, but your willingness to kill him for me is very sexy."

Light as angel kisses, his hand cupped her face and his gaze met hers. "I would do anything for you."

The devotion in his face made her nervous and like always, a one-liner to lighten the mood almost popped out, but he was being serious. He cared about her and instead of making a flippant remark, she held his gaze and kissed him.

"You're too good to be true." She didn't want to label the feeling she had for him . . . not yet. It was too soon and she wasn't going to make the same stupid mistakes she'd made in the past.

"Nope. You're the one who I can't figure out why you're letting me hang out with you. You're too good to be true." His eyes were giant aqua pools of sincerity.

The nervousness melted away and she could actually feel her heart smile. He thought she was as wonderful as she thought he was. It shouldn't have been a shock to be in a relationship as an equal partner, but it was.

A knock sounded at the front door.

Cinco looked away, dropped his hands, and stepped back. "Crap."

"What's wrong?" She glanced at the doorway that led to the hall that led to the door. "Who's here?"

"No one." He walked to the fridge, opened it, and pulled out two bottles of Shiner. He twisted off the caps and tossed them in the trash can under the sink. "You're going to need this."

"I don't understand. What's going on?" She took the beer and drank deep. "Is someone at the door or not?"

"Nope." He drank deeply and swallowed. He didn't meet her gaze. "That was a little message telling me that Lefty is done."

"Oh, so he finally came to his senses and put the tires back on my golf cart." That was easier than she'd thought it was going to be. Good, she wouldn't have to use Connie when going back and forth to the cottage.

"Not exactly." Cinco took another drink.

"What do you mean?" Something wasn't right. She headed to the door. "What did Lefty do?"

Cinco was close on her heels. "Now remember, he's an old man and he's lived a hard life."

She made it to the front door first, but his long arm reached around her and grabbed the knob.

"Do you have any weapons on you?" His gaze raked down her coral cotton T-shirt dress.

"Do I need some?" She went for the knob, but he didn't budge. "Let me out."

"Not before you take a couple of deep calming breaths." He took a couple of deep breaths as if to show her.

"Let me out or I'm going to knee you where it counts which I'm going to regret because I plan on using that area later, but that won't stop me from doing it now." It must really be bad.

"Just remember, I'm Switzerland in this." Slowly, he turned the knob and opened the door.

She stepped out into the evening sunshine and . . . life as she knew it didn't end, nothing gross dumped down on her head, and nothing exploded. She looked around. In fact, she couldn't find anything wrong. She scanned the front yard and the golf cart still up on blocks, but when she got to Connie, the slightest sliver of alarm shimmied down her spine. She shaded her eyes from the sun. The interior looked bluer than the blackest-gray cloth it had been. She walked down the steps and then around the car.

Son of a bitch. The interior was jam-packed with small blue rubber balls. If she opened the door, they would all topple out. "Where in the hell did he get these damn balls?"

"They go in the ball pit for the Fourth of July county-wide picnic we have here every year." He sat on the top step and sipped his beer. "Consider this payback for Betsy."

She took a step closer to the car, meaning to look into the passenger-side window, when her foot slipped out from under her and she landed with a splat on her ass. There was a sheet of clear plastic on the ground in a ring around the car. On top of the plastic was some clear goop that felt a lot like petroleum jelly.

"Are you okay?" Cinco was at her side and pulling her up, but she slipped again, grasped the edge of his belt buckle, and pulled him down on his ass. "He greased the grass around the car. It's hard to see under this shade tree."

"That little shit." She struggled to get to her knees, slipped again and face-planted right in Cinco's lap. She rolled off him and into the grass, which stuck in clumps to the gel all over her body. "I hate him so much. I was going easy on him with the brown M&M's, but this"—she held up a goop-covered hand—"this shit just got real."

"No murder or maiming. Anything else is fair game." Cinco rolled off of the clear plastic sheet too.

"Can I download your playlists? Lefty's about to get a heavy dose of Katy Perry." If Lefty thought she would back down just because of some blue balls and gel, he wasn't the man she thought he was. If he wanted to go old school with the pranks, she was down with that.

CHAPTER 22

"You've got to do something." Lefty paced back and forth in front of his office two days after the blue-ball incident. "She's gone too far." He pointed to his black eye patch that now sported a multicolored rhinestone butterfly.

"It's really pretty. When the light catches it just right, it kind of looks like it's flying." Cinco grinned. CanDee not only knew which one of Lefty's buttons to push, she was holding that button down for maximum stress.

"Don't get me started on the eye patches. She went and sparkled up all three of mine. I ain't figured out how she did it, but I'm gonna. Now I have to wear them until I get my new ones I ordered from the Amazon." He ground out a sigh.

Cinco had tried many times to explain that Amazon was a company and the Amazon was a rainforest. He was pretty sure that Lefty thought the things he ordered came directly from the rainforest.

"If you're not mad about the eye patches, then why did you call me down here?" Surely the brown M&M's wouldn't warrant an early-morning screaming call to get down to Lefty's office pronto.

"You're not going to believe it." He pushed open his office door and Lady Gaga's "Poker Face" blasted out.

So this was why she'd wanted to copy his playlist. It was pretty funny.

"It just plays over and over. I can barely hear myself think." Lefty yelled over Lady Gaga. "I can't make heads nor tails out of them lyrics. I'm pretty sure they ain't talking about poker."

He shut the door and the music stopped.

"Why don't you disconnect the wire?" He scanned the doorframe for whatever she'd used to rig up the music. "Or keep the door closed."

"Somehow, she's made it work while I'm in the office even with the door closed. And look at this." He pulled open the door and Lady Gaga went to work. Lefty pointed to his desk and yelled, "She glued all them drawers shut. I can't get to my paper clips. How am I supposed to work without no paper clips?"

He put his hands over his ears and stormed out of the room. Cinco looked around the room and found the small motion detector. CanDee was good. He nodded to the beat and headed out. He closed the door after himself and Lady Gaga disappeared.

"She brought me a bag of Peanut M&M's with only the brown ones. That ain't right. You know I hate the brown ones." Lefty resumed pacing.

"You shouldn't have greased the area around her car. She could have gotten hurt." In his opinion Lefty had started things and he deserved everything CanDee could think up.

"I'm going to have to go big in retaliation." Lefty shook his head like he just didn't have any other choice.

"Just be ready for whatever she comes up with next. Just so you know, she's very resourceful." He liked that CanDee could hold her own. An independent woman was a thing of beauty, but he wouldn't let these pranks go too far. If he had his way, CanDee would spend the rest of her life here with him, so she and Lefty needed to find a way to get along. But he was willing to let them have their fun.

A slow, devious smile crept across Lefty's face and he snapped his fingers. "I've got it. I ain't got no more time for chatter. I gotta head to town. Need anything?"

"No, I'm good." Cinco bit his top lip to keep from smiling. He hadn't seen Lefty this fired up in a very long time. In a way, CanDee had breathed new life into the old man.

Cinco followed Lefty out of the barn door and then closed it behind him. He had a few errands of his own to run in Fredericksburg. The first one being with his attorney to find out what, if anything, could be done to help CanDee out with claiming the rights to her first book. Phillip Harcourt was an asshole who deserved so much more than what he was probably going to get. CanDee might be okay with sitting back and letting karma deal with Harcourt, but Cinco was not. She might not be financially able to go after the bastard, but Cinco had plenty of money.

He opened the driver-side door of his pickup and climbed in. He did have plenty of money—eight figures to the left of the decimal, nearly nine—so he really wasn't happy with CanDee buying his groceries, but he knew better than to offer her money. Surely she had to know he had money. The Texas Rose might be the second largest cattle ranch in Texas, but it was by far the most profitable. That's why Naomi had targeted him. Clearly, money wasn't that important to CanDee. It wasn't really that important to him. He had everything he needed. It had been very important to Naomi.

As long as he lived, he'd never forget how his ex felt it necessary to assign dollar amounts to everything. Like the evening after their engagement party and she'd sorted the gifts by dollar amount. Only people who'd spent at least a hundred dollars rated a thank-you note. She'd done the same to him. Only when he'd brought her an expensive present did it rate a kiss from her. Now he realized how small that had made him feel. She'd been out to see what she could get for herself because money and things made her feel important and loved. It occurred to him that nothing he could have done would have changed that.

He didn't like anyone seeing only dollar signs instead of him. He was his own person and wanted to be judged based on his actions and not his credit rating.

He was going after Harcourt because it was the right thing to do and money had little to do with it. He would like to see CanDee get what was owed to her because it was hers. He wanted her to have all the fame too. Not that she wanted it or even craved it, but she had created a very successful novel and she deserved the bragging rights.

He threw the gearshift into reverse, backed up, and rammed it into drive. Every time he thought of Phillip taking from her and leaving her destitute, he wanted to wring that guy's neck. CanDee was smart, funny, and pretty as hell. How could anyone take advantage of her?

Then again, he'd learned the hard way that there were people who only cared about themselves. The thought had probably never occurred to Phillip that he was hurting someone else. There were so many terrible things Cinco wanted to do to Phillip Harcourt, the least of those desires was ruining the bastard.

Cinco decided not to tell CanDee about what he was doing to help her. He wanted it to be a surprise. He loved her and wanted the best for her, and he was willing to do whatever it took to give it to her.

"What are you doing?" Cinco walked into the kitchen a little after six that evening to find CanDee typing away on her laptop.

"Just putting the finishing touches on a Craigslist ad for a Chewbacca-roaring contest." She made it sound like that was a completely normal thing.

"I give up. What's a Chewbacca-roaring contest?" He opened the fridge and pulled out a beer. "Want one?"

She looked up from her computer. "No, I'm good." She grinned. "For the contest, people are supposed to call Lefty's cell number and roar loudly and then hang up. Brilliant, right?"

"Why would anyone do that?" He unscrewed the cap and tossed it in the trash can.

"For the fifty-dollar prize money." Her voice held a whole lot of *duh*.

"How is Lefty going to judge a contest he doesn't know he's having?" Cinco loved the mischievous smile on her face.

"That's the beauty of it. The contest ends in a couple of weeks, so hundreds of people will call, roar, and then hang up. Then those same people will call back to find out what they've won and get mad when they find out there's no contest. It's a twofer." She nodded. "Awesome, right?"

"Your creative genius never ceases to amaze me." He bent down and planted a kiss on the top of her head. "How about going out for dinner?"

Not that he would enjoy driving back into town, but he wasn't in the mood to cook.

"I was thinking we could have meatloaf sandwiches and a tomato-basil-buffalo mozzarella salad." She reread the ad, deleted something, and typed a new sentence. "I bought sourdough bread and fresh mozzarella the other day."

"That sounds perfect." He'd spent the better part of the morning and most of the early afternoon with Jack Simms, his attorney, trying to figure out what could be done for her. He needed to find out if there was a way to prove that she'd written *Murder, Mayhem, and Madness*, like notes, or whether she had a copy of it on her computer. "Anything new from Phillip?"

She looked up, confusion on her face, and then understanding dawned and she shook her head. "I don't know. I blocked his number."

How did he ease into this conversation? "So . . . um . . . do you still have a rough draft or something of your first book?"

"I think I have a paper one back at my apartment, but that's all. Phillip stole my novel off my old MacBook." She turned back to the computer and placed the ad.

He didn't know if a paper copy was enough proof. Jack had checked; she hadn't filed a copyright with the Library of Congress. Cinco would figure something out. She'd done the work and deserved the credit. Maybe her friends? Maybe she'd discussed the book with them prior to it being published. He'd find a way to talk to them . . . somehow. There had to be a way.

"I'll get the dinner started." He turned back to the kitchen. "You said something about buffalo mozzarella?"

"In the fridge." She pushed back from the table. "I'll get the sandwiches together."

"Deal." He liked working in the kitchen with her. Naomi had never wanted to do anything with him unless it involved shopping with his credit card. With CanDee, he felt like he was part of a team.

"Tomorrow, I need to go into town again." She nodded to the pad on the fridge. "Do we need anything?"

She opened the refrigerator door and pulled out the plastic-wrap-covered meatloaf.

He liked her using *we*, and the best part was, she didn't seem to notice that she'd done it.

"I don't think so. What do we want to cook this week?" He slipped the *we* in there for good measure.

"I don't know. Meatloaf and pancakes are really my go-to meals. Beyond that, I eat yogurt and the occasional fried egg." She stared at him. "It's weird. Since meeting you, I've hardly eaten any yogurt."

"That's because I feed you." He smacked her lightly on the ass. She was wearing another one of those short cotton dresses that she favored and her hair was curled. God, he loved how feminine she was. He loved how she had three kinds of shampoo and four types of conditioner all lined up in his shower next to his one bottle that did both. "I make a mean chicken Marsala."

She walked up to him and kissed him on the cheek. "I love chicken Marsala. Write down what you'll need and I'll pick it up tomorrow." She walked back the island, uncovered the meatloaf, and cut two thick slices.

"About the groceries . . . I think it's my turn to pick up the tab." He tried to be nonchalant.

"I'm good." She set a medium-sized cast-iron skillet on top of the stove and lit the burner.

"But I want to." He knew that pressing was probably a bad idea. "I can afford it."

"I didn't say that you couldn't." She forced a smile. "But I can afford the groceries too. You're letting me stay in your house and use your shower—who I named Jezebel, by the way—so the least that I can do is buy the food."

He had never thought of it that way. For now, he'd let her buy the groceries, but next time, they were on him.

"Why Jezebel?" He sliced a tomato and reached for another one.

"Because she's a slut. She's willing to rain pleasure down on whoever turns her on, she's not picky." CanDee laid the two meatloaf slices in the pan. While they sizzled, she headed to the toaster and popped in four slices of sourdough bread.

"I can't argue with that." He headed to the fridge for the mozzarella. With the same knife he'd used to slice the tomatoes, he sliced the ball of cheese. "What do you need from town so soon? Did you forget something?"

"I need several reams of bubble wrap and a dozen rolls of tinfoil." She flipped the meatloaf slices.

"Do I want to know?" Either she had a tinfoil fetish or this had something to do with Lefty.

"Probably not." She reached around him for a couple of plates.

"The motion-sensor music was genius. It will take Lefty a while to figure it out, but he will." He picked a few leaves of basil and chopped them.

"I knew he'd figure it out eventually, but I hope he puts the tires back on my golf cart first. I know he won't, but a girl can dream." She pulled the toast out of the toaster and laid two pieces on each dinner plate. She scooped in several spoonfuls of meatloaf gravy into a bowl to warm up in the microwave.

Heavy knocking came from the front door.

Cinco glanced at her. "I'm not expecting anyone . . . You?"

He wiped his hands on a dish towel and made his way to the front door.

Through the frosted glass, he could make out Lefty's figure. "It's for you. Your playmate is here." He called over his shoulder as he pulled open the front door.

"I'm right behind you." CanDee said from the kitchen doorway.

"I brung CanDee a peace offering." Lefty winked and nodded at Cinco as he held the pink package of Double Stuf Oreos.

"She'll love them." He was going to advise CanDee not to open them. Something was fishy. Lefty wasn't a quitter.

"She'll love what?" CanDee slipped an arm around Cinco's waist and eyed the Oreos. She leaned over and sniffed them. Slowly, her head shook from side to side. "You replaced the double stuff with toothpaste." She sighed dramatically. "Really? You're better than this. I'm so disappointed."

"Now, you wait. This was a perfectly good prank . . ." Lefty's cell phone rang so he fished it out of his back pocket and checked the number. "Give me a minute. I don't recognize this number."

He answered the call and someone Chewbacca-roared loudly and then hung up. "What the hell?" He stared at the phone.

CanDee bit her bottom lip to keep from laughing. "You're going to have to step up your game to keep up with me, or you can admit defeat right now and replace my tires." She stepped back and slammed the door in his face.

"Damn you, woman." Lefty stomped down the front porch steps. "I'll get you. Just you wait."

His phone rang again. He answered it to hear someone else roar and hang up.

CHAPTER 23

At noon the next day, CanDee crammed the last of four giant rolls of bubble wrap into her trunk. She had more than enough foil and bubble wrap to make Lefty's world metallic and crunchy. She'd picked up everything needed to make chicken Marsala plus some other goodies, which were all stored in the cooler in her backseat. She was headed back to the ranch. Her stomach growled and she remembered the red cinderblock building she'd just passed had some of the best barbeque she'd ever tasted. She flipped a U on Highway 87 and turned in to the parking lot.

The line out the door wasn't nearly as long as the one for Franklin in Austin, and Franklin wasn't half as good as Cranky Frank's. She parked and got out of the car.

She pulled out her smartphone and texted Cinco to ask if he wanted anything from Cranky's. Her phone buzzed. He wanted a pound of sliced lean brisket. She could do that.

"Funny meeting you here."

The hairs on the back of her neck stood to attention. She turned around.

Phillip was standing right behind her, invading her personal space.

"Following me?" That was beneath even him. Fear prickled her spine. She'd never been particularly scared of Phillip, but his eyes were hard. Her instincts were leading her to fight instead of taking flight like before.

"Just here to try the barbeque. Cranky Frank's is one of the top twenty-five barbeque places on the planet, according to *Texas Monthly*." He was all smiles, but there was something under it. Desperation? A desperate Phillip could be uncontrollable. She'd seen hints of it more than once.

"So you drove all the way out here for barbeque?" In her experience, there were no coincidences. "How did you find me?"

Was he following her?

"I was in town and noticed your car." He was all controlled charm. "You know how much I love barbeque. I drove out here to try Cranky Frank's. Well, that, and to see you." He leaned into her and she glared at him. She stood her ground and didn't back away. No more backing away . . . that was her motto. He'd never been violent, but he did like to bully her. "I saw you turn in to here and thought that I'd kill two birds with no stone. Maybe we could talk over lunch?"

Over her dead body. He was trying to intimidate her and she wasn't about to let that happen. She'd learned a lot since she'd seen him last and it was high time she showed him the new woman he'd made her.

"I'm getting mine to go." But by God, she wasn't running away. She was hungry and she wanted barbeque. It was Phillip's turn to run . . . oh wait, he'd already done that while she was out of town. She turned back around. "I know you don't care, but when you moved out without paying my rent with my money, they sold my things . . . including the things that belonged to my parents."

"Let me write you a check." He reached into his left breast pocket and pulled out a checkbook.

Who actually had a checkbook on them these days? He'd probably picked it up thinking that he'd offer her money. What an ass.

"Why do I even bother? Why didn't I realize before that you're a textbook narcissist? You won't hear anything I say except what you want to hear. No doubt you think what you did to me was okay, because in your screwed-up world, everything revolves around you." She tried to turn back around, but he grabbed her arm. "Let go of me."

Like hell was he going to push her around. Now that she was with Cinco and saw what a sane, normal relationship looked and felt like, she truly saw how messed up her life had been.

"We need to talk." His tone was a harsh whisper but his face held nothing but charm. His fingers bit into her upper arm.

Why hadn't she noticed that before—charm on the outside, but evil on the inside.

"CanDee, is this man bothering you?" It was Lefty. He was ten people ahead of her in line. "'Cause it looks like he's bothering you."

"I just need a moment of her time. That's all." Phillip appeared to be just another man charmed by a pretty woman, but his eyes flashed mean.

Lefty stepped out of line and went to CanDee's side. He was almost a foot shorter than her, but with his legs spread wide and his arms folded over his chest, he seemed to take up take up twice the amount of space. "Son, take your hand off the lady."

Phillip's grip tightened as he leaned into Lefty and bit out, "Mind your own business, old man."

Now the real Phillip reared his ugly head. He was capable of anything. How had she missed that before? Or maybe she hadn't missed it, just ignored it.

"Son, you need to step off. If you don't drop CanDee's arm, I'm going to punch you in the throat." Lefty was as calm as she'd ever seen him.

"Are you threaten—"

Lefty's fist moved so quickly she couldn't track it. He hit Phillip squarely in the throat.

Phillip dropped her hand and grabbed his throat while he wheezed in air. "I'm . . . going . . . to . . . sue—"

"Son, I've got twenty men who will testify that you laid hands on a woman. I don't know where you're from, but here in Gillespie County we don't manhandle women. So right now, you need to slink back to that fancy red car"—he pointed to a brand-new Porsche—"before I get mad."

Phillip wagged a finger at Lefty and wheezed out, "I'll get you."

"Did he just threaten me?" Lefty glanced back at CanDee. "I think he just threatened me."

"You know, it's hard to tell. He might have said, 'I'll bet you,' but that doesn't make any sense." CanDee rubbed her arm where Phillip had grabbed her. "Now that I think about it, he did threaten you."

"Boys, this man just threatened me and you saw him grab Miss CanDee." Lefty watched Phillip. "I told you I could handle this on my own, but I'd like for you to escort Mr. Fancy Pants to his car and then I'd like for you to drive him to the county line. If he ever sets foot on the Texas Rose, you have my permission to shoot him for trespassing."

CanDee hadn't noticed the twenty or so men gathered behind her. Phillip's eyes were as huge as moon pies. "I'm . . . going."

He sounded like Darth Vader on a respirator.

CanDee hadn't realized her hands were shaking until Phillip pulled out of the parking lot. Lefty's arm came around her and she slumped against him.

"Who was that a-hole?" Lefty shouldered her weight without breaking his stride. He walked her over to a picnic table outside, across from the front door.

"My ex-boyfriend. His name is Phillip." She sat down on the bench.

Lefty sat down across from her and covered her hands with his. "Your hands is cold." He rubbed them together trying to warm her up. "One Eye, can you get us a couple of them Dr Peppers, please?"

"Sure thing." A man with two perfectly good eyes and a mouthful of mismatched teeth charged into the restaurant to get them some drinks.

"Thank you." She should have said that right off, only she'd never been this scared.

"I ain't mixed it up in years. It was kinda fun." He grinned kindly. Beneath his gruff, the man had a heart of gold. "You need to tell Cinco about your ex when you get home. Promise me."

"I will. He already knows about Phillip, but I'll tell him about today." That wasn't a conversation she was looking forward to, but she wasn't one to shy away from things . . . not anymore.

"Good. He's going to want to make sure you're safe. He likes you . . . a lot." Lefty's unicorn-bedazzled eye patch caught the sun.

"Why did you help me?" It was out before she'd thought about it. It was kind of insulting. "I don't mean to offend you, but I just wanted to know."

"You're family. While you and I may have a disagreement, we're still family. No one messes with my family . . . ever." Slowly, his hands slid away.

They weren't family. She opened her mouth to say so, but nothing came out. The ranch wasn't her home, but it was beginning to feel that way. And Lefty, for all of his being a pain in her ass, would have been so much fun to grow up around—he'd have been that crazy uncle that parents despise, but kids watch for out the front window hoping he'll bring a pocket full of candy and teach them how to play poker when mom isn't looking. "I like being part of the family."

"I don't mean to pry, but what are your intentions toward Cinco?" Lefty leaned forward, prying anyway.

"I don't know. I didn't expect to . . . you know . . . meet someone." For someone who made her living using words, she was certainly short on them right now.

"You didn't mean to fall in love with him. I get it." Lefty grinned.

"But, I didn't . . . I'm not . . . we're not . . . oh." She just sat there and let it sink in. She was in love with Cinco. When had that happened?

"I can tell by the look on your face that you had no idea." Lefty's laughed sounded like a tree branch scraping against a window screen. "Good for you . . . good for him."

"I told Frank what happened and he made y'all up some sandwiches to go with them Dr Peppers." One Eye set two red plastic baskets down—one in front of CanDee and one in front of Lefty. "Slide has them Dr Peppers."

A short man with Post-it-note-yellow hair and a pockmarked face set two Styrofoam cups down.

"Did Frank make mine a Paul?" Lefty glanced at CanDee. "The Paul has double meat. I don't know who Paul is, but he likes him some meat."

She looked down at the enormous sandwich in front of her and then at the even bigger one in front of him. "I think you definitely got the Paul."

Thirty minutes later, Lefty walked her to her car. "Just 'cause I like you don't mean I ain't still mad at you."

"I couldn't agree more." She leaned down and gave him a one-armed hug.

"I'm so glad you said that." He hugged her back and then stepped back and opened her door for her. "You really shouldn't keep your car unlocked. Someone could steal it."

"I wish . . . no, really I can't afford a new car." She sighed. "The door lock is broken, which is good because the only key broke off in the ignition."

"Well, that's not good." He eyed the lock like he was mentally ordering the parts to fix it.

"I'll see you back on the ranch." She closed the door and then rolled down the window. "Thanks again."

"My pleasure." His eye patch winked in the sunlight.

She rolled up the window. Gray clouds were gathering on the horizon and it was turning muggy. She turned the black plastic stub of a key sticking out of the ignition and the car hummed to life. She turned on the air conditioner. A cloud of gold shot out of the vents.

Lefty had glitter-bombed her car.

With her eyes closed, she felt around for the window lever and rolled it down again. She blew the glitter out of her mouth and wiped her eyes. "Good one."

Finally, an opponent worthy of her devious mind.

Lefty danced around as he pointed at her. "I got you. I got you. I got you."

"I'm so proud of you." She blew more glitter out of her mouth. "I was a little worried after yesterday, but this time, you stepped up to the plate. This is exactly the high-quality prank I expected from you."

His phone rang and he pulled it out of his back pocket and answered it. Someone Chewbacca-roared and then hung up.

"Payback's a bitch." She blew him a kiss and pulled out of the parking lot.

CHAPTER 24

Cinco didn't want it to seem like he was waiting at the front door for CanDee, but he was. He looked out the window beside the door, watching for her car.

CanDee had texted that she'd run into Phillip and that her phone battery was about to die and she didn't have a charger. When she got home, he was supergluing a charger inside her car.

Lefty had also texted him that she'd had a run-in with her ex, but the damned old man wouldn't give him the specifics. Cinco was going crazy with worry. Something was wrong, he could feel it, but that wasn't the worst of it. Some small part of him wondered if CanDee still loved Phillip and if she had to choose, would her ex be the one who came out on top? Considering all that Phillip had done to CanDee, it wasn't logical for her to feel anything but hate for the man, but love wasn't logical. He shook his head. It seemed that Naomi was still mind-fucking him.

Until he'd met his ex-wife, self-confidence had never been his problem, but the stakes had never been this high before. He loved CanDee and was ashamed to admit to himself that made him vulnerable. He wasn't sure that CanDee felt the same way about him.

Damn it to hell. He pulled open the front door and walked out onto the porch. He'd just pass the time in the porch swing. People sat in porch swings some of the time. It didn't mean that he was waiting on her or worried or worriedly waiting on her.

He checked the clock on his phone. She'd left Cranky's almost an hour ago. She should be here any minute. Using his foot, he pushed the swing back and forth. Just another lazy afternoon spent swinging and watching the road to his house like a hawk. He checked the clock again. It was still the same time. Not even a minute had passed. Screw this.

He got up and paced the length of the porch and back again. After five more rounds, he checked the time again. Two whole minutes had passed. He paced some more and finally, her car turned onto the dirt lane that ran to his house.

Without thinking, he hopped down the stairs. As soon as she parked, he was at her door, opening it for her. He practically pulled her out of the seat and into his arms. He hugged her tight. She was safe now. She was home.

"Sorry about the charger." She leaned back. "I wish I'd charged my phone before leaving."

She looked tired and—he squinted—sparkly? He dropped his arms and stepped back. "Why are you covered in gold glitter?"

"Lefty." She smiled. "He was trying to make up for the Oreo debacle so he glitter-bombed my air conditioning vents. He did a great job too, because he got all of that glitter in the vents without spilling any."

There was pride, not venom, in her voice.

"Okay." He had no idea why she wasn't mad.

Yes, he did. Deep down both CanDee and Lefty liked the challenge. They were a lot alike.

Cinco didn't ask if she needed any help unloading, he just opened the back door and pulled the Igloo cooler off the seat.

"I got all the stuff for the Marsala and some other things," she said lamely. "Phillip . . . I didn't know he was going to be there."

He wished his hands weren't full of cooler so he could fill them with her, but he nodded toward the house. "Why don't you tell me while we put this stuff away."

She nodded as she walked to the trunk and popped it open. "There's not much to say. Phillip claims to have seen me turn in to Cranky Frank's and followed me in so we could chat like old friends. He grabbed my arm and Lefty punched him in the throat. Lefty's kind of a badass, but I'd appreciate it if you didn't tell him that I said so."

"Your secret is safe with me." He followed her to the trunk and looked down. "Why do you have four large rolls of bubble wrap and—is that a crate of tinfoil?" He shook his head. "On second thought, I don't want to know."

"That's probably for the best." She picked up one roll and stuffed it under her arm, and then another. "Lefty won't know what hit him."

"You like him, don't you?" Some people bonded over drinks or poker, others over practical jokes. Who was he to judge?

"Very much." She leaned into him. "Again, I'd prefer you didn't tell him."

They climbed the porch steps in silence and headed to the kitchen. Along the way, she left the bubble wrap in the parlor. In the kitchen, he set the cooler on the island and opened the top.

There was something he wanted to know badly. He had to ask, even though it cost him some pride. "Do you still have feelings for Phillip?"

His world stopped waiting for the answer.

"Yes and no."

His heart cracked wide open. At least she was honest, that was something. The hell it was. Now he wished she'd lied. Wait, no, he didn't.

"I don't love him . . . I don't think I ever did, but I wanted to . . . I wanted to love him." She leaned against the sink. "Do you know what I mean?"

He breathed in and out . . . in and out. His heart rate returned to semi-normal. She didn't love Phillip. "I know exactly how that feels. I wanted to love Naomi, but she wasn't the one for me. Wanting to love someone and being in love with them are completely different things."

He was staring at the woman for him and he wondered when exactly was the right time to tell her. Surely, unloading chicken and—he glanced down—frozen green beans from a cooler wasn't exactly romantic.

"After seeing him today, I want to bang my head against the wall and ask myself why I didn't see him for who he really is." She shook her head and reached into the cooler to pick up a bag of baby spinach. "I've never thought of myself as particularly gullible, but clearly I am. I made excuses for his behavior to everyone, including myself." She put the spinach away in the fridge.

"I've never really thought of myself as weak or a victim, but I allowed him to bully me. I can see that now." She looked up at him, and the heartbreak on her face had him setting the chicken and beans on the counter and wrapping his arms around her. "I've never understood the whole domestic-violence thing. You know, every time I saw something about it on TV I'd think to myself, why doesn't she just leave or buy a baseball bat and defend herself, but I get it now."

His heart dropped to his stomach. "What did he do to you?" He swallowed down the bile. "Did he hurt you?"

She shook her head. "No, nothing like that. It's just . . . I just . . . it was the beginning. Now that I look back on things, I can see that. It started with little jabs to my self-confidence and slowly built until I was asking him his opinion on everything I wore and did and said. I went out of my way not to make him mad and if I did, he had me believing that it was all my fault. As bad as it sounds, I always thought that victims of domestic violence were weak or raised in a household where violence is the norm." She hunched her shoulders. "That may be true in some cases, but not in all. I was raised by a strong female role model who taught me to never take crap from anyone, but I did and I have. I have no idea why. Now that I think about it, Grammie didn't have the best taste in men. She dated one loser after another, but she never let them push her around. Mooch off of her, yes, but never push her around. I didn't grow up seeing her victimized, not that I see myself as a victim, but I get it now. I get that victims aren't born, they're made. It starts small and snowballs into something ugly and violent."

He tried to keep his voice steady, neutral. "Was he ever violent with you?"

"No, but looking back on it, I think the control he liked to have over me would have escalated to violence if I hadn't backed down. I'd like to think that would have been my wake-up call and I wouldn't have taken it, but honestly, I don't know. That's the worst part, I don't know for sure that I wouldn't have made an excuse for his behavior." She sounded so sad and disappointed in herself.

He led her to the table, sat down in a chair, and pulled her onto his lap. "Here's what I think. You're a good and strong person so when someone like Phillip entered your life, you only saw the good in him because that's what you do. It never occurred to you that he could be anything other than kind, because that's what you grew up seeing. Because you are kind, when he started doing things that made you doubt yourself, you knew there was something wrong and, not being able to see the darkness in someone, you naturally thought it was you. That's how Naomi got me. Never in a million years did I ever think that she would lie about being pregnant. It was so foreign from the belief system I was raised with, it never entered my mind. Here I was, buying teeny-tiny little cowboy boots for our little one, and not once did I think that she was just using me. And then there were those men she slept with. My parents have been married and I assume faithful to each other for close to forty years. I had no idea she was cheating until it was too late. Because we come from good families with good role models, that's what we expect in others. It makes us easy targets."

It hurt to admit it, but he needed her to understand that she wasn't the only one who'd become someone they didn't recognize just to please someone else.

She kissed him gently on the cheek. "It must have been awful. Getting ready for a baby and then finding out there wasn't one. I can't imagine."

It had hurt then and he realized that it still hurt. "I can say this now—things worked out for the best. She would have been a terrible mother, and I'm not sure the version of me that she brought out would have made for the best environment to raise a child in. I want you to understand that I know what it feels like to look into the mirror and not recognize the person staring back at you. It's a terrible thing to hate the person you've become."

"And look at us now. Both able to look back and learn from our mistakes." She snuggled into him. "Aren't we the grown-up civil couple?"

He liked that she saw them as a couple. He did too. His love for her doubled.

"Time gives you a clear head. Also, we're both people who want to understand what went wrong so that we don't make those same mistakes." He had a kinship with CanDee that he'd never had with another human being, and something had changed between them tonight. She'd opened up without him prodding.

"You're right, I'm learning from my mistakes, or at least trying to." She circled his chest with her arms.

She pressed herself into his chest and he was disposed to believe that all was right in the world.

"You know . . . I don't think I could look back on Phillip and be this insightful if it wasn't for you." She kissed the spot right below his ear. He loved when she did that.

"Why?" He didn't care why; all he cared about was her lips on his skin.

"Because for once, I'm with a good guy. Well, apart from your hatred of Double Stuf Oreos and the fact that you mistook me for a stripper, you're a good guy." She sucked on his earlobe.

"I thought we were over the whole stripper thing." He buried his face in her hair and got a nose full of glitter. He sneezed. "If you ever do start stripping, the glitter thing could be your in."

"I'll keep that in mind." She laughed and the deep, rich sound made his chest downright sore with happiness. Would it always be this way? Would she always have this effect on him?

Good God, he hoped so.

"If you weren't such a good man, I wouldn't have seen what a shit Phillip is. I'm in a healthy relationship with a smart, caring man with a killer body, and I love him. That's more than I'd ever hoped for, and I have to say that it's nice. It's nice to be happy with you and with myself."

He took both of her hands in his and kissed the glittery backs of each. "I love you too."

She got very still and then her eyes turned huge like she'd just figured out what she'd said. "I love you." She sounded a little shocked. "It's too soon, but I do."

She didn't sound particularly happy about it.

"I'm sorry it's a bad thing." He hadn't meant for that to sound so snippy, but it hurt.

"It's not bad, only I didn't . . . I mean . . . I never thought I could be this happy. The negative part of me is waiting for the other shoe to drop." She shook her head. "I wish I could change that . . . One thing at a time."

"I love that you can acknowledge your faults and are willing to work on them." He kissed her loudly on the mouth.

"I feel that I must tell you that I've loved you longer." Her voice was smug. Not that she was competitive . . . no, not at all.

He grinned.

"Really? I figured it out last night. How about you?" His hand was slowly inching up her side and was now resting under the curve of her breast.

"You made that up." Her eyes narrowed. "I'm not going to lie, I figured it out at Cranky's today. But if you need to feel superior and think that you loved me first, I guess I'll have to let you."

"It's the truth." He would have crossed his heart but he cupped her breast instead. "Let's go wash off that glitter."

He glanced down. There was a nice trail of it coming from the hall into the kitchen. As far as he was concerned, Lefty could clean it up. It was his mess. He noticed her rubbing her left upper arm.

"Did you hurt yourself?" Carefully, he rolled up her sleeve. A bruise was blooming on her arm. Actually, it was four small bruises all lined up like the pads of a man's fingers.

CanDee lowered her gaze. "That's where Phillip grabbed me . . . but to be fair, I bruise easily."

Slowly her head turned to him. "I just made an excuse for him, didn't I? Oh my God. I can't believe I just did that."

He'd never wanted to kill anyone as much as he wanted to kill Phillip right then. The bastard had marked her. He'd caused her pain. This was not something he could ignore. Phillip would pay for hurting her. If it was the last thing Cinco did, he'd make Phillip pay.

CHAPTER 25

At ten the next morning, CanDee rolled back on her haunches and rubbed her lower back. She'd finally finished the timeline that was spread out across the parlor floor. Usually, this was the time she liked best, when everything came together, but there were some inconsistencies.

And then there were the diary entries.

She opened the diary in question and reread the passage.

> *I know what we did was wrong, but the alternative was much worse. In a world run by men for men, legal options for women are few. Even in Texas where married women may own land, we still cannot inherit it without explicit language in the will.*

The entry was dated May 27, 1915, which was two days after the fire. CanDee picked up the photocopied obituary from the Roseville Gazette dated April 2, 1920.

MILDRED ZENETTA SLATTERY DIES AFTER A GREAT FALL

Roseville sustained the sad loss of one of its finest residents from one of the most highly respected families in the death of Mildred Zenetta

Slatter, at her home in this city. She left this world for her heavenly reward at the age of thirty, three months, and twenty-four days. Sunday evening, March twenty-first, after a joyful and very uplifting sermon by Pastor W.I. Townsend that lasted long into the night and successfully brought to Jesus Mr. Harold Alvin Jackson, Mrs. R.L. Huntington, and Mr. Elijah Rose Slattery, Miss Slattery fell while climbing the steps to her home at 127 Main Street. While the fall was not immediately fatal, it did inflict a lingering head injury of a grievous nature. Miss Slattery took to her bed and was attended in loving Christian generosity by Mrs. Henry Tinney, Miss Aldora Throckmorton, and Mrs. Josiah Genstry until her last breath around five-thirty in the afternoon of March thirtieth.

For the love of God, old obituaries were wordy and full of inconsequential detail and strangely put together. She guessed that an education in a one-room schoolhouse didn't make for Rhodes Scholars.

The funeral was held at the family home . . .

CanDee knew that in small towns funerals were held at home, but yuck. It was just hard to imagine that practice today. People tramping in her house to pay their respects to Great-Aunt Whoever propped up in the living room. She guessed that if someone asked where the bathroom was, she could tell them to take a right at the dead body and then it's two doors down on the left.

She skimmed down.

Miss Slattery was a native of Mississippi, but traveled to Roseville by wagon train at the age of two with her family to open a hotel. Her father, Mr. Edgar Buckner Slattery, along with his wife, Gertrude, opened a hotel on the corner of Main and Rosemont, which is still in operation to this day. Mr. Slattery is most known for his rescue of the infant James Lucas Karo during the well-remembered cattle stampede of aught eight. Mr. Slattery sustained many injuries during the stampede including a lingering partial paralysis of his tongue and an apoplexy of unknown origin.

CanDee rolled her eyes and skimmed to the bottom.

> Miss Slattery is survived by her sisters Mrs. S.L. Medford of Roseville and Mrs. John Ullery of San Antonio, and her parents Mr. and Mrs. Edgar Slattery of Roseville. She is also survived by her son, Elijah Rose Slattery, who thankfully came to Jesus on the very the night of Miss Slattery's fall.

So Miss Slattery had a son and wasn't married? No husband was mentioned, alive or dead. Based on this extremely long and amazingly super-uninformative obituary, CanDee was sure a husband would have been mentioned . . . a lot and in great detail.

CanDee picked up another of Edith's journals and skimmed down.

> *That Slattery woman was here again today. In her delicate condition, I feel very sorry for her, but I cannot help her. She says that the child she's carrying belongs to Deuce and while I believe it's possible, there is nothing I can do. Deuce has denounced her and Mel refuses to see her, but I cannot in all Christian generosity turn her away. Her family has insisted that she give the babe up, but she has refused. If it comes down to it, I will have her move in with us and Mel will have to accept it. I will not stand by and watch anyone be turned out of her house to live on the street.*

CanDee flipped to a few months later.

> *I have been to the Slattery house to pay my respects to the newborn baby boy. Miss Slattery seems to be in good spirits, as is her father. He seems to love and dote on the babe, which is good. Miss Slattery asked me again to speak on her behalf to Deuce and I assured her that*

I will, but he is a hard man who will not be swayed. She is young and believes herself in love with him, but I hope it will pass. Deuce cares more about whiskey and carnal pleasures and I doubt will marry again even though his Roberta passed away last December. My heart goes out to the fatherless babe. I will do what I can.

CanDee had little choice. She picked up her legal pad with the Rose family genealogy and added a box under Lacy Kendall Rose Jr. She wrote *Elijah Rose Slattery born 1910, married 1940 to Mini Thomas*, and *died 1978*. Under Elijah, she made one box for his child and wrote *Timothy Thomas Slattery born 1942, married 1980 to Lisa Marie Evans*, and that they had a son named Trent Slattery in 1981. She added a box for him.

Did the Rose family know that more than likely, they had a whole illegitimate side? She had a feeling that they didn't. In the genealogy, she couldn't leave out the connection . . . or could she? Elijah Rose Slattery was never recognized as a Rose. She needed to find proof that either he was or wasn't. She wanted her genealogy to be accurate, but she didn't want to hurt the man she loved. If her suspicions were correct, there was something even worse than the Roses' possible illegitimate side.

She rolled onto her knees, stood, and stretched her back. She walked through the kitchen to the doorframe of the summer kitchen that held the slightly faded but still legible pencil marks Edith had made at each point in Tres's life. It seemed that Edith and Mel were the doting aunts that replaced his mother even before she died. According to Edith, Roberta never recovered from the baby blues and often left Tres with her for days at a time. Edith had written many, many pages about her beautiful sweet-tempered nephew. And then things had changed when he'd turned fourteen. He'd become wild, drinking the day away instead of working. Edith had used the word *drunkard* several times and worried about him constantly. She even thought that he might be smoking opium, although she'd never seen him do it.

An incomplete thought tugged at her brain. She was missing something. Something about whiskey. Hadn't Cinco told her a story about Edith making Tres drink the rest of a bottle on his seventeenth birthday? But she commented several times about his drinking that started at age fourteen. By all appearances, Edith had been meticulous, so the inconsistences regarding Tres didn't make sense.

CanDee touched the pencil mark that read, *Tres, age 15*. It was a good foot shorter than she was. She glanced at the one three inches above it that read, *Tres, age 14*. So he'd hit a growth spurt and shot up and then he'd gotten shorter? Did that explain why he was three inches shorter after the fire? In a journal entry, Edith had been very specific about the measurements she'd taken for the new suit she was making Tres two weeks before the fire. After, she'd also written down the measurements of the new pants she was making him. CanDee scanned the doorjamb but couldn't find a measurement after Tres turned fifteen.

Was that on purpose or simply an oversight?

She walked back into the parlor and glanced at the journals. Edith didn't do oversights. She had to be the most organized woman CanDee had ever met . . . well, not met, but it felt like they'd met.

CanDee walked over to the 1915 pile of things on the timeline and picked up the photocopied article on the fire. There was a drawing of the main house as a burned-out shell and a brief article stating that a fire "of unknown origin" spread through the house, killing Lacy Kendall Rose Jr., Carlton Rose Jr., Thaddeus Bartor Rose, and Loco Hernandez, a ranch hand. It had been Christmas Eve and everyone was home for the holiday.

She needed to find out about Loco Hernandez. Maybe the ranch had some employment records?

What were the odds that the ranch would have a picture of Loco? Who was she kidding, they wouldn't have a picture of him.

She needed a way to prove or disprove her theory because the evidence she had was pointing to one horrible conclusion: Loco hadn't died in the fire, Tres had. The man who'd survived the fire and claimed to be the heir to the Texas Rose was actually a ranch hand named Loco. The inconsistences in the heights and the pictures of Tres all pointed to Loco taking Tres's place. She picked up the one of him at fourteen and set it beside his wedding photo. True, they were decades apart and one was covered with scars. Their hair color was the same, but the bone structure was different.

And it might have been Edith's idea.

CanDee scrubbed her face with her hands. She was a writer in between a ranch and a hard place. How much of this did she include? On the one hand, her clients were paying her, so she wasn't sure they'd want the story out, but on the other hand, they hired her to write their genealogy and this was part of their history. Besides, if she didn't include it, she was in some part helping to do the same thing to the Slatterys that Phillip had done to her . . . stealing something that belongs to another.

Out of ideas, she googled *Loco Hernandez*. Apparently, there was a fighter by that name and some British actor who'd been born the year that Loco had supposedly died in the fire, but no picture of a ranch hand who'd died in 1915.

If she didn't take her work so seriously, she'd just skim over Loco Hernandez and go on her way, but this was her livelihood and her reputation. Maybe the family museum would help? She closed her laptop, shoved it in her leather bag, and headed to the family museum.

After closing the front door, she glanced toward the tree where Connie was parked and—son of a bitch—she was gone. Lefty had better have car-napped Connie so he could vacuum out that glitter. She scanned the area for any sign of Connie, but there was nothing.

Sunlight winked off her golf cart and she jumped back. It had tires. She walked down the porch steps to admire the tires. It had all four. Cautiously, she approached in case it was booby trapped, but nothing gross rained down on her head, exploded, or shot out at her, so she figured the coast was clear. She sat down and waited for more glitter to burst out, but nothing did. With a prayer that the engine worked, she turned the key. The engine fired to life. She hit the gas and the golf cart took off.

Did this mean that she'd won?

Smiling to herself, she turned onto the dirt road that led to the main house and the family museum. She bumped along at a good pace, turned the corner, and could see the outline of the buildings when her golf cart coughed, belched, and died.

Stomping on the gas pedal, she expected the engine to jolt her back, but nothing happened. She turned the key to off and then turned it back on again. Nothing.

Damn it, Lefty, he'd given her back the tires and then shorted her gas. She shoved her leather bag onto her shoulder. That was fine. Two could play that game. She stared at the front of the cart but couldn't find a latch or anything, so she walked around to the back, found the latch, and popped up the little hood. While the workings of an internal combustible engine mystified her, she recognized the battery, which seemed like the best way to disable the cart long enough for her to get some gas. She wasn't giving up and she wasn't giving in and she wasn't going to take this lying down. After unhooking the battery, she picked it up and glanced around for a good hiding place. There was a copse of trees to her left with lots of brush covering the ground. She tucked the battery deep inside the brush, dusted off her hands, straightened the skirt of her dark green T-shirt dress, and held her head high as her sandals slapped the dirt road on her walk to the museum.

By the time she stepped into the museum, found the air conditioner control panel, and switched it on to high, she was dusty and had sweat rings under her arms.

"Where in the holy hell did you put my golf cart battery?" Lefty crossed his arms in the doorway.

"Where in the hell did you put my gas?" She grinned. "And she's my golf cart. Her name is Rita."

"Her name ain't Rita, it's Penelope, and she don't like you." Lefty continued to stare at her. "You okay?"

He was talking about yesterday. "I'm fine. Better than fine."

"Good to hear." He turned around to go.

"Do you know anything about a ranch hand named Loco Hernandez?"

Lefty froze and the look of horror on his face was almost comical. "No."

It was her turn to cross her arms. "You're a terrible liar."

"Am not." He looked honestly offended. "I'm a wonderful liar."

"Tell me about Loco Hernandez." She was being pushy, but she needed to know the truth.

He took a deep breath and shook his head. "I can't. The Rose family has been good to me. They picked me up, dusted me off, and made me part of the family. I ain't gonna betray that." He held her gaze for several seconds. "I can't."

"So it's true." She swayed a little and put a hand out to the wall to steady herself. This was major and could potentially ruin the Texas Rose Ranch.

"Yes." His voice was a choked whisper.

This was bad. While her mind had known that Tres was really Loco, her heart hadn't believed it until now. She shook her head. "What do I do?"

He walked to her and took her hand. "I got no idea."

Recently, she'd been leading with her head and now it was time to follow her heart. Her career as a genealogist wasn't as important to her as Cinco. Besides, who was actually going to read the damn book anyway, so who would know that she'd left out a fairly significant detail like, oh, um, say, the ranch actually didn't belong to the Rose family.

"I'm going to pretend that Loco really was Tres." The words felt heavy in her mouth.

"I'd say that was the easy way out and I'm not sure you're one for easy street." He led her to the chair and nodded for her to sit down. "Tres was like a father to me, nicest man you'd ever meet. Give you the shirt off his back if he saw you needed it."

He smiled, lost in memory. "My little boy had just died. He was two . . . name was Jimmy. My ex was drinking and got behind the wheel—killed herself and Jimmy. I drowned my grief with the bottle." He shook his head. "Whole chunks of time I can't remember. I don't even know how I got to Fredericksburg, but I ended up behind the wheel of my old Chevy Apache pickup. I didn't know who I was or where I was, but I was going somewhere. This was before drinking and driving was against the law. I pulled onto the highway and crashed into Tres's pickup truck. No one got hurt but our trucks was all messed up. I stumbled out of my truck looking for a fight. I saw them scars on his face and hesitated. Tres just looked at me and said, 'You look like a man who needs a second chance. We all have scars. Yours are on the inside.' He drove me to the ranch and I've been here ever since."

"Why are you telling me this?" Not that it wasn't nice, but it did seem out of character.

"Because I want you to know who Tres Rose was. He weren't just some name on a piece of paper, he was a man who saw the good in everyone. Whether he was born into the Rose family or not, he loved this land and the ranch was better for it." He smiled sadly. "You're a good person, and leaving out a big thing like this is going to weigh on you. I just thought it would make it easier to know that he was more of a Rose than the man whose place he took. Miss Edith didn't have the best of things to say about her nephew."

CanDee sat up. "You knew Edith?"

"Yes. She died a year after I come to live here. She was feisty as hell. Kind of like you." He pointed to her. "She and Mel were quite a pair.

Always picking at each other in the way that some old married couples do, but there was love there. Mel was lost after Miss Edith passed. It was hard to watch."

"I would have loved to have met her . . . well, both of them." CanDee felt like she already knew them.

"Miss Edith was a fine lady. Always had her hair done and her dresses were pressed. She loved to cook and made homemade birthday cakes for everyone on the ranch. She was the type of lady who smiled and remembered your name, but if you got mud on her floor, she would give you so much hell that you'd get all teary eyed." Lefty had loved Edith, that much was evident.

CanDee put her hand on his. "Thanks. I'm going to leave it out. I can't stand the thought of the Texas Rose not being owned and cared for by the Rose family." It wasn't only because she loved Cinco that she would omit such a huge detail, it was because she loved Edith and Mel and in some way respected their wishes. More than any other place, this ranch felt like home. Generations of blood, sweat, and tears shed by the Roses and, well, Hernandezes on this ranch and the tender, loving care they took of the land and livestock would all be for nothing if the ranch changed hands. If she told the truth, she'd be dishonoring the past instead of honoring a rich Texas legacy.

She didn't have any other choice. Edith and Mel had done the right thing and she refused to undo their work.

CHAPTER 26

"Is this a bad time?" Cinco saw CanDee and Lefty holding hands. Based on his history, this little domestic scene should unnerve him, but he knew that Lefty and CanDee holding hands likely meant they were arm-wrestling or one of them had that buzzer handshake thing that shocked people.

They dropped their hands and turned around.

He saw no guilt—not that he was looking for it, but it was nice there wasn't any.

"I was just telling the hellcat about Miss Edith." Lefty shook his head and then nodded at CanDee. "She's so much like her."

"Thank you." CanDee grinned. "Edith's pretty high on my list of dead people I'd love to have dinner with."

"She's dead. That gross." Lefty waved. "Gotta go. I got an engine up on blocks and I gotta figure out why she ain't working."

"How about you look at it after you fill Rita up with gas?" CanDee leaned down and kissed the old man on the cheek. "You may find that your life works better if I have gas and tires . . . at the same time."

"My life's just fine the way it is." His faded brown eye gleamed. He shuffled out of the front door.

"He gave me back my tires but shorted my gas." CanDee grinned. "Tonight, I'm going to rearrange his tools. I can't wait."

She practically vibrated with excitement.

"Your relationship with Lefty is interesting." He slid his arms around her and pulled her in tight. He'd missed her today. Not stopping by for lunch because he had a long call from his attorney had made him mad and surly this afternoon.

Today, Cinco had filed a suit against Phillip Harcourt on her behalf. Now all he had to do was tell her. He opened his mouth to spill, but nothing came out.

"So, I was thinking that we could make French bread pizzas out of the stale French bread I bought the other day. Sound good to you?" Her voice was muffled because her face was tucked into his shoulder.

"That sounds perfect." This was what he'd always wanted—she was the life he wanted. Just standing here holding her soothed his bad day away. He could do this forever.

Unfortunately, they needed to talk about life after she finished her book, but he wasn't a hundred percent certain if that would go in his favor. He didn't doubt that CanDee loved him, but asking her to move down here permanently was altogether different. While she loved the ranch, he had no idea if she wanted to make it her home.

"How's the genealogy coming along?" He decided to start off slowly.

Under his hands, she stiffened.

Something was definitely not right.

"Good . . . fine." Her voice was overly bright. "I had no idea that Lefty knew Edith."

"Apparently she loved nothing more than a second-chance story." With her head rested on his shoulder, he was disposed to think that right now all was good and kind in the world. "I don't know the story, but I think he was an alcoholic."

"He told me that after his son died, he tried to drink the grief away." She patted Cinco on the back, loosened her hold, and stepped back.

"Lefty had a son? I never knew the particulars." Clearly Lefty really liked CanDee and had confided in her. To his knowledge, the old man hadn't disclosed that information to any of Cinco's immediate family.

She shifted from foot to foot. She was acting strange.

"Something wrong?" Cinco's hands balled into fists. Had Phillip tried contacting her again?

"Yes and no. I've run into a little snafu with the genealogy." She sucked in her lower lip. "Are there any more family pictures anywhere?"

Good, it was just the book and nothing major.

"Maybe. When I was a kid, my grandmother, Susie, showed me a huge brown Kirby vacuum cleaner box full of old photos. I haven't thought of it in years. Maybe it's in my parents' attic or even here?" He pointed to the ceiling.

"You Roses sure do like attic space." She glanced at the ceiling and the smallest glimmer of anticipation sparkled in her eyes.

He looked around until he found the trapdoor in the ceiling. It was close to the front door. "Let's see if there's a fold-down ladder."

He grabbed a chair, positioned it under the trapdoor, and climbed up. There wasn't a string hanging down, which made him think that there wasn't a ladder. A small brass drawer pull served as the opener and he felt the weight in his hands. He yanked and the attached door with a small wooden ladder attached squeaked open. He jumped down and extended the ladder.

CanDee grabbed the ladder and stepped on the first rung, but he put a hand on her shoulder. "Me first. I don't know how safe this is and I don't know what's up there. Plus, you probably have on tiny underwear and that would distract me."

"I've never met a man more interested in my undergarments." A sexy smile curled on her lips. "I'll just wait down here and watch your ass in those tight jeans."

"My jeans aren't tight." He tried to look behind himself and did the whole dog-chasing-its-tail routine.

"You know, you have a great ass and I'm so glad your jeans are molded to the fine piece of work." She smacked it lightly.

He knew he was wearing a stupid grin, but he couldn't help it. She liked his backside. He knew that she loved him, but it certainly was a boost to the old ego that she liked the look of his body. With an exaggerated hip shake, he stuck his boot on the first rung and tested it. It held his weight. He tried the next one and his foot didn't fall through so he tried the next one and the next until he made it to the top. With one hand holding on to the ladder, he felt around with the other hand for a light switch. After some flailing, he finally found it and flicked the switch. Mainly this was a cavernous open space of nothingness, except for a few boxes stacked in a corner.

"There are some boxes. I'll get them and hand them down to you," he called over his shoulder. He had no idea what could be in the boxes. They kept the ranch files and paperwork in a storage building, so it couldn't be ranch business.

Careful to only step on the wooden rafters, he made his way to the left back corner of the attic. One by one, he brought three boxes to the trapdoor opening.

"I'm going to hand them down to you one at a time," he called down to her. He eyed the V-neck of her dress and grinned. "From up here, I can see down your dress . . . nice."

"Goodness me, it's hot in here." She pulled her neckline out. "Does that give you a better view?"

"Yes, ma'am. Are you going to show me more of that red bra later?" Not only was he in love with CanDee, but he really liked her too. Even digging around in a stifling hot attic with her was fun.

After handing her the boxes, he folded up the ladder and closed the trapdoor.

"I think we struck out." She tossed a deflated football in the air and caught it. "Unless you want me to include your dad's old football trophies, a very extensive baseball card collection, or a turntable and some speakers that might have been the height of technology when Ronald Reagan was president, I don't see anything of historical value."

"Trophies?" He went over to the box and sure enough, there were lots of football trophies, ranging from peewee to high school. "I'm sure he'll be happy to get these back. My mother won't. She's probably the one who put them up here in the first place."

"Should we just quietly put them back and forget we ever found them?" CanDee folded the flaps of the box back in.

"No, I think he'll want them. He has an office and I'm sure he can sweet-talk my mother into letting him display them there." Now that he had what his parents had, he understood a little more how their relationship worked. Love based on mutual respect and affection was something beautiful. He hadn't had that solid foundation with Naomi.

"Why are you smiling?" She glanced down at the boxes like she couldn't see what was making him happy.

"Because I love you and that makes me smile." He slid a hand around her waist and pulled her into him.

"You're not getting sappy on me, are you?" She gave him a big smacking kiss on the lips. "Because I like it and I love that you love me."

"I love that you love that I love you." He returned the smacking kiss.

Gagging noises came from the doorway. "You two are so sweet that my blood sugar just spiked."

It was Rowdy.

"You're just jealous because all you have to keep you warm at night is Elvis." Cinco grinned.

"Elvis Presley?" CanDee glanced up at Cinco.

"No, my basset hound," Rowdy said. "I named him Elvis because he looks like the King of Rock and Roll in the fat years after a two-day bender. Cinco's just jealous because Elvis hates him. He started out as

Cinco's puppy, but once he met me, he packed up his dog toys and moved to my house." Rowdy hunched his shoulders. "What can you do? The dog clearly has taste."

"Taste, my ass. That dog is psycho and has a stupid name. When he was mine, his name was Merle. That's a perfectly good basset hound name."

"Not according to Elvis." Rowdy glanced down at the boxes. "Found some more moldy old records that just make your little hearts go pitter-pat?"

"Don't make me kill you in front of company. Mom would be so mad." Cinco slid his hand down to CanDee's lower back. "Did you come in here just to piss me off or did you have a real reason?"

"So much hostility. Where's the love?" He looked at CanDee. "He's so negative. It just breaks my heart."

"Are you almost done?" Cinco made a big show of checking his watch. His brother was one of the most infuriating people on planet earth. He was pretty sure even Mother Teresa would have lost her patience with him.

"I just came to see if her cousin found CanDee." Rowdy nodded in the direction of the cottage. "I saw him knocking on the door and sent him to your place." He waggled his eyebrows. "I told him that you were hot and heavy with my big bro."

"Cousin?" Her brows scrunched up. "I don't have any cousins. Both of my parents were only children."

The hair on the back of Cinco's neck stood up. "What did he look like?"

"Um . . . I don't know. Tall, blond, average looking. He drove a sweet red Boxster Spyder." He looked from Cinco to CanDee and back to Cinco. "I don't understand."

"Phillip." CanDee shook her head like she just didn't believe it. "He really must need the next book badly."

"I think it's restraining-order time." Her ex was stalking her and Cinco wasn't about to stand for it. The worried look on her face made him want to use her ex as a speed bump.

CanDee was as tense as a baling wire.

She opened her mouth to argue and then closed it. "He's getting desperate."

"Who's Phillip?" Rowdy went into protection mode. Cinco's little brother wouldn't let anyone mess with his family and clearly, he thought of CanDee as family. Cinco'd never loved his brother more.

"My ex-boyfriend." She dropped her gaze to the floor like she was ashamed.

Cinco pulled her in closer. It tore him up. This was not her fault.

"Was he the guy Lefty punched at Cranky Frank's?" Rowdy's brow flattened . . . yep, he was itching to mix it up.

"Yes." Cinco should have told his family about CanDee's ex, but he thought Lefty had taken care of the problem. Phillip had balls to show his face on Rose property.

One of Rowdy's eyebrows arched and he shot Cinco a look. "Let's go see if he's still around here somewhere."

It wasn't a question but an order. Rowdy may have been a pain in the ass, but there was no one more loyal. If someone messed with his family, he was ruthless.

"That is an excellent idea." Cinco could feel a nice rage simmering through his body. His hand dropped from CanDee's waist and he kissed her lightly on the forehead. "Go to the main house, find my dad, and tell him what's going on. Stay there. I'll come and get you after I've made sure that he's gone."

He didn't give her a chance to argue. He nodded to his younger brother and then stepped out into the sunny spring afternoon.

CHAPTER 27

CanDee hated that everyone was going to so much trouble just for her. After lunch the next day, she sat in the parlor, alone—finally—as Cinco had reluctantly left her to go to work.

He, his father, and his brothers had organized the ranch hands into roving patrols. The guards manning the front gate where tourists gathered for ranch tours were on the lookout for Phillip, and she was in the process of filing a restraining order against him. This had all happened in the last twenty-four hours.

There was a knock at the front door and she glanced out the parlor window. The twins, Dallas and Worth, stood side by side. The one on the left held a plastic-wrap-covered plate out in front of him.

She opened the front door.

"We just wanted to drop by and tell you that everything's going to be okay." The twin on the right grinned and then pointed to the plate his brother was holding. "Worth made you some cookies."

Worth smiled shyly and extended the plate. "I thought these might cheer you up."

She wasn't particularly depressed but it was nice that Cinco's family had rallied around her. So this was what it was like to have brothers? It was awesome. Anyone who wanted to bring her cookies was good people.

She took the plate. "Thank you so much. I love cookies. Come in and we'll see if we can scare up some milk to go with them."

"Well, I don't mind if I do." The twin that she now knew to be Dallas stepped inside.

Worth followed and she closed the front door.

"I know I bought some milk the other day—"

"We have an unauthorized black sedan at the quarry." The voice was male and came from the vicinity of Worth's front left jeans pocket.

He pulled out a walkie-talkie, held it to his mouth, and pressed the button on the side. "Say again."

"There is a black sedan parked behind the shed at the quarry. I can't see who's inside." The voice was male, but she had no idea who it belonged to.

Worth depressed the button. "Okay, we'll be right there."

"Rain check." Dallas held his hand out for her to shake.

"Anytime." She took it and pumped once.

The walkie-talkie buzzed and then the man said, "Want me to go into the explosives locker and grab some ANFO and blow up the car?"

Dallas and Worth shared a look.

Worth pressed the button. "Um . . . no. I don't want you to blow up anything. No aluminum nitrate–fuel oil. Got that? No ANFO."

Dallas shook his head. "Marshy's new and a little overzealous. This is his first manhunt. We'd better go."

"I think that would be best." Manhunt? The Roses took her security very seriously. Not only did she feel safe, but cared for too. "Thanks for the cookies."

He turned on his heel and headed for the door.

Worth nodded, tipped an imaginary hat, and followed his brother out the front door.

Back in the parlor, she set the cookies down on the coffee table and picked up her laptop and then opened it. Maybe some work on her novel would clear her mind enough so she could tackle the genealogy outline or even a synopsis. Absently, she clicked on her email.

Fifteen items were currently unread in her inbox. Starting from the top, she deleted emails. Once she'd deleted everything from Groupon, LivingSocial, and all of the Yahoo! Groups to which she belonged but didn't actually participate in, there were only five emails remaining. She really needed to unsubscribe from things she didn't read. Of the five she recognized four of the email addresses, but the fifth one was a mystery. The title was blank. She clicked on it.

> I know your little secret. Meet me today at three at Java Ranch in Fredericksburg or I go to the media and the whole world finds out that the Texas Rose Ranch doesn't belong to the Roses.
>
> P.

She reread it two more times just to make sure that what she was reading was right. Holy crap. How could Phillip know about the ranch? She rubbed the tense muscles in the back of her neck. So it was going to be the ranch for her next book. What about the next one and the next one? How long would he hold Cinco's legacy over her head?

Forever.

And she'd give Phillip the next book and the next one and the one after that because she loved Cinco and the ranch was his life. Complete helplessness saturated her soul. If she went to Cinco, he'd tell her to call Phillip's bluff, but she knew that her ex wasn't bluffing. He'd do whatever it took to keep himself on top and if that meant hurting people, all the better.

This was an impossible situation. Man, she went from one impossible situation to another. She checked the clock on her computer. It was almost two now. She'd have to leave soon in order to meet Phillip.

Someone knocked on the front door and CanDee jumped about a foot in the air. Like a spy hoarding state secrets, she slammed her laptop closed and tossed it on the sofa beside her. She stood and went to answer the banging on the door.

After peeking out of the window next to the door and finding Lefty, she pulled open the front door.

"I fixed the door lock on your car and got you a new key." He handed her a car key rimmed in black plastic. He scanned her face. "What's wrong?"

Absently, she took the key. "Nothing. I've got to go."

"Something ain't right." Lefty intentionally blocked her way. "You look scared."

"Nothing . . . I'm good." She didn't want to slam the door in his face, but she needed to get out of here soon. Where was her purse? She looked around. Oh yeah, the parlor. Not intentionally meaning to be rude, she turned on her heel and walked back to the parlor.

"The hell something ain't wrong." Lefty followed her into the parlor.

"I've got to go. I need to meet . . . someone in Fredericksburg at three." She grabbed her purse and headed back to the open front door.

"I'm going with you and you can tell me what's going on in the car." He stepped to the side and let her go first out the front door. He followed her and then shut it.

"I'm good—"

"Either we ride together, or I'm going to follow you. I'm good either way." He shot her a look that said this was nonnegotiable.

"Fine." She rolled her eyes and as she walked to her car. "You're a pain in the ass."

"I try." He marched past her and opened the -passenger-side door for her.

"I'm driving." It was her car.

"The hell you are." As though he realized that good manners were about to cost him the driver's seat, he shot to the other side of the car. "I ain't never ridden in no car with a woman where I wasn't driving."

He practically knocked her out of the way and jumped in the driver's seat. He was fast, she'd give him that. He grinned as he slammed the driver-side door.

"Damn it." She stomped to the passenger side and got in. "You're such a pain in my ass."

She leaned over and shoved the key into the ignition.

"You're starting to repeat yourself." He shoved the key into the ignition and the engine turned over. "Now, tell me who we're meeting and why."

He backed out of the yard and pulled onto the dirt road that led to the main house.

She told him about her first book and what Phillip wanted now. By the time they passed into the Fredericksburg city limits, they had a plan. Lefty dropped her off a block from Java Ranch.

She checked the clock on her phone . . . she had two minutes. She slipped her phone into the right pocket of her dress and walked at a brisk pace to Java Ranch. She pulled open the glass and wooden front door and found Phillip sitting at a table right in front by the coffee station. He wasn't even smart enough to conduct his illicit business at a back table.

She took two deep breaths and walked to him. Angry nerves rattled through her. If she could just stick to the plan, she'd be rid of him forever.

He looked up from his laptop and she noticed that he was wearing a turtleneck, no doubt to hide the nasty bruise on his throat Lefty had given him the other day.

"Sit." He ground out the word.

She huffed out a sigh and pulled out the chair across from him.

"I took the liberty of ordering you a latte." His eyes were mean, but he kept a smile on his face and his voice to a whisper so that the rest of the world saw only a nice man buying a lady a cup of coffee.

She hated lattes, but he loved them so that was all that mattered to him. To her, coffee should be black and hot and strong enough to tar a roof. "So civilized. Why don't you cut the crap and let's get down to business."

"You want to get down to business, fine by me. My lawyer just emailed me." His hand covered hers and his short nails bit into the back of her hand. "You bitch."

Cinco was going to see his lawyer today. It appeared that everyone had an attorney but her.

"You think you can sue me and get away with it?" Phillip's whisper was cold as ice. "You're nothing without me."

"I don't know what you're talking about. I've never sued anyone . . . ever." She tried to pull her hand away, but he held tight. "Let go of my hand or so help me God, I'll walk out of here."

She was tired of being bullied. No one was ever going to bully her again.

Phillip's mouth twisted in a vicious grin, and he didn't release her hand. "You were so much more fun when we were together. I don't like the new you."

"I'll take that as a compliment." She didn't know if she bought into that whole load of crap about bullies really being scared and insecure. This bully was just an asshole.

"How's the book coming? Is it finished?" Phillip had changed into congenial-friend mode.

Psycho much?

"Second draft is done." She couldn't believe that she was about to give up her dream . . . again.

"Adrian is the killer?" His eyebrows raised.

"No, Mandrell." This was a conversation she'd never foreseen happening.

"Damn, I didn't see that coming." He nodded.

"Of course you didn't. You can't write yourself out of a paper sack, much less a novel that anyone wants to read." The only way to get what she needed was to piss him off.

His eyes turned mean again as he grinned up at her.

"We both know that I'm the brains. I took your pathetic story and turned it into a best seller. Without me, *Murder, Mayhem, and Madness* was a rambling pile of horseshit and you know it." How he was able to keep the smile on his face and his voice low enough that only she could hear it was proof that he was crazy.

"So that's why you're blackmailing me into giving you the next one . . . because I can't write? The saddest part of this whole thing is that you truly believe that you're talented. It's just so pathetic." While she really didn't need to lay things on quite so thick, payback was a bitch and she was enjoying this immensely.

Every muscle in Phillip's body tightened and he gritted his teeth so hard she wondered if he'd grind his teeth to dust. "You . . . I am . . . I'm so much better . . ."

Outside, brakes squealed and then a horn honked, drowning out whatever he'd said.

"You can't even create full sentences. I believe that you're actually getting worse." She leaned into him and mirrored the hatred seething in his eyes. "Here's the deal. You will email me right now confessing that you stole my first book and that you're blackmailing me for the second. After I get that email"—she pointed to her smartphone, which was facedown on the table—"I'll send you the manuscript. If you ever try to contact me again for any reason or if you go to the press about the Texas Rose Ranch, I'll go directly to your publisher with the email."

"You bitch . . . you can't do this to me." His hands were shaking with rage.

"Watch me." She sat back and smiled. "I'm guessing you've already spent the advance they gave you for the second book? It would be real shame for them to demand their money back when they find out that I wrote both books. Just think, you'd have to go back to mooching off women to live, or worse, you'd have to get a job, and everyone who worships you now will know that you're nothing."

His face was turning a nice shade of mad. Bullying the bully was a hell of a lot of fun.

He knew he was backed into a corner so he turned back to his laptop and typed. A few seconds later, her phone dinged with a new email. She picked up her phone, pulled up the email.

Murder, Mayhem, and Madness was written by CanDee McCain and myself. She is giving me her next book of her free will.

"Do you think I'm an idiot?" She made to get up. "I'm out of here."

Her stomach dropped to her knees. She was calling his bluff and unfortunately the Texas Rose stood in the balance.

"Fine." He banged on the keyboard and a couple of seconds later, she got a new email.

Murder, Mayhem, and Madness was written by CanDee McCain and I took the manuscript without her knowledge or consent. She is giving me the rights to her next book—title unknown—of her own free will.

"That's all you're going to get from me." He closed his laptop and laced his fingers together on top. "Take it or leave it. Just remember, your boyfriend's ranch is at stake."

"Here you go." She picked up her phone and forwarded a copy of the outline she'd emailed to herself on the way here. She wasn't sending him the finished product. He could fend for himself . . . or not . . . either way, she didn't care.

She stood as his phone buzzed, and walked to the door.

"This is only the outline." He called after her.

"I know. I wrote the last one; this time you're on your own." She stepped out into the afternoon sunshine and smiled. She was rid of Phillip. It had cost her the publishing rights to her book, which made her a little sick to her stomach, but she loved Cinco and had saved his home.

Now that she saw Phillip for who he really was—a spineless asshole—she knew without a shadow of a doubt that he wouldn't come after Cinco's family. He wanted to stay on top for as long as he could, and now that she had leverage, he'd back off.

Without the weight of Phillip holding her down, she was ready to take the next step in her life. She wanted to marry Cinco and have some babies. It was quick, but it was right. They were meant to be together.

Someday soon—after she worked up the nerve—she'd shock the hell out of him by doing the asking. She couldn't wait to see the look on his face.

Cinco stood outside of the Java Ranch and stared at the cozy scene unfolding before him. From across the street, he'd seen CanDee walk in, so he'd jaywalked to have coffee with her, but she'd sat across from Phillip.

Right now, the man's hand was covering hers and he was smiling up at her.

Cinco waited for her to jump up and storm out, but she just sat there. His heart twisted in his chest. She didn't seem to be angry or surprised to find her ex. In fact, it looked like they had a date.

This didn't make sense. She loved Cinco, but she had a date with her ex? She didn't like Phillip and was scared of him. Only she didn't look scared right now.

That niggling sensation in the pit of his stomach that he'd ignored reared its ugly head. This situation had shades of Naomi. She'd met with plenty of men behind his back. But CanDee wasn't Naomi and she wouldn't do that. Only she was meeting with Phillip and she certainly hadn't mentioned it to Cinco. There were tons of reasons that she could be meeting with her ex, but off the top of his head, he couldn't think of one.

His gaze stayed on CanDee. She leaned closer to Phillip and said something that made him smile.

Cinco could actually feel his heart break. He couldn't watch anymore. He turned around, walked across the street, got into his truck, and started the engine. He pulled into traffic and someone slammed on their brakes and honked their horn at him. He could have cared less.

CanDee was meeting Phillip of her own free will. Why would she do that? He turned onto Highway 87 and headed home. Were they getting back together? His heart screamed no, but his head couldn't deny what he'd seen.

She loved Cinco, she'd told him so . . . but then, why meet her ex?

It was likely something innocent, he reasoned with himself. Maybe some unfinished business? If this man really had cost her everything, then why meet with him? Especially after she'd been so rattled by seeing him at Cranky's.

And why hadn't she mentioned her meeting with him? Cinco would have been happy to go with her. Hell, they'd spent the morning and some of the afternoon together. Now that he thought about it, she must have left right after he did.

None of this made sense. There was probably a perfectly good explanation for this and he needed to let her explain. That was it—he wouldn't pass judgment until he'd heard her side of the story. He hit the phone button on the control panel, pulled up his recent call history, touched her number, and hit call.

Her phone went straight to voicemail. So she'd turned her phone off. Why would she do that?

He wanted this to be something innocent. More than anything, he wanted that to be the case, but things weren't adding up.

Through the car's speakers, his phone rang. He checked the number. It was CanDee. See, here she was calling to explain.

He hit answer. "Hello."

Relief flooded his system.

"Hi there. I saw that you called. Sorry, I was on the phone." She sounded so happy.

Okay, it was possible that she'd taken a call while she was meeting with Phillip, or maybe she'd left him and then had taken a call. It could happen.

"No problem. Where are you?" He could turn around and meet her for coffee. True, she'd already had coffee, but he could meet her for more coffee and then she could tell him in person why she was meeting her ex.

"I'm on my way to the library in Fredericksburg and then I need something from Walmart. Need anything?" She sounded overly bright and cheerful. Naomi did that when she was lying.

All of the air went out of his lungs. "No, I'm good, thanks."

CanDee was lying. Rage tinted with heartache pounded through his system. He couldn't stand the lying. Not again . . . not with CanDee. She knew how important honesty was to him.

"Okay, well, I'm almost there. I need to go. I love you."

"Goodbye." He pressed end.

If she lied about meeting Phillip, was she lying about having feelings for him? Once a liar, always a liar. At least, that had been his experience. But CanDee should have the chance to explain her side of the story. He wasn't passing judgment until he'd heard her side.

CHAPTER 28

Two days later when she still hadn't mentioned her meeting with Phillip, Cinco knew that she was hiding something. He cut another piece of steak, brought it to his mouth, and chewed. Dinner, just like lunch, had been heavy with silence.

Waiting for her to confess was killing him. Yesterday, he'd picked a fight with her over something that he couldn't even remember. The makeup sex had been fantastic, but then again, that had never been their problem.

CanDee liked to use sex as a way to avoid talking about serious things. Just when he'd thought he'd gotten her to open up, she was keeping something from him.

He couldn't take it anymore. "Why did you lie to me about being at the library when you were really meeting with Phillip?"

Her mouth fell open. Thank God she'd just finished swallowing or macerated steak would have fallen out. "I'm sorry."

She'd been caught in a lie and she knew it. Naomi had always started by apologizing. At first it had worked, but after a while, he'd been able to see it for what it was worth . . . a hollow word that meant nothing.

Slowly, CanDee picked up her napkin and wiped her mouth. She looked up and caught his eye. She wasn't a coward, he'd give her that. "I agreed to give him my novel."

If she'd slapped him, he couldn't have been more stunned. "Why?"

She rubbed the muscles at the back of her neck. "It's complicated."

"Since you think I'm an idiot, uncomplicate it for me." He wasn't shouting, but he was using his outside voice.

She sat back and crossed her arms. "Don't take that tone with me. No one's pushing me around again . . . ever."

Following her lead, he slowly wiped his mouth and gathered himself. "I'm trying to rein in my temper, but when you lie to me, it pisses me off. You know that honesty is my deal breaker."

"Really? Honesty? And you've been completely honest with me?" Her condescending tone was making it hard to keep calm. "How about the lawsuit you filed against Phillip in my name?"

It was his turn for his mouth to fall open. He stared at her. Okay, so he hadn't remembered to tell her. That was different than intentionally lying. "Is that what you were discussing at your intimate little coffee date the other day?"

She took two deep, frustrated breaths. "No, as a matter of fact, I was negotiating his leaving me the hell alone forever. I bought him off with my manuscript, but I now have leverage against him, so it will be the last thing he takes from me." She tossed her napkin on the table. "I need for you to drop the lawsuit. I'm giving him the rights to the books."

He was missing something because he hadn't figured her for a coward. "Why?"

"So he'll leave us alone." She dropped her gaze. Again with the lies.

"Stop lying." Was she intentionally trying to hurt him?

She closed her eyes and sucked on the inside of her cheek like she was gathering herself. When she opened her eyes, they were hazy with tears.

Immediately, he felt like an ass, and then he wanted to kick himself for feeling like an ass. Naomi had used tears to control him.

CanDee swiped at them. "I found some things out about the Texas Rose—Phillip must have overheard me talking about them with Lefty."

Women. They were frustrating as hell. He folded his hands in his lap and refused to go to her. He wanted the truth, damn it, and he'd have it. He was done begging for forgiveness for things he hadn't done. "What are you talking about?"

With the back of her hand, she wiped more tears away. At least she didn't make a big production out of them like Naomi had. "Phillip overheard Lefty and me talking about your grandfather, Tres. The man who survived the fire wasn't your biological grandfather, it was Loco Hernandez, a ranch hand. After the fire, the ranch should have gone to Deuce's biological son, Elijah Rose Slattery."

"What?" Something clicked in his brain. "That's why they paid off the Slatterys." He stared at her, trying to make sense of everything. "As a child, I remember overhearing an argument between my grandfather and my father. It's the one and only time I've ever heard my father cuss. He said something like 'Damn it, Dad. You don't always have to do the right thing. You didn't do anything wrong.'"

Her eyes narrowed. "So, I gave that bastard my book for nothing?"

The pieces were beginning to fall into place. He was out of the chair and kneeling in front of her. "Phillip blackmailed you . . . didn't he?"

"Yes." She nodded. "I lied about where I was because I thought I was saving the family ranch. If I'd told you I'd met with Phillip, you would've wanted to know why. Since I didn't think you knew about your grandfather, I didn't tell you. It turns out that it was all for nothing."

Cinco wanted to kick his own ass. He hadn't seen a little cozy coffee date, he'd seen the woman he loved and who loved him bargain with the only thing she had left because she thought he might lose his home.

"I am such an ass." He wanted to touch her, to hold her . . . but he didn't feel like he had the right.

"And I'm an idiot, so we make a good pair." She just sat there and didn't reach for him.

Had he screwed things up so badly that things would never be the same again?

"Can you forgive me for not trusting you?" He should have trusted her. She wasn't Naomi and had never given him any reason to believe that she was anything like his ex. "I'm so sorry."

It seemed like too little, but hopefully it wasn't too late.

"Can you forgive me for not trusting you enough to mention what I'd found out about the ranch? I fell in love with you and your family and I couldn't stand the thought of being the person who took the Texas Rose from you." Her hands remained on the arms of the chair. "I'm sorry."

"You have nothing to be sorry for . . . let's just agree on honesty from now on." He sat back on his heels. "Will . . ." His voice cracked. He cleared his throat. "Will you let me touch you?"

With her right index finger, she reached out and pressed it lightly into his kneecap.

"Touched you first." She grinned. "I love you."

This was it. This was the moment. His father had told him that he would know and this was it.

"Wait, stay right there." He practically jumped up and ran to the pantry. Where the hell was the damn oatmeal box? He moved bottles, canisters, and boxes of things out of the way until he found that red, white, and blue cylinder of dry oats. "Got it."

"God, I hope you're looking for the chocolate syrup so we can have some crazy makeup sex right here on the kitchen floor. Since it hasn't been mopped since I've been here, I call top," she said from the kitchen table.

He hauled the oats to the kitchen island, ripped the top off, and upended the oats into a mountain on the granite.

"I can't imagine what you plan on doing with those, but I'm willing to give you some creative license just as long as it doesn't involve me eating them. I mean, I guess I can choke some down in, say, an oatmeal cookie, but other than that, whatever oat fantasy you have may not come true." She leaned forward to get a better look at what he was doing. She stood.

"Sit." Cinco pointed to her chair. "I'll be right with you."

He sifted through the oats until he found the plastic sandwich bag that held the most precious thing he owned. He shook the oats off and pulled the bag open. Inside was the ring that he hoped CanDee would accept.

He hooked the ring around his left pinky finger and tossed the bag on the island. With the ring behind his back, he knelt in front of CanDee.

"What are you doing?" She tried to look over his shoulder. "What's behind your back?"

"Nothing. Just wait and see." It occurred to him that he should be nervous, but he wasn't. This not only felt right, but it felt like he was finally starting the life he was meant to have. He looked her straight in the eyes. "I know this isn't the most romantic place, but it feels right. Will you marry—"

"Wait a minute." She slid down from the chair and knelt in front of him. Her eyes were huge. "Are you proposing to me?"

Nerves just about swallowed him whole. "I was thinking about it."

"Well, stop." She was completely serious. "I'd decided a couple of days ago that I wanted to propose to you. You can't propose to me first."

"Yes, I can." He actually wondered if someone could die from happiness. "Do you have a ring for me?"

"No." She tried to look over his shoulder again. "Do you?"

He grinned as he brought the wide, heavy gold band around from behind his back. "I do."

He held it out for her. "CanDee McCain, will you marry me?"

She stared down at the ring. "It was Edith's, wasn't it?"

She'd made the connection before he'd gotten a chance to tell her. "Yes. Mel had it made for her."

He held it up so she could read the inscription. "*Forever.*"

She mouthed the word and the tears started up again. She nodded.

"So?" He needed to hear her say yes.

She launched herself at him as her head bobbled up and down. "Yes, damn it. I'll marry you. But for the record, I thought of it first."

"Not true. I knew you were the one for me when you climbed on my back in the lookout tower." A lifetime wouldn't be enough with CanDee, but forever sounded just right.

"Isn't that when you discovered my thong underwear?" She held her finger out for him to slide on the ring.

"That had nothing to do with it. Your choice of undergarments was just icing on the cake." He slid the heavy gold band on her left index finger. "I figure we can take a trip to San Antonio to pick out your engagement ring."

Edith's ring was way too big.

"It's huge." She closed her fingers to keep the ring on. "Edith had enormous fingers."

"We can have it sized down for you." His father was right. He'd remember this moment for the rest of his life.

"So you keep your valuables in dry food. Good to know." She grinned. "If a bracelet falls out of the macaroni and cheese, I call dibs."

"I love you." He kissed a tear rolling down her cheek.

"I loved you first." She cupped his face and brought it to hers.

"I love you forever." He kissed her tenderly on the mouth.

A cool breeze wafted across his cheek and he could swear he smelled roses. If he didn't know any better, he'd say that Edith had just given them her blessing.

ACKNOWLEDGMENTS

I would like to thank all of my fans. Your emails keep me writing. Thank you to Jane Myers Perrine for helping me plot out this book and for always finding the easiest way to fix the giant messes that I create. Thank you to Marlena Faulkner for offering to do my Myers-Briggs assessment. It's good to identify the crazy. I'm so glad we're friends. Thank you to Emily McKay, who brings calm to my life. Thank you to Catherine Arvil Morris, who dropped everything to take care of me after knee surgery so that I could finish this book. Thank you to Melody Guy for her patience, fantastic insight, and wonderful vision. Lady, your awesomeness knows no boundaries. Thank you to Kelli Martin for making this happen. I'm so glad you didn't choose the *General Hospital* or Formula 1 options. As always, thank you to my sweet husband and lovely daughter . . . you both take such good care of me.

ABOUT THE AUTHOR

Katie Graykowski likes sassy heroines, Mexican food, movies where lots of stuff gets blown up, and glitter nail polish.

She is an award-winning and best-selling author of three series: The Marilyns, The Lone Stars, and The PTO Murder Club.

Katie has been married for more than twenty years to a very loving, patient, and tolerant man. She has one human kid and three canine kids. She lives on a hilltop outside of Austin, Texas, where her home office has an excellent view of the Texas Hill Country. When she's not writing, she's scuba diving.

She'd love to hear from you. Visit her at www.katiegraykowski.com.